GENISOVA

GENISOVA

RANDY KOVICAK

GENISOVA

Copyright © 2018 Randy Kovicak.

All rights reserved. No part of this book may be used or reproduced by any means, graphic, electronic, or mechanical, including photocopying, recording, taping or by any information storage retrieval system without the written permission of the author except in the case of brief quotations embodied in critical articles and reviews.

This is a work of fiction. All of the characters, names, incidents, organizations, and dialogue in this novel are either the products of the author's imagination or are used fictitiously.

iUniverse books may be ordered through booksellers or by contacting:

iUniverse
1663 Liberty Drive
Bloomington, IN 47403
www.iuniverse.com
1-800-Authors (1-800-288-4677)

Because of the dynamic nature of the Internet, any web addresses or links contained in this book may have changed since publication and may no longer be valid. The views expressed in this work are solely those of the author and do not necessarily reflect the views of the publisher, and the publisher hereby disclaims any responsibility for them.

Any people depicted in stock imagery provided by Getty Images are models, and such images are being used for illustrative purposes only.
Certain stock imagery © Getty Images.

ISBN: 978-1-5320-6125-7 (sc)
ISBN: 978-1-5320-6126-4 (e)

Library of Congress Control Number: 2018912818

Print information available on the last page.

iUniverse rev. date: 11/05/2018

Year   **2140**

GENISOVA SPACE STATION #3

Master Seisha pondered the question for a few moments, then she turned and looked out across the space between her and Earth admiring the beautiful blue planet that none of these children had ever set foot on. Why do humans kill one another? Where to begin answering such an innocent question that could take an entire day to explain? She had been alive long enough to know so much about the history of humanity to adequately answer the question, but she was born in a time when life up here had become somewhat isolated from that down on earth.

The place she calls home is the third of four self sustaining space stations, the first of which began having permanent residents about 80 years ago. She was born on the first space station and has only been to earth a couple times in her entire life. Humans have come so far in these last 100 years, but there was still a long way to go. The truth was that humans still do kill each other down there on planet earth, although something like that has never happened up here. In fact there was hardly any violence to speak of in the lives of the people who lived in these orbiting sanctuaries.

She sat on a short round platform in the front of the class. The thick wall of glass behind her was all that separated them from the vastness of space outside. The children sat spread out on the floor, each wearing a different, brightly colored robe. They looked up at her, eager to hear every word she had to say. She wondered what made this child as this question. It was such a foreign thought for all of these people, the Genisovians, especially for the children.

Seisha began, "Well, you see, once upon a time life was more of a struggle for humans. On earth, animals of all kinds would kill each other for food. Humans were not far removed from these wild animals and they needed to eat, so they, too, would kill animals to eat for survival."

"You mean, humans would kill animals for food? Why?" asked the little girl.

"Since those times we have learned of other ways to create food. There is now no need to kill an innocent animal to survive. Before we learned how to do this, humans would eat animals as a source of meat," replied Seisha.

The Genisovians, and most all of humanity, had now developed the technology to create food that was just as good or better than before. Meat that tasted like meat, but wasn't meat. New varieties of fruits and vegetables that were easily grown in space. There were humans that still hunted or raised animals for food, but that was practiced less and less. Especially since the evolution of virtual reality, where people who wanted to hunt could now do so virtually.

"I heard my parents talking about how humans killing each other happened all the time long ago. Why would someone want to kill another person?" asked another little boy.

"It is true that even today down on earth people still kill each other," began Seisha, "but since the beginning of Genisova it happens less and less. People have fought since the dawn of time over just about anything from land to religion to politics. The evolution of the consciousness of humans has begun to help us move past those old barbaric ways. Today, as you all probably already know, the people of Earth have much more to worry about than killing each other. The suns harmful rays have made life incredibly difficult, nearly impossible for most on earth."

"What happened? Why did people stop killing each other?" another child asked.

"I wouldn't say that humans have exactly stopped killing each other. The answer is very complicated, but eventually, you could say, our spirit began to have more say than our brains. For Genisovians, one man decided to do something about this human predicament. He was an enlightened man that had a vision of what humans were truly capable of. He was not the first person to try and bring a new message or way of life to humanity. Many before had tried to help evolve the collective human consciousness. You may or may not know some of these people."

One girl shouted out, "Jesus?"

Another little boy said, "Buddha?"

"Yes, these were both important figures that had great influences on many people, and there have been plenty more whose names we will never know that have all helped in moving humans forward towards enlightenment."

"It has been an ongoing, slow process, but it is still coming along just fine. All you need to worry about is that things are changing for the better and many of those old traits are no more. Life is now more peaceful up here in the sky, but humans still have much work ahead of them."

"I heard people used to use these things called guns? What are guns?" one curious little boy said in an innocent voice.

"It is something very similar to what we call a parastun. They were originally made by humans to hunt animals with, but eventually they began to kill each other with them. At one point they reached an epidemic of sorts, but, thankfully, a new creation that came from a Genisovian helped to reduce the number of guns used in the world," Seisha replied.

Master Seisha paused. "I realize this is a lot to understand, but all that you can see and feel around you came about because a small group of people grew tired of the old human condition and their ways of doing things. Finally, when a scientific discovery was made that humans would not be able to live on earth for as long as we once thought, there was a drastic shift in the way some people thought about the future of mankind. One man saw an opportunity within this problem that confronted all of humanity as a chance for change. This group of people, who we now call the Council of Genisova, began their story on earth in the original Genisova. It began as an idea in one man's mind and turned into a revolution that has altered the course of humanity, perhaps saving all of us from extinction."

Master Seisha changed the subject and continued on with her daily lesson for the children. These questions lingered in her mind and brought back some memories of long ago, ones that someone close to her shared about the beginnings of Genisova.

Year 2038

Landau was pretty fired up as he began this conversation with one of his best friends, Charles. "The sun, the source of all life, has turned its back on us," he began. "We have to do something or else all is lost. But there may be a silver lining in this dilemma. We need to do something that no one has ever had the patience or courage to do. I have had a vision and it is pretty clear. The world is ready for change, a big change. I can feel it and see it when I look around. People are ready to take the next step, but no one knows what to do. They all just need some direction. So let's give them some direction."

Some years ago several scientists who studied the sun noticed some unusually high amounts of solar flares occurring on its surface. This was not completely abnormal, but this activity lasted much longer than usual. This odd behavior triggered the launch of a probe towards the sun. The data came back suggesting something was amiss. Our sun is essentially a giant thermonuclear fusion reactor which gives off heat and light as a byproduct. For unknown reasons, the rate of nuclear fusion in the sun's core was increasing, meaning it was not only getting hotter but was also giving off more intense, harmful UV rays. Of course, the data said it could happen slowly, so most humans interpreted this to mean, "Tell me when it's a real problem." The scientific community, conversely, tried to warn the rest of the world to prepare for something more serious.

"I have spent the last five years of my life searching for answers. I have traveled the earth, I have climbed mountains and crossed deserts. I have studied the stars and planets, quantum physics, general relativity. I have experienced all the different religions, I have fasted, I have prayed, I have meditated, I have had about as many different types of experiences as you can have and they have all pointed me in the same direction. I don't want to waste anymore time searching for clues, I want to do something about this human dilemma."

"What is it you are going to do, and how does this involve me?" asked Charles. "How can two people change the course of history?"

His curiosity was slightly piqued, however; he knew Landau well and was used to these deep discussions about anything and everything. Landau was wealthy and handsome, and he also had a vibe and energy about him that permeated any room he walked into. He had dark brown, wavy hair and crystal blue eyes. He was attentive, genuine, and people felt as though he could see deep inside their soul. He had a slim but muscular build. Unless he was in deep thought or conversation with someone, like his friend Charles, he usually had a smile on his face. Charles and Landau had first met right out of college and discovered they both had many of the same interests in life. The two men met at Landau's request. It was the first of several conversations that he would be having with all his close friends in an attempt to convince them of his idea.

"I need to find enough people who are willing to help me create this vision I have that will hopefully enable humans to move past the stage of evolution we are stuck in. There are so many people out there who want more than what the world is giving them right now. They think the same thoughts that I do but do not have the means to do something. I have more money than I could spend in my entire lifetime, but I know it means nothing in the end. It cannot buy happiness or contentment that will last. And now, something has to be done. Humans have to start planning for the future of our species or else our species will become extinct."

"The facts are that the sun is changing, the earth is getting hotter, and the ultraviolet radiation we are receiving will most likely begin killing us and drastically changing the face of the earth within the next 100 years. We will have to adapt or move off from this planet. Mars or Titan or Enceladus are future destinations, but they are too far from the resources of earth to be an option in the near future. No, I think we should build a space station that is large enough to sustain millions of people, and this will become a stepping stone to the next land. But what good is it to build a safe haven in the sky if we are going to keep on hating and killing and consuming? We must first help everyone reach their potential and if they can show themselves resolute and willing to partake, then they can join our refuge from the sun."

"So, let me get this straight," Charles began, "you want to create a place to change human behavior first and then move them to a city in a space station in orbit around the earth? How will this ever work?"

Charles was Landau's best friend and partner in crime, or at least in many of his adventures. He had a bald head and wore nerdy glasses proudly as if it were the latest style. Neither of them worried much about their appearances and were comfortable with who they were.

"Don't you see? This is our chance. We have to get it right. The motivation is there for people to begin to make the changes necessary to take the next step. We create this new world and begin to set things right again. Or, at least, we move it in the right direction. People are ready for this. People want this. They just need the resources and guidance to do it. Let's take away their daily stresses and let them focus on what we are all supposed to be doing here on earth, living fully to our potential."

"It sounds pretty crazy, but if you can convince enough people we would have the resources, and we certainly would have the technology. Ultimately, someone has to do something about the sun. I can't see anyone else taking this kind of a risk. It would be of the utmost importance that you showed all involved that you were 100% in. Then, all we really need is believers."

"Believers, eh?" Landau laughed. "Like starting a new religion. But that is the last thing I want to do. It's precisely the opposite."

"We can't just sit idly and do nothing while the sun continues to change and our world becomes more dangerous. Even if there are still so many people who don't believe it is real. There are many people who want to help, they want to do something, they just don't know what it is. Even I want to do something to try and save us. We could give them something to live for, to contribute to and be a part of something bigger than all of us. I think this could actually gain some momentum. Where would we begin?" Charles asked.

"We would need to gather together enough like-minded people who have the same ultimate goal. We would begin small, careful, and calculated. Then start to work together to devise a plan. We would need property and lots of it. It would need to be ideally located to provide for the future. We would need to build the basic infrastructure to support the entire plan eventually. Things could be added on later, but there would need to be enough to begin with to support everyone. We would need to think ahead and plan for all the different scenarios that could go wrong."

"I see where you are going with this. What happens if it doesn't work? What if no one goes for it?" Charles was trying to be optimistic.

"We will have to be prepared for the worst. I have reached a point in my life where I have nothing to lose by trying to make this work. I have nothing to gain from going back to my old life of consumerism and self preservation. I am willing to commit the rest of my life to this endeavor. But I can't do it alone. What I am requesting of others is definitely a huge ask, with no guarantees of success. But what else can we do? Keep on doing nothing? Sit back and watch the earth continue to heat up and kill everyone?"

"That may be the convincing point in the whole thing. Sometimes in life people need a little extra motivation. It would be essential to have several key people in place to help get something like this off on the right foot. The proper people helping to plan all the different areas of development. People to help design the physical structures and people to help guide those who will be making this new world go."

"It will not happen overnight so everyone will have to be in it for the long haul. I have a vision for what I see it becoming, but getting there will most certainly be an adventure."

"One more thing, have you told Lu?"

"Why would I tell her about any of this?" Landau snapped. "She made it pretty clear that she really didn't want this kind of life."

"Well, I know for a fact how you still feel about her— how you really feel about her, anyway. And those types of feelings don't just go away."

"I think she has moved on. I think she is actually engaged to someone else now. That didn't take long." You could feel the sarcasm in his voice. He hardly ever got rattled, but mentioning her name did the trick.

"She is a very highly sought after woman. You knew that men would be lining up for her the moment after you split up. "

"That's okay. As much as I loved her, and maybe still love her, it doesn't change the facts. It doesn't change the huge fundamental difference between us. All that I wanted to accomplish, all of the difference I wanted to make in the world, she had no desire to take part in. That is a major problem, despite how we both felt about each other."

"How do you know she wouldn't have been okay with all this? I think she may have actually been very interested in it. I just think she was a little overwhelmed by some of your ideas."

"The ideas that have been building up inside of me for all of my life are way too important not to share with the rest of the world. I am not sure I could ever live with myself if I never even tried to share this. She knew how important all of this was to me and I don't think they are the type of things that should be a deal breaker in a relationship."

"You pretty much gave her an ultimatum. "

"I look at it the other way around. I am not a selfish person."

"Well, as a friend, I think you should try to contact her and let her know what is going on. I mean, this is kind of a big deal."

"I am not even thinking about dating anyone at this point in my life. If she wants to talk to me, she knows how to find me. And I don't think she will be looking for me anytime soon. I appreciate the concern, but onward and upwards."

Charles got up to leave. There was one more thing on Landau's mind, but he wasn't sure if he should mention it. He decided at the last second to ask him something.

"Hey Charles, have you ever heard of quantum entanglement?"

"Yeah, why?"

"Isn't it fascinating?" Landau had a sparkle in his eyes.

"It certainly is. What angle are you working on this?"

"That connection, what is that connection? Something is hiding there and I have been thinking about it for a long, long time. Anyway, another conversation for another time."

"Right. Well, see ya."

More conversations about his vision began to take place and Landau eventually had a small core of 10 people. Most of these being friends who were very well off or of some particular expertise in their fields. They all brought something valuable to the table, whether it was a specialty in technology or psychology or engineering or spirituality. A few still had reservations, but he was determined to persuade them of his overall vision. Those he chose were deeply compassionate, intelligent, successful, and influential. They cared about the fate of humanity and saw the big picture, realizing that there was something catastrophic waiting ahead for planet earth. But most important, they were trying to achieve a higher level of consciousness. They were individuals who were not only trying to advance their careers and passions but also their self-awareness. Call it spirituality, call it faith in a higher power, call it simply a belief that there is more than we can see guiding this universe, they were all chasing this elusive entity.

This mysterious guide was key to the whole process, because without it, it wouldn't work. Now they were not going to try to define what it was, but just acknowledge that it exists. It is true that many people would just call this God, but for most of them that was putting a label on an unknown identity and putting it in a box. And that was not what they were trying to do. There had been much more research by respected scientists making a connection between the visible, physical world and the invisible quantum world. It was beginning to change the way we see our reality. Landau was very interested in the connection here and wanted to take it to a higher level of understanding. It also helped in the campaign for his cause with new members.

Soon enough a council was formed and they began laying the groundwork for this endeavor. Property was purchased and designs were begun. It was in a secluded area on the edge of the Rocky Mountains. A curriculum of sorts was laid out and word was sent out to people who they felt were ideal candidates for what they were looking for. The council spent years planning and editing and laying out the details of how to proceed with the plan. A name was created for the project, Genisova.

During these first years of planning they were receiving much response from people who were very interested in joining the cause. There were already a vast amount of people in the world looking for a reason to commit to a cause like this. But their hands were tied. What could your average everyday Joe do on a greater scale to help change the fate of humanity? Pray? Sure. Help their neighbor? Alright. Donate some money to a charity? Okay, that would not be worthless. These things do help make things better. But the whole situation continues to go on, round and round on this wheel of suffering. These things are truly just band-aids placed on the massive wound of the human predicament. Maybe in the eyes of the God of their particular religion this would be all that matters. Maybe some individuals could overcome the difficulties of this world and find true contentment and happiness. Maybe. But what about the vast majority of humans? What could be done to help change their fate? What could be done to give them a chance, a shot at something more, something higher? And, what about the most pressing problem: where do we live when earth is no longer an option?

This opportunity was available to all those who would be willing to make some changes and make some sacrifices. This could possibly change the fate of humanity. What an opportunity! As word began to spread that this new "city" on earth was beginning to take life, there was actually quite a few people ready and willing to leave behind their life as they knew it and join the cause. It began with about 25 people, then 100, then, over the course of a couple years, it was thousands. The basic infrastructure was built in place with the entire design for the future included. In the beginning the volunteers were eager, excited, and willing to do whatever it took to make this world work. The job of qualifying then teaching and training people was easy at first. As the numbers began to grow, however, and word continued to spread, the job became a little more challenging. New ideas were necessary to adapt to the variety of people wanting to partake in the cause. New positions were needed to continue to keep everyone productive and contributing.

How would all the pieces fit together harmoniously? This is what was so wonderful about Genisova. It was fluid and flexible and adaptable. The people appointed to teach and train had to know their students and learn from them what would work best. Patience and understanding were key to making this all work together. They were exploring unchartered water and needed to be entrepreneurs as they continued on this daring endeavor.

Year 2046

"Have you heard of this place called Genisova?" asked Jacob. He was meeting with his friend Julianne for a drink after work. It was Friday evening. They met at their usual place at the end of their work week and sat outside on the patio. Jacob was 25 years old. He was black with an average build, with a gentle way about him. Julianne was Korean with long dark jet black hair, beautiful eyes and a slender, pretty face.

"No, I haven't, what is it?", she replied.

"I'm not really sure. I heard a friend of my cousin signed up for it, or joined it, or something. My cousin said she is a little different, but she basically quit her job and left for this place to join this city or group of people and she's not sure she's ever coming back."

"Really? Wow! That's crazy! Like a cult or something?" Julianne inquired.

"Yeah, but she said it's not exactly like that. You don't have to stay or sign a contract or make any kind of commitment. You can leave whenever you want. And it is like a new job and everything. I don't exactly understand much about it."

"Well, what is it then? Why would she quit her job?"

"Not sure. My cousin said she may do it too, but she's not sure yet and wants to wait and see what her friend thinks first. She said it is a group of people who are trying to make a change in the world and have decided to start their own little city, I guess. Some super rich people started this whole thing and supposedly there are quite a few people who live there now."

"Seems really suspicious to me. Rich people creating an elite society and trying to brainwash them into believing in some weird new religion. There are enough crazy religious zealots running around here as it is."

"I know, it does sound highly suspicious. But, my cousin is actually fairly normal for the most part which makes me wonder about all of it. She seemed sincere and said she may actually really consider doing it some day."

"Hmmm. I don't know but I'm a little curious now. I'm going to have to look this up on the Internet and find out more about it."

They finished their drinks and went home, wondering what this curiously strange place was. Julianne did go home and look it up and did find out some more information, but it was generic and limited. She was mostly content with her life. She worked for UPS delivering packages all over the city. It was hard work, but it paid the bills. The hours weren't the greatest but she got time off occasionally and, all in all, she was happy with her life. Jacob on the other hand was not as content as Julianne. He worked as a nighttime custodian at St. Jude's hospital. It paid very little and he was always struggling to get by. He was not married and not even dating anyone, and he could afford to do very little beyond the basics of living life. He wondered why his cousin's friend, who had a great job as an architect at a large firm, would up and quit and leave her seemingly good life behind? This was starting to bother him more and more. He needed to have another conversation with his cousin.

He never went to college. It was never really even in the picture. His parents we're divorced at an early age and life was always tough. His brother had been killed in a gang related shooting in which some questionable events occurred with the police. This tore his family apart even further. He just wanted to get away from everything as much as he could. Education past high school was not encouraged or discussed. It's too bad, because he was actually a bright child. He was never pushed to get good grades in high school and so he just slowly faded away getting a job, paying bills and making ends meet. His dad was never really in the picture and his mother had very low expectations for him.

His best friend growing up was an outstanding athlete but got so-so grades. He played football at a small college but cared very little about his studies. He did just enough to stay eligible to play football. He was not the best influence on Jacob. Jacob dreamed of a different life but had not the faintest clue how to make it happen. Instead, he just kept doing what he was doing. He had no short or long-term goals. He wanted to get married and have a family, but he felt inadequate, as though he could not provide for a family. What was this Genisova? Was it hope for a better life? He resolved to have another conversation with his cousin.

Suzi was an astrophysicist and professor at a major university. She was a scientist through and through, a self-proclaimed atheist, and felt there was absolutely no wiggle room for anything else. She was tall and thin with red hair, bangs, and freckles peppered across her face. She was plain, rarely wore makeup and without fuss. But still cute, nonetheless. Her fiancé, Darius, was a financial advisor for a small finance group. Super clean cut, preppy, dapper looking. Blonde hair slicked back and the sweater arms crossed over the front. They both did pretty well for themselves. They had dated for quite a while and just recently gotten engaged, but no one was making any plans for the wedding yet. That's because they were so busy being professionals that it was difficult to see what came first in their lives, their jobs or their relationship.

A colleague of Suzi, Marcus, was leaving his position at the university and going to Genisova. Together they had been helping map the night sky of the deep universe, searching for planets that were similar in size, position, and other qualities to that of earth. The so-called Goldilocks planets that were in just the right position to possibly harbor life. In some ways you could say they were searching for aliens. He told her that an amazing opportunity for his career awaited him and that even though he would likely be making some sacrifices in his life, the rewards of that position outweighed them. He said it was something big, but would not elaborate.

He had come back to the lab to get the rest of the things from his office. Suzi knocked on his door and let herself in. "Why," she asked, "are you giving up all you have been working on here for some unknown shot in the dark? I just don't get it."

He replied, "If this is what I think it is, nothing I ever could do here would compare to what they are trying to do. Did you know Kristopher Andersen left his position for Genisova? He approached me at our last conference and told me to look into it."

"Why would he do that? This is crazy. What's happening to my fellow scientists?"

"I guess there are some of us out here that feel like there is maybe another approach to all of this."

This was shocking to her. She had heard whispers and rumors about Genisova, but it seemed like a bunch of hoodoo voodoo stuff to her. She had no intentions of looking deeper within herself for any answers to life or the universe or anything else for that matter. Everything she needed in life could be found in the laboratory or through a telescope. Hard scientific evidence was all there really was to her world. Probably why she had very little motivation for picking a wedding date because there really wasn't any hard evidence pointing her in that direction either.

She did wonder why Dr. Andersen had recruited her colleague and not her. She thought she was more accomplished in the field and known better throughout the world of astrophysics. She would never sign up for something like this anyway, but she had to admit that part of her pride was slightly offended by this. What could they be working on at this Genisova that was so big? She hadn't heard of any new developments in their field that we're groundbreaking. She was extremely competitive and lived for her work, so this whole thing was beginning to bother her more than she had anticipated.

Marcus was good at what he did and he was going to be a challenge to replace. He had a slightly different approach to life then she had. He did not see things as black-and-white and left open room for wonderment. He had always discussed how he felt there was more to life than what we could see. He knew they were searching the night sky for answers, but he felt like there was something missing from their search. Like there was potential for some divine hand in everything.

Would she ever consider going to another place if it meant that it would further her career? What exactly did they do at this Genisova? She did know that there was a lot more to it than just a job. It was like a training school for life where they tried to revamp the way you look at life. This was not for her. But the rest of it did seem at least intriguing. It would be at least worth listening to what Marcus had to say after he had been there for a while. She had made up her mind that after some time she was going to contact him and ask him for some insight. Can just anyone join this place or do you have to be accepted? What about her fiancé? What would he say? Just have to see.

Andrew turned and looked at his boss, "So you want me to go and investigate this Genisova, eh?" Andrew was 34 and worked for a major news corporation. He was tall, with sandy brown hair that was a little too long, and pale blue eyes. He looked like the guy who went to the gym occasionally. Just enough to stay somewhat in shape but more so to check out the girls and give the appearance that he cared about his body. His office was downtown New York atop one of the towering skyscrapers with a spectacular view of Central Park.

His boss, who's name was Evan, replied, "We think it would be a great story. We hear some interesting things about it, but there is so much skepticism in the general public, we really don't have much concrete evidence as to what goes on there. From what it sounds like, pretty much everyone that starts there stays there. Very few ever leave. And those that choose not to stay don't have a whole lot of things to say about it good or bad."

"What do they say? How could they just say nothing?"

"They just say, it wasn't for me, or give very few details. Not much goes on at the beginning of the program. They're pretty much assessing the individual for how they will create a program around them. I get the sense that they know early in the process if someone is going to stay or not and then they really don't share a whole lot of information with them."

"So, what you're saying is, I need to convince them that I am a good candidate for the long-haul and hang in there long enough to get more insight as to what is actually going on there? How long are we talking about here? What does the program run, like a few months or so?"

"A year," said Evan.

"A year?" Andrew exclaimed. "You want me to put my life on hold for a year?"

"I guess, sort of. It is not like you won't be doing anything. You're not married or not involved in any serious relationship that I'm aware of. You can leave if you want, it's not prison. There are quite a few higher profile names and leading professionals that are essentially foregoing their lives to sign up for this place. I mean, I think, it could be a big deal. I even heard whispers about space travel and space station city type ideas. What if this is really about some new high-tech scientific discovery that is top secret? A breakthrough in AI finally? There are theories out there as to what is going on, but we have no solid information to speak of. You can't really do a story on much of anything but hearsay."

He was starting to get the feeling Evan wasn't taking no for an answer. But he wasn't going down without a fight.

"I get it. It sounds like a great story, perhaps something big, but this is quite an ask. You want me to give up my current life for an indefinite amount of time in order to get a story? Is there going to be some extra compensation for this? How are you going to make it worth my while? This is kind of like going undercover, or going into protective services or something like that."

"Look Andy, you are one of our best young reporters, and you were chosen out of a very short list of eager newcomers with lots of potential. If this all goes well, as we predict it could, this could be very big for you. It's like going on assignment to cover a war or something along those lines. You are put out of your comfort zone for a little while, you work on your story, you have some new and potentially exciting experiences, and then you come back to your old life with all sorts of possibilities at your fingertips. This could be a great move for you."

He began to fidget with his fingers and pace back and forth. He wasn't really sure if this was a chance at a promotion or a punishment.

"What exactly are you looking for out of this whole project? Is it going to be a highlight or a special report? How much information do you need, how deep do I need to dive into this abyss?"

"I don't have a concrete answer for you. If you agree to do this you would have a lot of freedom to do as you see fit. You would pretty much be in charge artistically of how you want to approach it, within some boundaries, of course. You have to come back with something, obviously, that we could use as a story, or else what's the point of it? I think the longer you stay, the better. It appears that they are pretty good at reading people and may know right away what you are up to. You would need to have some kind of alibi, shall we say, as to why you are really there. Apparently they don't turn anyone down, that I'm aware of, so they can't say no. I don't believe they have ever kicked someone out. They just won't let you go any deeper into their secret Batcave until they feel you are ready, or you just quit, give up, I guess."

"Man, you make it sound kind of brutal. They seem to be very on top of it, like they have done their homework and have their approach down pat."

"The original founder, Landau is a unique, intelligent individual. And a billionaire, I might add. You don't get to be where he is by not knowing what you were doing. The rest of his council are all amazing people and I actually can't believe that this hasn't received more publicity than it has. But like I said, they know what they are doing. They have kept things under wraps as much as they can. Why? I don't know what they are hiding."

"I have to admit I am starting to get a little more curious about what they're up to. Especially the part about some of the more interesting figures that have just quit their successful careers and left it all behind. For what? Why? What is the deal here? There has to be some catch to all of this. There has to be some grand prize at the end of it all. People don't just pick up and leave their entire life never to return for nothing. So there has to be some major incentive. But what? I haven't heard of any grand, luxurious lifestyle being handed out to those who go in there. I guess, nobody is coming out for us to question, so we really don't know what the end game is. OK, I'm talking myself into this as we speak. I'm in. Where do I sign up?"

The Maxwell family had found out about Genisova through an acquaintance. They had been well informed about many details of Genisova, what its purpose and mission was, why it was formed, and what was expected of potential candidates. But how did the scenario work for a family with two children, aged nine and seven, that needed to be in school? When they first heard about it, Theresa and Jonathan both fell in love with the idea of Genisova and wondered if there was a way for it to work for all of them. Theresa was shorter, petite with long auburn colored hair and green eyes. She was an elementary school teacher. Jonathan was an aeronautical engineer and looked like a middle linebacker on the football team with a square face and a matching haircut. They realized that a possibility would be a home-school situation, but they really wanted the kids to develop their social skills with peers their own age.

They had struggled with many different things in their previous situation. Both were successful professionals but had a hard time fitting in. They saw so many other parents that were interested only in superficial things like the size of their house or whether it was lakefront property or not, or what type of car you drove, or where your kids went to school, what fancy vacation you went on, and the crowd you hung out with. You had to act a certain way, look a certain way, and be popular with certain people or you were not included in these little cliques that you would have thought adults would have left behind in high school—but, apparently not. People continued to be cliquey and judgmental and materialistic, and Jonathan and Theresa would not buy into any of it. They focused on family and their own lives and didn't care what other people thought. They were not popular and not included in a lot of things because of this. They did what was best for their kids most of the time and stressed the truly important things in life like respect for others, embracing diversity, and inclusion of everyone. They spent Saturdays at the library and went to museums and art fairs. Their children had lots of different interests in life and were very well rounded.

They liked the community they lived in but would shed no tears when they left. They were ready for a change and ready for a fresh start with other like-minded people. Genisova was a daunting transition from the outset, but there were so many attractive parts to it that in the end the decision was easy. Their children understood, for as young as they were they listened in on many conversation their parents had. Conversations about their life and the issues they had with other people, and despite the fact they would leaving some friends behind, they were excited about a change, too. Jonathan and Theresa loved to experience new things and were constantly embracing any opportunity to do so. They had met by chance one day at the local farmer's market and had discovered they had much in common. They both loved fresh local produce, for starters, and then they just hit it off.

Turns out when Genisova first began, there were no children there. However, of course, the council had the foresight to know they would create their own school eventually. At first it was difficult because there were not enough kids to form a school. The children of any Genisovian had to commute to the nearest school, which was about a 30 minute drive one way. They did not want to discriminate in any way, but the reality was that this was a problem of sheer numbers. From the outset their intentions to grow the community slowly and carefully presented a little bit of a tricky problem. For a family to desire to participate in Genisova, both parents would need to be on board. It also meant that you would be making decisions for your children that would impact the rest of their lives. Everything would need to line up correctly for the entire family dynamic to work here.

For the Maxwells this is what happened. They had lived their lives in a very similar fashion to how Genisovians approach life. With a teacher in the family, education was obviously important, but they were also both concerned about the environmental changes going on. They strongly believed that all of humanity should be taking the issue at hand much more seriously. As you could've guessed, the majority of people living on planet earth, were not very concerned about the predictions scientists had made about the sun changing. And maybe some did really believe in what they foretold, but weren't too concerned at the moment because the immediate changes were minimal.

But the scientists predictions were fairly serious, and they would turn out to be correct. Unfortunately, human nature is to procrastinate. And aren't the problems of today, the ones sitting right in front of our face, enough to handle as it is? Lucky enough for Genisova, there were in actuality many people who cared passionately for the future of our planet. And these people, once they were found, were truly interested in what was going on at Genisova. These were the people who began to consider their life situation and see if they could make the changes necessary to join the cause. The Maxwells had heard about Genisova several years earlier and were aware of the lack of numbers for a school.

The first school age children brought to Genisova were home-schooled. And actually they were receiving an amazing education because the environment they were surrounded by was incredible for learning. Being the first children there, they received a great deal of attention wherever they went. Everybody loved them and wanted to teach them the skills they already knew. But they didn't have other children to play with or just goof around with. It was hard, but someone had to be the first. There were three children in this family so they did have each other, but it wasn't enough.

The next two families came in together. They had known each other beforehand and made the decision together to come so as to help ease the children situation. The next few families already had parents there, commuting, and so, as the numbers begin to grow, they felt more comfortable bringing their children on site. By the time the Maxwells were considering moving to Genisova there was a small school of about 150 kids total, in grades K through 12. They had some of the extra-curricular activities a smaller school would have and if they didn't, the students could commute to the nearest school. With time the school continued to grow, and eventually, after about 10 years, the school was able to offer everything a conventional school could offer.

—⚉—

Mohammed had been born in the United States at a time when Muslims were looked upon with suspicious eyes by many Americans. He was tall and skinny with dark messy hair and matching dark brown eyes. He dressed like your typical sharp dressed computer savvy guy. The unrest in the Middle East had continued to be fairly volatile despite there seeming to never be an origin of the violence. The mindset of these terrorists of the time continued to evolve and adapt to the rest of the world. They would strike somewhere and lives would be lost. The victims would try to adapt and change their security measures and the terrorists would change their approach. There had not been a major attack on a US city in years and then it happened. It was at a professional football game. Thousands died. They hit Americans where it hurt the most. This murderous event re-created the animosity within a lot of people who remembered 9-11. It also re-instilled fear amongst many Muslims, some of whom were the most peaceful people on the planet.

Mohammed's parents were very concerned for their children and when he voiced interest in Genisova, they were weary. He was not as concerned. He was excited. But he knew the environment surrounding Muslims could be contentious. He wondered, would he be accepted there, or would people be suspicious of him? He experienced discrimination all the time in his daily life. Most often when he went in public places, like the grocery store, sporting events, or busy restaurants, he could to see, even feel, people look at him with different eyes, judging, suspicious eyes. He knew this feeling well. He hoped that Genisova would be free of these looks.

He was a practicing Muslim, but not your textbook practicing Muslim. There were definitely things about Islam that he did not agree with. As with most every religion there are so many different interpretations of the correct way to practice. Human beings can be very proud and very egotistical, and this can be true with religious leaders. He always wondered who was right. How could anyone really know for sure? Some Muslims interpreted the Koran to quite an extreme and this is what had led to so many problems with Muslims. He had a hard time believing that any religion supported any form of violence. If it was divinely inspired, then it would certainly need the touch of human hands to change it into something evil. Regardless of what people thought, he still believed in a God and Islam was his medium to that God. He felt it to the bottom of his bones that there had to be more to this life, more to this world than just what we see. Islam worked for him and had value for him. It helped him to see the world through the eyes of God. That's all that mattered to him. He hoped when he joined Genisova his life would be better and he could still hold onto his faith.

Landau and Charles had continued to be good friends and as Genisova went from a dream to reality, they began to be swept away into this new city and way of life that they had created. There was little free time to do much of anything. They had worked diligently to ensure that Genisova would persevere despite all the critics and doubters. It was not all smooth sailing, but their thoughtful design and attention to detail paid off as it continued to slowly grow and prosper. Landau was showing some board members plans for a new division of Genisova they were getting ready to launch. He could tell something wasn't right when Charles went out of his way to approach him.

"What's up?" asked Landau.

"I got a call the other day from someone inquiring about Genisova. She didn't say who she was at first, but I figured it out after a couple moments."

"Who was it?" He was now intrigued.

"Lu."

"What?" replied Landau surprised. It had now been years since her named had been mentioned by anyone. Was he hearing him correctly?

"I know."

"Well, what did she say?" Landau's heart rate began to accelerate just a tad, and he became a little anxious.

"She pretended at first that she didn't know who I was, acted like just another person inquiring about Genisova. She asked some basic questions and I gave her the same typical responses we give to everyone."

"After a long pause one time, I just said, "Lu?", and she replied, "How did you know it was me? It's been so long since we last spoke. "

Charles then began to recount the conversation. I said, "How are you? Is there something else going on here, or are you truly inquiring about Genisova?"

She replied, "I'm not sure…" and then broke down and began crying. "I don't know what came over me. It's like I was possessed and just picked up my phone and called."

"Is everything okay? You sound a little upset."

"I'm okay, I just miss him sometimes and it can be hard."

"Aren't you married to someone else?"

"No."

"Oh. But I thought…"

"It never happened. I called it off." Lu said firmly.

"Why, what happened?"

"I'm not sure. This is very difficult. I just, you know, life has been different ever since we went our own ways. I thought things would be better actually, but they weren't."

"Lu, that was a long time ago. I think Landau believed you moved on. You seemed so mad, and unhappy and looking for something completely different than what he wanted. You know, I really shouldn't be talking for him. You need to talk to him."

"I can't. I'm not sure what I would say."

"Are you seriously considering Genisova?"

"Maybe? What's it like? Really."

"What are you looking for— Landau? Or yourself? It's a big commitment either way. This is not the place to find many of the world's luxuries, as you might have guessed."

"I still don't fully understand the point of depriving yourself of all the wonderful things this life has to offer."

"Like what?"

"Pick a café on the Seine, or a play on Broadway, or a beach in Bali, shall I go on?"

"If you have had those things a hundred times, what does 101 matter? In a hundred years you won't be able to go to any of those places ever again. How many times can you drive a $200,000 car or eat a $200 steak or drink a $500 glass of scotch before it grows old? At some point in life, for some people, those things no longer matter? Then what? Where do you search to fill the void in your life? And, by the way, we are not as deprived as you may think."

"I really don't know what goes on there, I just know Landau and what he stands for. Ironically, of all the people of the world, he has more money than he knows what to do with and he doesn't even really want it."

"I would think it almost heroic to be able to have that much money and not let it control you and take over your being, as it does with most people who have it. It is nearly impossible to have it not affect you like it does not affect him."

"He should just give it all away then."

"He is, in essence. Just not the way the rest of the world thinks you should give it away. He has found a different way to use his wealth to affect people. He is also trying to figure out a way to save our planet from the sun. Can't get any bigger than that."

"I heard that was part of the reason people were coming here. Is it true what they are predicting about the sun?"

"Yes, I believe so. If you understand how to read the information, it points to a very grim future. The rest of the world should be paying attention, but they are not, as you would suspect."

"Why isn't anyone paying attention? Don't people realize what this means?"

"The world is such a mess in so many ways right now, most people and governments are too caught up in their own problems to even start thinking about it. Did you believe it? Did you even know about it? And you are an intelligent, educated person."

"Most people don't want to believe it's true. Life is hard enough as it is for most people," Lu confessed.

"If it were true are you ready to start doing something about it? What would it take to make you try to help save the world?"

"Well, when you put it like that, it seems very convincing."

"So, what are you going to do?"

"Can I have his number? I do want to talk to him first, you just sort of put me on the spot. Is he even involved with someone else?"

"No, he's not, but I have to talk to him first about this. He would never stop you from joining because it goes against the whole principle behind this place. But I think it is only fair that I give him heads up that you called. Okay?"

"That sounds good, can you give him my number?"

"Yes, but I'm not going to promise anything."

"Take care Charles, it was so nice to talk with you again," and Lu hung up.

"So I thought I needed to let you know about all of this," Charles said to Landau.

Landau sighed and put his head down. "That's a lot to take in. I'm not even sure what to say."

"Well, you don't have to say anything. She's probably just having a moment. But I did take her number down, so you can do with it what you want."

"I think I'll pass. I'm a little busy these days, in case you haven't noticed."

"I agree, but I do wonder ever if you are a little lonely. I know you and you don't even show interest in anyone anymore. Did she hurt you that bad?"

"I trust that life will guide me in the correct direction in all ways, including this. I will look and listen for signs. It never fails me."

—⋘—

After six months or so Suzi did talk to Marcus to find out how it was going, and what it was like. The conversation was an unexpected surprise, but left Suzi wondering what she should do next.

"Hey Marcus, so was it a good decision to leave the university? I am very curious as to what could've pulled you away from our work so easily."

"I wouldn't say it was such an easy decision, but, yes it has turned out to be a life-changing decision, one that has impacted me in ways beyond what our work could have ever done. Have you considered coming here? We could certainly use someone like you."

Suzi found this statement caught her way off guard. She was not expecting someone to extend an invitation to make her feel wanted like this. "I am not really sure that place is for me," said Suzi. "I'm not like you. I don't believe in a higher power or in divine intervention or any of that kind of silly stuff—just science."

He replied, "No one ever said you have to believe in those types of things to come here. There are plenty of people who have begun their experience here thinking the way you do."

"What do you mean, began their experience like me? You say it with a hint of—and then they change their way of thinking."

"Well, yes, you could say they have changed, but everyone here changes. I don't know exactly what their beliefs or anyone's beliefs here are, but I know what I see and what I feel. And I know that everyone has a similar purpose with similar intentions. The people here are all still very different, but they have found a common ground."

"What? What has everyone there so connected?"

"Just that basic fact that you simply stated, that we are all connected."

"That's it? We're connected? That's not going to convince me to go anywhere."

"You could work with Dr. Andersen."

"I just don't know. It would be amazing to work with him, and you, again. Your replacement still has a long way to go before learning the ropes."

"I think you might be surprised."

"So what's the compensation like?"

"Well, that's a little bit harder to explain. There is no money here, all of your needs and desires are taken care of. May seem a little odd, but it is actually a big part of the purpose of being here."

Suzi was trying to not reveal the shock on her face. "What do you mean, there is no money here? Like, you only use credit cards or some other form of electric currency? Or, there is NO money there? Like, you don't get it paid for what you're doing?"

"It's a new way of thinking. It is a complete paradigm shift and it only works here in this isolated community, away from the extreme materialism and consumerism of the outside world. But, if you want something, pretty much you can have it. It is a long, slow process of sorting through each individual person and what their desires are and what they truly need for fulfillment in life. If you want or need to have tons of things in your life, this place is not for you. It will help you come to the realization of what you really need and want in life. I can't say enough about this process."

"I feel like everyone is slave to the system or whatever you want to call it, like being brainwashed to think a certain way, convincing you to want less than what you actually deserve."

"Some people here may actually get more than they deserve. What do you really think you deserve? How do you really equate that to something tangible? Let's have an honest conversation about the people of the world who actually, truly, get what they deserve. How many people do you know in the world who work way harder for less compensation than people who do very little and are overcompensated? How do you put an actual true dollar value on what you do? So many people get filthy rich in our world selling or doing something that has a little or no value towards enriching our society or world. Then there are so many other people who pour their heart and soul into their work and continue to struggle to get by. You are fairly well compensated for what you do, but you are an intelligent person who understands how the system works and how to make the most of it. And, by doing something you enjoy. On an even playing field, equal for everyone, who should make the most money? What is the criteria? Should the surgeon who saves your life make less than a stockbroker who types a few strokes into a computer, moving money from one fund to another? Should the elementary school teacher who we entrust the lives of our little children with make so much less then a pretty woman on a magazine cover? How do you call any of it fair? I could go on and on but I hope you at least begin to see my point."

"I can see where you're coming from, but how does this Genisova fix any of it?"

"It is an attempt at a clean slate. It is complicated, but at the same time simple. It only works if the people who are participating are willing to buy into it. Everyone who begins here realizes there will be some sacrifices, the hope is that the end goal is worth the sacrifices. If money or prestige or status are that important to you, then it will most likely not work. That is why the majority of the world does not care about Genisova. It's not for them. However, there may come a day and sooner than you think, when people may wish they had changed their mind."

"I'm not really sure what would be in it for me. If I'm not compensated monetarily then it would be purely for my work. I am not looking for anything spiritual from anywhere in life." She paused for a little while. Then she said, "I have to think about it. How do I know what I will be doing once I get there?"

"You are evaluated once you decide to enter. There is a team of people whose sole purpose is to help you find your place at Genisova. It is an open conversation where you get to help in making that decision. There's a period of concentrated discernment to help the process. I can't tell you what your options will be. Only they know what there is available at the time. All I can say is that there is definitely something bigger going on than what the rest of the world thinks is happening. If you start the process and there is nothing that interests you, you then can decide to leave. You can also do something different, maybe something you don't want to do until the position you desire is available or created. It really is a fluid and flexible process. In the meantime all your basic needs are taken care of. You can leave for short periods of time, but of course you have to return to finish the process."

Suzi sighed, "Well I have a lot to think about. I am very curious about some things and would have to decide if the other issues I have are a deal breaker."

"Okay, well let me know if you need any more help with making your decision."

"I will. Good talking with you."

―⚏―

Jacob had made the decision to try and see what Genisova was all about. After several conversations with his cousin he did a lot of soul searching and in the end thought he had nothing to lose. She got him in contact with the right people and then they began to contact him and give him some basic directions. They sent a small device about 2 by 4 inches in size and with a camera-type lens on the side of it. It came with some basic instructions that told him how to turn the device on. He set it down, turned it on and a hologram image popped up from the lens and a man began to talk to him. The man gave a basic welcome speech and then went into some details and inquiries for him. The first thing he asked was, "Are you okay leaving your job and house and car and many of your material possessions behind for about a year and then possibly longer after that if things go well?" This made Jacob really think hard about leaving behind his life. Things like playing a pick-up basketball game or going out with friends to the bar. There would be new friends to be made and they did have a basketball court there.

It made him nervous to think about leaving it all behind. There was some basic paperwork to fill out online and a profile form that asked a lot of questions about who he was and what he was looking for in life. He could tell that most all of the questions had a purpose. He was told that he could either sell his home and car, or keep them and return later to deal with it if he wanted. If he did choose to keep his home and ended up staying indefinitely, they would arrange to have his house taken care of. He rented, so that wasn't a problem and he decided to sell his car. It wasn't anything special, so it really wasn't a big deal either. He lives a fairly basic, boring life.

He wondered what would he do at this place? What type of work would they assign to him? There were so many questions, and he was very nervous about all of it. But, he was also excited and curious about this new experience he was about to begin. His cousin did set him at ease and really she was the only reason he agreed to even think about it in the first place. It was kind of like sky diving, jumping out of an airplane with no idea what was going to happen. It made him anxious and eager to get started all at the same time.

Since he decided to sell his car, he had to arrange a bus ride to the nearest major city and then someone was going to come pick him up from there. He was told to bring a certain amount of money just in case, but that as soon as he arrived at Genisova he would no longer need it. That idea seemed crazy to him. He figured he would probably have to start working right away in order to earn his keep, but he was told he actually would not start working for quite some time. He wondered what he would be doing?

He packed his suitcase with all the things they recommended bringing and then was told he could bring a certain amount of extra things with him. It was challenging, picking out the clothes and items that he would be bringing with him. He packed up all the stuff he couldn't bring and gave some away and then left the rest with his mother. She was a little concerned about him leaving, but in the end didn't really care a whole lot. She said he would be back in a couple weeks and she would see him then. He tried to explain that it was at least a year, but she just laughed and said, "Yeah right!" He would be living in a fairly decent sized "dorm room" but with access to quite a bit of other living space. There would be plenty of common room areas, but there were also a decent amount of more private areas where one could be left alone if need be.

Going into this, he had absolutely no expectations whatsoever. He hoped all the things his cousin had said were true. That this place would be life changing for the better and that it was going to be part of something bigger than all of us, something that would change the world as we know it. Those were pretty bold statements. Sounded too good to be true. Although it did make him curious to find out what was going on. It sounded way better than what was going on in his life at this point in time. He had no purpose or goals and was going no where in particular. Just spinning his wheels waiting for something to happen. He just made up his mind that this was the thing that was going to happen.

He was told that when he reached the final bus stop to look for a man in a red sweatshirt. That was it. He would be looking for him so it shouldn't be an issue. The bus ride took quite while and he figured that they were headed west. When they finally stopped he got off and got his two large bags out and stood there waiting for his ride. After a couple minutes of searching a middle aged man came up and said, "Jacob?"

"Yeah, that's me," he replied.

"My name is Cedric. How are you? How was the ride?"

"Not too bad. It was nice. There were some scenic areas that were beautiful and I have never been this way before. Where are we?"

"We are about a half hour ride to Genisova. Are you ready to begin this next step of your life?" Cedric asked.

"I'm not sure, but I think so. How does anyone really ever know here? It seems like a big mystery."

"C'mon, let's get your bags and start making our way to our destination."

They packed their bags in the trunk of a midsize car and made their way west.

"I guess you could say that it is a mystery of sorts, but you will find right away that there is very little to be afraid of. It's normal to fear the unknown, but your mind will be set at ease right away and then it will turn into a form of excitement. You'll see."

"I have never been a person of adventure or one who takes big gambles in life. "

"Are you looking for adventure? Do you know what you are looking for?"

"Not really. Happiness, I guess. I don't even think about it very much. I just get up and go through the motions. Isn't that what everyone else does? You get up, go to work, have a little fun when you can and then repeat."

"Yes, I would say that the majority of humans do approach life this way. But what if I told you there was more to life than you thought? What if it was just a matter of changing the way you look at things?"

"That seems like it would be too easy."

"I didn't say it would be easy. As with most things in life that are worthwhile, there has to be some time and effort put into it. But in the end, isn't that part of what brings us satisfaction? Is the person who builds their own house from scratch more proud of their house then the person who simply shows up and buys it? The same goes for everything in life. If you build it from scratch, it has more value to you. Everything from making a pizza to building a house."

"Yeah, I guess you are right. So, what are we building from scratch?"

"We will start with you, then move on to the next thing," he said with a smile.

"How are you going to build me from scratch? That makes me nervous. It makes me think you are going to try to brainwash me into believing things the way you do."

"Well, for starters, I don't know what that would be. I don't believe the same things as the other people at Genisova. Everyone has their own way of thinking and believing. We are not here to try and convince you to think a certain way. More so to listen to what your own mind and body are trying to tell you. That's all."

"Interesting. I don't really think I have a belief system."

"Oh, you do. You just may not know it. The whole process begins by simply listening, not speaking or thinking. It is wonderful."

As they continued to get closer to Genisova, Jacob could sense a feeling of ease coming over him. He never paid much attention to any of his feelings like this. Of course, he had had them before, but he couldn't tell you what made him feel like that in the past. He had no idea what this place looked like. The pictures online did not give away much. As they approached what appeared to be the gates or entrance to this place he could see some of the buildings off in the distance. There were lush green fields in every direction and you could see the mountains behind everything. They pulled up to the entrance and stopped at what appeared to be a security guard. There was no fence or gate that was visible and he wondered if there were boundaries that may or may not be crossed on the property. The guard said hello in a very friendly voice and then told them to pass on through.

They drove past some buildings that looked like typical red and orange brick buildings that belonged in a midwestern small town. There were no skyscrapers visible, nothing that seemed domineering. It was nice, quaint, sorta picturesque, like a jigsaw puzzle. They drove to a larger building that was more modern looking, with straight lines and geometric shapes. It seemed to be an apartment complex. There were a few people walking around and they seemed to look like normal people walking around a downtown area. Nothing seemed out of the ordinary.

They parked in front of the apartment building and Cedric helped Jacob with his bags. They began walking towards what was apparently his new place.

Cedric told him, "You will get a security key card for getting into the building and to get into your room. It's pretty much just like a hotel key card. I will show you where the central office building is and if you have any problems that is where you go. Let's take a look inside."

They went inside and there was a simple, clean looking foyer with some chairs and tables for sitting at.

"Your room is on the second floor. It is nothing fancy but you will have access to all of the other common areas in all of the housing buildings."

"Does everyone live here or in buildings like these?"

"No, there actually is quite a variety of places that people live in. As you learn more about this place you'll see how the housing assignments work. It becomes more of a what-fits-your needs type decision that you will come to at some point. This will work for now until you get a little more oriented."

As they walked up the stairs Jacob was taking all of it in. He saw some other rooms off from the vestibule area that appeared to be exercise rooms or just larger hang out areas. Cedric lead him to his room and opened the door to let him in. There was a fairly decent size living room with a nice kitchen off to the side. A hallway led to a bathroom and bedroom. Sunshine radiated the room through the plethora of windows. It was a modern looking apartment. No television or computer could be seen. Beautiful photos of amazing, tranquil scenes and other contemporary sculptures were thoughtfully placed throughout the room. You could tell that the room was decorated to help set the person making this transition at ease and relaxed. The feeling was subtle, but there.

"It is very calming. Who did the decorating?" Jacob asked.

"There is actually a member who is in charge of decorating the living areas and other things along those lines. She does an amazing job. She was actually given some information on you and custom designed this living space for you. Do you like it?"

"I do. She actually designed it thinking of me? How did she do that? I mean, I actually find that incredible, like she could read my mind."

"She is very intuitive and good at what she does. Her work here is felt deeply all around. You have had your first taste of how this place works." Cedric got out some papers from his bag and gave them to Jacob.

"Here are some instructions for where you are to go tomorrow. The refrigerator and cupboards are stocked with food. You will eventually be able to get food at our local grocery store or any of our restaurants spread throughout the property. Genisova is set up like a small city so you will have access to whatever you need at the various stores. One area that is set up like a small college or educational center, which is where you will be going tomorrow. There are other areas, which we call villages, that are designed for things like medical, engineering and agriculture."

He then touched a control panel on the wall and a hologram-type image popped up over a desk area. It looked like a virtual computer or TV.

"This is your computer, which also functions as a TV, which we do not exactly encourage people to use that much."

"Okay, I don't watch that much anyway. Am I going to be going to school here? What is the plan? I know that I will go through a period of evaluation and then be given a job. What else is there to this?"

"You will be given many instructions tomorrow for what is to come. Genisova is sort of like a school for how to live life. Not that we know the best way to live life, but we give you the means to help you figure out how you should live your life best. As you will find out, besides trying to reach the goal of discovering what is best for you, there is a bigger goal that we are all working towards together. The longer you stay here the more you will find out what that goal is."

"It all sounds great, I just wonder what I am going to be doing. I was a custodian before, so I assume I will be doing something along those lines, right?"

"Did you like your job?"

"Not exactly. I mean, I was good at it and a hard worker."

"Did it help bring you purpose in life?"

"No. At least not that I am aware of," he said with a laugh.

"I don't think you will be doing that here. I think you will just have to find out what is in store for you. I don't know what you will be doing, but I will say that you won't be doing anything that you do not like doing."

"Does anyone take out the trash here? I mean, no one likes taking out the garbage."

"We all take out the waste here. And it is not a problem. You will see. Maybe no one loves taking out the trash, but some things have to be done. It is not a burden for anyone. We all help get it done and it is just fine. Maybe you can help with making it a better process for everyone. That could be part of your purpose. You will just have to see."

"I am beginning to see a little bit of what you mean."

"I think you are going to be just fine here, Jacob. I can see that already. Do you have any more questions? I think everything you need for now is provided for here."

"No, I think I can figure it out at least for now. Thank you for your help. I appreciate that you took the time to help explain things as best you could to me. It helps make me feel more comfortable."

"I will see you tomorrow at nine in the morning."

"Great."

Mohammed got up early that morning and had his sister drive him to the airport. He was leaving today for Genisova. He had left his job at a major computer company where he was a programer. He was from a big family and had received mixed responses from them about this new adventure of his. He enjoyed his job but was looking for a change of scenery and possibly even a change in life altogether. Something was festering inside of him that he could not exactly explain, but he knew it was there, pushing him outside his comfort zone. A friend of his from college that worked for another computer company had told him about Genisova and thought maybe he would be a good fit for it. He had said that there were certainly jobs in technology available there and that it was free from any prejudices, unlike anywhere else he had ever been. His religion was important to him and the fact that he was Middle Eastern made him uneasy most everyday.

After they had been driving in silence for a little while, his sister finally blurted out, "Are you sure this is what you want to do? I do support you, but it seems a bit extreme to me all the same."

"Look, I am searching for something more out of life and I am not getting it where I am at. Have you ever felt like that?"

"What are you looking for? Why can't you get it anywhere? Why does it have to be in this isolated, weird place away from the rest of the world?"

"I don't know that I can find it there, but I have a funny feeling about all of it."

"A good funny feeling, or a bad funny feeling? Most people say funny feeling when they are unsure about something."

"I just know that it is going to provide something different from what you can get anywhere else. And I believe I can keep doing a job similar to what I am already doing."

"I get it, I get it. I know how you feel about being Muslim in our world. It really bothers you, or at least it bothers you how others make you feel about it. I feel it too, but I am not running away from the problem."

"I'm not running away from it. I am sure there will be some people in there that will look at me as if I am a possible terrorist. It will be just as hard to gain people's trust in there as it is out here. But, what if? What if, it's not like that? What if the people don't care who I am or what I believe?"

"That would be great, but I just don't have that kind of faith in humanity. People are people wherever you are."

"Well, let's hope that this place can put the trust back in humanity," he said with a smile.

"I love you Mohammed," his sister said with a sigh.

"I love you too."

"I'm going to miss you. When am I going to get to see you again?"

"It may be a little while, but I can leave, you know. I am free to leave whenever I want."

"Okay, but don't wait like a year before coming to see us."

"I won't."

She dropped him off at the airport and helped him with his bags. She gave him a big hug and kissed him on the cheeks. A little tear started down one of her cheeks as she began to wipe it away.

"I am sad to be going and will definitely miss all of you, but I am very excited for a new chapter in my life. I hope that you and the rest of our family will understand this and support me," he said.

"We all love you and do support you, albeit in varying degrees. You can't expect mom and dad to be that open to something like this. But they do understand to some extent. And, like you said, you can leave whenever you want."

When the plane landed and after he got his luggage his driver was waiting for him outside. His name was Curtis, and was Japanese. He seemed like a very sharp looking individual by the way he was dressed and carried himself. They get into the car and headed towards Genisova. His driver was welcoming and asked him several questions about how his flight was and if he had any problems. Mohammed said everything was fine and then cut to the chase.

"What is so secretive about Genisova anyway?" he asked.

The driver paused for a moment and then responded, "Why do think that it is secretive?"

"Well, you just can't find out that much about what goes on there, besides the basic information. It makes it appear as if they are hiding something."

"It is true that some things are not as public as others, but if you stay long enough, then eventually you will know everything there is to know."

"Why is that? And how do they keep everyone who does know from telling everyone else?"

"It really is not that much of a secret. The people who do know are not told, per se, to not talk about it, they just understand that it would do no good to do so. And then they choose not to say anything. Anytime anyone does something that could have a large affect on the rest of the world, there will always be people who feel it is controversial. They will disagree with what is being done and will want to try and stop it or make a big deal about it."

"You see, that makes me think there is a huge deception of sorts going on," Mohammed replied.

"Let's just say that we like things quiet and non-controversial here, and the more publicity things get, the less quiet things become. If Genisova goes out and proclaims everything it plans to do, it would make its ability to do those things that much more difficult. There are well thought out reasons for pretty much everything that goes on here, as you will see. I think with time it will all begin to make sense."

They finally began to approach what appeared to be their destination. From what he could see he liked. After going through the security gate they pulled up to his building. He was shown to his room and explained how the beginning of the process works.

"Is it true that part of the goal is to make a livable space station? Is that the only reason that some people come here?"

"There are many reasons that people choose to come here. For some it is a chance to start over. For others it is to find peace and happiness. Many are here to help solve the problem that will confront humanity in the near future. There are lots of reasons that people come here, all of which are acceptable. There are some that have come with no intentions and we help them find their purpose. It is different with everyone, and that is okay."

—ɷ—

Landau had so much on his plate, but now there was something else beginning to find its way in through his armor of business. It was Lu, short for Lucina. Somehow, with all this going on, she was still in the background, somewhere. What had happened? Once upon a time they had seemed so in love. But he knew something else was unsettled in his heart and he wanted to go search the world for answers. It wasn't like he just up and left. They had many discussions about these things, but she was just too distracted by the rest of life. As sweet and gentle and compassionate as she was, she still couldn't let go of all of those things that immense wealth can buy. And who could blame her? How many people could just walk away from that type of life that easily? Not that Landau wanted to just up and leave and give it all up, he just didn't care as much and was not attached to any of it. Did he like nice things? Sure, who doesn't? But he could also do without. She struggled with it and didn't want to give up the lifestyle, so they grew apart. As their relationship began to struggle, he left to search the world for answers. She took it as him leaving her, and he took it as her not wanting to be with him.

That was a long time ago. It seemed liked forever ago and now, she calls out of the blue. Landau had other women vying for his attention. But now he was so focused and busy with everything that the deeper they got into all of this, the more he took the responsibility upon himself as the shepherd of the flock. He felt like he owed them all that he had, and a relationship was the last distraction he needed. And as some women would try to gain his attention, they saw he would have nothing of it and they respected it. Unfortunately, this really started to isolate him in some ways. His friend, Charles, was one of the only people who could really approach him on a much more personal level and speak frankly with him about these types of things.

—ɯ—

The Maxwells were excited that there was finally a good core of children enrolled at the Genisova school and had decided to make the move after the end of their current school year.

The day had finally arrived and they were ready for their new adventure. This was not the typical situation as this was an entire family that would be making the move. They had decided to sell their house and most all of their larger possessions, likes cars and furniture and treadmills. There was really no point in keeping anything that they couldn't bring with them. They could have put it all in storage but decided that if Genisova did not work out they would just buy a new house and replace everything they got rid of. Everything they needed would be provided for them when they arrived there. The children brought many of their favorite toys and things that children like to have. It was no problem at all. They would be living in an attached condo which was pretty much like a small house. It was not all that different from where they lived before. The big questions for them would be what would the children do with themselves beside go to school?

They were told to rent a vehicle and given directions to Genisova. They arrived with no problems and were welcomed as everyone else was on their first day. They knew that they would be beginning the program the next day but it would be as different for the children as it was for the adults. School had not begun yet, but there was a modified program for the kids to attend in the summer time. The children at Genisova actually went to school most of the calendar year with a little bit longer break in the summer. It was the suggested time for people with kids to come to Genisova. It really made the transition much easier on everyone. Jonathan and Theresa wanted to do everything they could to help with this huge life change they were all going through.

Jonathan spoke to both children, "Are you guys ready to begin tomorrow morning?"

Beatrice, who went by Beau for short, replied, "I am ready but not sure what's going to happen. I am a little worried about making new friends."

"I am sure you will make many new friends, but it may take a little time at first. People have to move all the time all over the world, so other children know that this is part of life."

"Do you know if they have a playground here? Do we get to go out for recess?"

"Yes, they have a great playground here, and you absolutely get to go out for recess."

"That's good, because I don't think I would like it here if they didn't."

Her mom and dad both laughed. "What about you Chase?"

"Well, I am excited about the science experiments they told us about. Some of the things they do we never do in our old school. It seems like school might actually be pretty fun, maybe. I do hope all the other kids are nice to us. You never know how kids are going to be. It seems like if people are here, then they are here for a good reason and that must mean they are at least sorta good people, right?"

"That is a good point, and I would hope you are right. Time will tell. We are all a little nervous and curious as to what is going to happen. We would have never agreed to come here in the first place if we didn't think it was going to make all of our lives better."

The family gets settled in and gets a good night sleep before they start their new adventure.

Andrew had to do a little convincing of his friends as to why he was taking this new assignment and basically disappearing for a short period of time, and potentially a little longer. He had many friends that he hung out with socially, but, in truth, had very few close friends in his life. Two to be exact and one was married and the other lived far away. He had never developed any close relationships in the time that he had been in the new city he lived in. He had been on quite a few dates and most all of them were short-lived. He would continue to date for physical reasons or would end it because he was not interested. There were also quite a few that never returned his calls. Either way he was not involved with anyone seriously. There was one girl in particular that he had really wanted to try and get closer to, but the feelings were not mutual. Her name was Astrid. They had been on several dates but they reached a point where she began to not show as much interest and it ended. He had moved on, but never forgot her.

He did not get rid of any of his things. He decided that he would continue to rent his apartment and that if he ended up staying longer than he thought he would sub-lease it until he was done. He had arranged for a friend to help with this if it ever were to happen. His flight landed safely at the closest airport and he was found by his ride pretty swiftly. He wondered if his paperwork had been red flagged because of who he was and if they would treat him differently because of this. His drivers name was Fiona. She was very attractive and this caught him slightly off guard. She was athletic with long dark hair and piercing, green eyes that belonged on a tiger. Andrew had figured they would send a man dressed in khakis and a blue button down with a dry personality.

"How are you today Andrew?" she asked.

"I'm quite fine, thanks for asking. And how are you?"

"I'm great. We are so excited to have you here. Are you excited also?"

He had decided that the story that he was going to go with was that he needed a break from the limelight and was doing some soul searching, maybe looking for something deeper in life, possibly even a career change. He would ride it out as long as he could and then just say he really missed his career, friends, and his lifestyle.

"I am eager to get started and see what this is all about, how this process works. I am hoping it will help me find the answers I am looking for in life."

"Well, we are hoping you find what you are looking for too," she said this with a twinge of—we know what you are up to, don't worry. But still said it with sincerity making Andrew wonder what to think about her.

"I think you will be surprised as to what you are going to find out about not only what goes on here, but also about yourself."

Once again, she had this tone of—I know something you don't know— about her.

"Oh, and why is that?" Andrew tried to sound unconvinced.

"I just do. I would tell you more, but why ruin the surprise."

Andrew was really not expecting a greeting like this. He had already imagined how it was going to go. They would not be nice and would not say much of anything. They would treat him like the enemy. An invader who was going to try and defraud them and what they were doing. This was not at all the welcome he thought he would get.

"That's fair," he replied. "I have to admit, you are much cheerier than I thought you would be."

"What did you think, we would just pick you up and drop you off like a chauffeur? You sit in the back with the window up between us? That's not at all how this works. You are sitting up in front with me and you are now a friend, hopefully one of us. We all can't wait to get to know you. We know who are on TV, but we also know that is not who you really are. That is not the person behind the face on TV. We want to get to know who you really are. So, Andrew, who are you?"

"Whoa, jumping right into it, are we?"

"Why not? Of course, we all know that you work for a major news corporation and are most likely being assigned here to get a story, but since you want something from us, we first want something from you."

"Okay...I guess we are jumping right into it. How do you know I am not here for other reasons?"

"We don't, and we hope you are. It really doesn't matter because we are going to treat you the same as anyone else that comes here. Like I said, I think you are going to be surprised as to what you find."

"What am I going to find?"

"For starters, you're going to find yourself."

"That sounds like a canned, cliche response if I've ever heard one," Andrew scoffed.

"That's true, but it is the truth. You'll see. I think I am going to stop here and just let the process begin to take shape. I am really looking forward to getting to know you. I hope you try and take all of this somewhat seriously. I'll share this one last thing. The people who work here are very good at what they do. They are very good at reading people and will not give you the information you are looking for unless they see some authentic effort on your part. Let's just say you won't be able to fake it. But, for what its worth, if you let it, it will change your life for the better."

As they approached the gate Andrew inquired about the security surrounding the property. There appeared to be no fence or wall to speak of, but as they got closer he saw something he didn't notice before. Spread about 50 feet or so apart were little pods about one foot in diameter just sitting on the ground.

"Are those for security purposes?" he asked Fiona.

"You could say something like that."

"Why, do they need to keep people out?"

"For the most part there is no reason to worry about keeping anyone out. But, I don't need to explain to you the world we live in, do I? There are things going on here or there will be things going on here that will most likely require higher security."

"Now you have my attention. But you keep talking about the elusive future. Is there really anything that important that's going to be happening here? Or is it all just hype to arouse curiosity."

"I know I keep saying this but you'll just have to wait and see."

The rest of the drive to his new place revealed nothing too out of the ordinary. Regular buildings set in a scenic setting, definitely carefully planned and executed to a T. Andrew went up to his room and wondered more about this interesting woman that had escorted him from the airport. He didn't want to admit it but he did find everything about her intoxicating. Geez, that's the last thing he needed to do was fall for the first person he met here. This was not at all going as he had expected. What next? He had kind of an unsettled feeling and yet, somewhere inside him he had this calm feeling that everything was going to be just fine. He was now somehow ready to open his mind and be open to whatever would come next.

—⟶∭⟵—

It had been quite a while since Lu had called and talked to Charles on the phone about Landau and Genisova. She decided that she was going to actually go to Genisova and see what would happen when she arrived. She did not want Landau to know about her coming, but was not sure if it was possible, considering his position there. She called back again and talked to Charles and inquired if it would be possible to show up without letting him know. He said he would have to discuss this with some other Council members behind Landau's back and did not feel very comfortable doing it.

"Charles, you know me, I am not some crazy lunatic trying to undermine everything you are doing there. I am just curious as to what it is actually like there. You are the one person besides Landau that knows me well enough to understand what I am doing here. It is completely innocent. I have reached a point in my life where I need to explore these feelings I have to make sure I haven't made the biggest mistake of my life."

"I just don't know how I could actually swing getting it by him. And I don't understand the secrecy to it. Why don't you want him to know? What if I say no?"

"I feel like if he knows that I am coming that he will act differently. I do know him, despite all the years apart. I know that it would change his reaction. I'm not going to lie, I want it to be a surprise of some sort. If you decide that you can't, then I will just go through the normal route and sign myself up."

"He already knows that you called me. We discussed our conversation. We are very open here about things like this. "

"Is there any real harm in not letting him know? I assume he will know the moment I get there."

"Do you know everything that is involved in coming here? Or, are you just planning on coming here for a day trip? It doesn't work that way. There is a method to all of this and there is quite a bit at stake here. We don't take things of this nature lightly. If you are serious about coming here for the long haul, then you better know what you are getting into."

"I don't know if it is something I want to do, but isn't that why people come and try it out?"

"Most people look into what this is all about first. There is a bit of a process to go through to come here and you should do some thorough investigating into what you are getting into. If you are really serious, I will send you a welcome package and you can decide for yourself if you want to take it seriously. If you make up your mind that this is what you want, and you're not just coming here to put on a scene for Landau, then I will listen to your intentions."

"That sounds like a fair deal. Send me the info and I will get back to you."

"Good bye Lucina."

Suzi was conflicted as to what to do with her life. Some of the greatest minds in her field were leaving their conventional careers for this Genisova and it was awfully compelling for her to join them. There were several issues that she would have to face if she were to make this move. Probably the most glaring one was her fiancé. She had mentioned to him several times about this place. He made it appear like he was listening intently, but then quickly moved on to the next subject, giving her the sense that he felt it was just a silly, little passing fad. However, this is how most of their conversations went. There was never really much depth to their conversations. Talk about their careers, which had entirely nothing to do with each other and then small talk about the weather, politics, whatever was on the front page of the news.

It never went much further than that. Someone listening in from the outside would probably never guess that they were engaged to be married.

Why were they engaged, she sometimes wondered? He was attractive, in shape, intelligent, successful in his career. They both made fairly good money and had taken several nice vacations together. They went to parties with their friends, played golf and tennis at the different clubs in town, went to concerts or the symphony, all the things that people of their status do, whatever that means. But they did all of it. It was a nice agreement between them. Their love life was moderately satisfactory, enough so that they both felt like it was good enough to say I do. She did sometimes wonder if there was something more to it, though. Should there be more to the intimacy or their conversations? It did oftentimes leave her with an almost empty feeling afterwards. But then, quickly on to the next thing, whatever would occupy their attention. All was well.

Essentially, things were okay, and there were no major issues, so why not go to the next step, which is marriage. The actual conversation they had about getting married someday went something along the lines just described. Neither of them got over emotional about it and it ended with a nod of the head, signifying that it was a done deal, just like that. When he did propose, she accepted very nonchalantly and then they kissed and moved on to the next thing. Not much flair for anything in their life. Except for their work. Let's talk about stars and planets and red shifts and supernovas...now we are getting worked up. Mutual funds, IRA's, hedge funds....now we are getting aroused. It's just the way they were wired.

But, now, there was something else going on inside of Suzi. She was very much considering trying out this Genisova thing, purely for advancing her career. How would she tell Darius? Would he take her seriously? She had decided that if she would do this that she would approach it as a temporary thing. She would explain it to him as though this was a chance to boost her resume and work beside some amazing and gifted people. Not an opportunity that comes around everyday. They had not made any plans for the wedding yet, so she could say that it could wait, even play it like if it's meant to be we will be just fine afterwards. If not, then it wasn't meant to be.

"So Darius, you know that Genisova I have been talking to you about?" began Suzi.

"Umm, I vaguely remember you mentioning something about it," he lied.

"Well, there are a couple of people working there that are at the top of my field, and I have been invited to work beside them." She didn't exactly know this for sure, but she had assumed that if she did make the move, they would have no other place to put her but beside these people. It actually was a perfect situation in that sense. I mean, where else would they place her, finance?

"And, what are you saying? Are you thinking about moving there?" he replied mockingly.

"Maybe. It would just be temporarily. It would be a bit of a risk, but how many times do you get opportunities in your field to do something like this? It really is the opportunity of a lifetime. I might regret this big time if it don't do it." She now had his complete attention.

"How long are we talking here? Can you leave and come visit? Is this the place you were talking about that is like a secret little town?" He is now starting remember whispers of their previous conversation.

"I do think I can leave whenever I want. But I think it is frowned upon to be leaving all the time, like every weekend. There are other aspects to this whole thing, parts that I am not as excited about, but may be willing to put up with if it provides me the opportunity to work with these people." Darius was now squirming in his seat a little bit and all sorts of things were flying through his mind.

"Wow, I guess I never really thought you would actually consider doing something like this? What about the wedding?"

"What about it? We haven't even planned one thing for it. There is no date, no anything. It could wait. Are you in a sudden rush? When were you thinking of getting married?"

"I don't know, I just thought those were the things that women got excited about and planned. I would just go along with what you wanted."

"Yeah, right. I got it. But I haven't planned anything yet. Maybe this is the reason why. If I do do this, then when I get back I would definitely begin planning everything." She had just decided that this could be her selling point.

"How long would you be gone? Do you have any idea?"

"Not really. I think the typical period of time is like 6 months to a year."

"Okay," he took a big breath, "that is a long time. This is a lot to process. I can't believe you are just going to up and leave for a job. We have a life together here. Who will I go to the movies with?"

Suzi did feel bad for him in some ways, but part of her was starting to feel like she was just a body, a robot, there to keep him from being lonely. "Is that all I'm good for is a movie partner? You can go to a movie with anyone. Call your sister or your mother. Really? The movies?"

"That's not what I meant. I meant we do so many things together, you know like couples often times do. They enjoy each other's company. At least I thought we did."

"I do enjoy your company and I do want to marry you, but I am not sure I want to pass up this opportunity. Is there any chance you would be interested in coming with me? I am sure there isn't, but I thought I would ask anyway."

"I feel like you have already made up your mind about this, like I was never even part of the equation. This really should have been something we both talked about before you made the decision on your own."

"I did mention it several times and you blew it off. Plus, I knew what you would say—no way! I knew there was no chance you would be interested in something like this, because I wouldn't either if I was you. There is no upside for you to go other than to be with me. And, this may not even turn out to be something I even like. I may start it and a couple weeks later decide it's not for me and then we both would have quit our jobs and have to start over. I have actually talked with my department head and he said that if I leave there is a slight chance I could come back to my job within a year's time. They could treat it like a sabbatical."

"Man, this is just crazy. You have already made up your mind without me."

"Sort of. I was just hoping you would be supportive. You could come with me, but like I said, I am not sure what you would do there." She is now just trying to appease him and make him feel better, although she feels like it would be a bad idea for him to go. "We could always see how it goes and if you decide in a month that you want to give it a try you could."

"Well, I think you should do what you think is best for your career. If this is the big opportunity you say it is, then you should go for it. I'm not really sure what I would do if I was offered a chance of a lifetime and it was on the other side of the country. I guess we would be having some big decisions to make then also."

They decided together that they would take it day by day, and week by week, and see how it goes. Suzi decides to contact Genisova the next day and see what they want her to do next. She is sent the paperwork to get started and begins taking the next steps on this unexpected new adventure.

—∞—

Lu did get the package and looked through everything. There was no denying that her true intentions were to try and get closer to Landau, and at least find out if there was still anything left between the two of them. She was now coming to the realization that this was the way of life he would be living from now on. This was not just a small commitment for him. There was no turning back. She was not sure Genisova would be for her, but this could be a great trial to see if it was. Could she handle being away from all the luxuries she was so used to? Life was good. Cushy. She was attractive and men would bend over backwards for her. She had plenty of money, mostly inherited through her father's family and she really never had to work another day if she wanted.

She had met Landau long ago at a party of one her friends. He was rich and handsome, and yet, very different from anyone else she had dated. He didn't talk about the things the other boys that she dated talked about. Lucina had piercing blue eyes and long, light brown hair with natural wave to it. He found her attractive and sweet and a little bit mysterious, but after their first conversation he was not that awestruck. It actually took some time. He moved on to another group talking about computers or science, and she was left standing there as though she didn't exist. She wasn't used to being passed over for someone else, and the someone else was not another attractive female.

He was not interested. But, he was this deep thought provoking man and clearly had his mind on other things. She knew he found her attractive, but he conveyed very quickly it would have to be about much, much more than that. Now that she thinks about it, it was there all along. He was like that from the start. She was the one who chased after him. She called her friend and asked more about him. She actually began pursuing him, and although he was used to women trying to throw themselves at him, this was a bit different. She became relentless, in a fun way, and eventually he agreed to go out on a date. From the get-go, he was very up front with her about his intentions in life, but she didn't listen very carefully. She just thought most of it was all talk.

They did have an intense chemistry, and their relationship flourished. It was a magical ride for a while. But they also both knew there was something off between them. Eventually they began to fade away from each other. Landau was more focused on digging deeper into enlightenment and she was more into her status of dating him. He had tried to have many conversations with her about his quest in life and she just thought it was cute.

One time he had asked her what she thought her purpose in life was, and she replied, "To live life to the fullest." This one sort of stumped him because in many ways it was true. She didn't seem to care about enlightenment because she was happy with her life the way it was, and she seemed to have found contentment in some form, although maybe not the type he was looking for.

Nonetheless, she was content, or seemed to be. In this way, her simplicity intrigued him. He wanted her to be more complex, because he thought that to have a more fulfilling life you had to have more depth to it. But, maybe he was overthinking things and it really was that simple. Of course, her life was simple because she had it made and has never had to face any adversity. She did go to a prestigious university and did work as an executive in a major clothing corporation, because she loved fashion. And, she was good at it, even though she was given the job because of who she was. Life at the top really is just about who you know and where you come from.

Landau on the other hand, came from much less, and had to work much harder to get where he was. He was extremely gifted and was always good at whatever he did. Things came easy to him and then at some point he realized this and wanted to make things harder for himself. He could never get away from a nagging feeling inside him. It was this feeling that he would keep searching his entire life for a greater understanding of the universe and come up empty in the end. He had to go deeper and find something more. He wasn't sure why, but something inside made him keep searching. There had to be something more to life. This was how his search for more meaning began.

Lu knew that there was more going on, but she also knew that he was this super savvy business man with some major technology corporations to run. He had to stay grounded to some degree. He couldn't just up and leave and go off on some crazy expedition to the corners of the earth. Well, boy, did she underestimate him. He started planning things a year in advance before his leave. He fully planned on being accessible while he was gone so he could keep things running as smooth as possible. He could also jet home in the wink of an eye if need be. But, when he decided to up and leave she still did not take him seriously. She reacted by putting more distance between them, even though it wasn't what she wanted to do. It was very difficult to leave her behind, but he felt like he had to stand behind his beliefs, and if they were meant to be, then the universe would bring them back together in the end.

For this group of newcomers their day began the next morning at 9 AM in a classroom in one of the learning and development buildings. Jacob, Suzi, Andrew, Theresa and Jonathan pretty much all felt like they were going to school again. This orientation would be much different then any class they had ever been to before. There were some basic instructions given by a woman named Lavender and then they were each given a standard issue of items all Genisovians received when they arrived. They were also assigned a time to go and meet with the director of security to be taught basic procedures and rules. This was also when their different signatures would be given to Genisova, like fingerprints, but also eyes and voice recognition, a strand of hair, and other things to help identify them. In the box of things there was a tablet/computer, a watch, a pair of goggle-type glasses and a few other items. Lavender told them they would be getting instructions on how to use these things and what they were for later.

Landau and his friends, Charles and Fiona, were sitting at the front of the room waiting for them all as they entered. It was not like the cold-sterile looking classrooms you went to at college or university. It was instead more like a living room with comfortable chairs, and once again well decorated to set the mood. Of course, not one of them knew what that mood was supposed to be. They were all going through a lot of different emotions, but somehow the room had a sense of ease and calmness about it.

"Welcome to Genisova," Landau began. "This is Charles and Fiona, and they both have been here at Genisova since the beginning. You will be seeing a lot of them and getting to know them very well during your stay here. We are so glad you have decided to come join us on this journey towards the future. You all have your own reasons for making this decision and I guarantee it is not the same for any of you, yet, you are all still here. This moment is the only moment that matters in your life right now and we are honored to have you here. We know you all have a ton of questions and you will have an opportunity to do so, but I want to begin by telling you a little about me and Genisova.

"You all know who I am, I think, and probably know most of the obvious stuff most people know about me. If not, then here it is. I grew up in a house the same as most, but what may have been different was the way my parents did some things. A love of knowledge in all ways, unconditional love without judgment of anyone and the pursuit of a deeper meaning in life. Ever since I could remember there was always talk about the bigger picture and the search for answers to the questions that evade us all. Eventually, I earned degrees in business, programming, and space engineering, along with a masters in philosophy and spirituality. Many don't know that. I went on to create three different companies, each with different types of products in various fields. You know most of these and they have created incredible wealth for me and many around me. But there is more to life to money and the desire went deeper.

"I decided that in order to find a greater understanding of myself and the mysteries of the universe I would need to leave my comfortable circumstances and look elsewhere for answers. Some time ago I began searching all around the world for a new understanding of the mysteries that evaded me and truly find the meaning to life here on earth and in this universe. This is the age-old question that virtually everyone ponders at one time or another in their lifetime. As I just said, my companies had brought me great wealth. This provided me with the means to do things that most people in this world do not have. If there was or still is anything in this world I want, I could most likely have it. Now I'm talking about things that can be bought, not things like love, happiness, and contentment. Such a tricky word, right? Contentment. What does make us content? When are we content and truly happy? Why am I telling you about my ability to buy anything the world would make available to us? Not to brag, but to make a point. Because it did not buy me love or happiness or contentment. Now, did I have moments of this in my life? Yes, of course. But they were always fleeting.

"Let me tell you that I used my means to search this earth for answers to my questions, and I'm not going to lie, money will let you go to some pretty great extremes in search of whatever it is you are looking for. I spared no cost in my search. And after a short while it became apparent to me that this search would require much more than money. It was going to require patience, time, effort, and most of all sacrifice. The answers to the greatest questions of all time would not come easy. This I began to understand. I had studied all the different religions of the world but realized there was a difference between studying and living. So I immersed myself in different religions seeking clues, and I did find many answers. I realized that the answer is different for everyone. We each seek answers on a different level.

"It is only recently in our human history that we have freed up enough time in our lives to have the freedom to actually sit and ponder the greater meanings of life. You may or may not actually care about any of the things I care very deeply about, and that's perfectly fine. One thing that I have learned is that judging people in any way serves no purpose whatsoever. And I strive to not judge others, but when the news was brought to my attention that there were sudden and severe changes taking place with our sun, something changed inside of me. I suddenly felt a new purpose in life and although I had made a pact not to judge others, I swore I would not sit back and do nothing. I won't judge others who do not care about what is happening with our planet, but I won't sit back and let their indifference keep me from doing something.

"I knew something had to be done, and sitting back waiting for our government or any other government to do anything would be futile. This is when I seized the opportunity to create Genisova and create an opportunity for hope. This place is open to anyone who wants to come and contribute towards that hope for our future, for this planet will not support life for us forever and it looks as though it may not support life for our grandchildren someday. But in creating this world we have decided that even though anyone may enter, we are going to try to ensure that you become all that you were meant to be. What does this mean? It is different for everyone, but it is a journey that we take together and you discover that answer for yourself. It is not always an easy, straightforward process, but since our inception we have found this process works for the most part, one way or another. All we ask is that you give it an earnest attempt and time for it to work."

He then gestured to his left. "Fiona." Fiona walked to the front of the room.

"Hi everyone. I hope your trip and stay thus far has been pleasant. I would now like to give you a little more detail and information as to how things work here. I was one of the first members of Genisova and I can say from firsthand experience that if you let it, it will change your life. And in the process we are all working towards building a new future and the means to survive the inevitable threat from our own star, the sun. Like Landau mentioned you are all probably here for different personal reasons but somehow your journey has brought you here to the same place. We hope that eventually we are all on a similar path to a similar goal. The basic principles as to how things work here are as follows. You will begin your process by following a carefully laid out plan that will be slowly modified as we get to know you better and find out what works best for each person.

"There will be a series of classes and assignments that you will complete. They will consist of things like improving diet and health, exercising, self discovery, meditation or prayer, stress reduction, time management, business, science, language, arts and music and many more. These are just a sampling of the types of the things you will be delving into. You will not be tested on these things and the direction that you will be taking will be individualized and different from everyone else. It is the overall well being self enriching part of the process. For why build a new hope for the future if the people involved in it are not fully prepared and at their best. During this process as we get to know you better, together we will be figuring out how each of you will be contributing to life here.

"As you may know, there is no money here. We have found that money is the source of most all of our problems as humans in this world. It is not an easy process to eliminate money from our daily lives. You all still have a bank account from the lives that you left behind. That money will still be there for you if you ever do decide to leave. But here, we think you will find that many of your problems will go away when you are not having to worry about money. Your basic needs will be taken care of and if you really desire something it can be obtained. We ask that you start simple, with just the basics that you need in life. Maybe a few things that you purely enjoy and maybe can't live without right now. As time goes by those things may stay with you or you may find that they fall to the wayside.

"How does it work with there being no money here? It certainly did not just happen over night. It has been a slow process. In the beginning we needed many things from the outside world. As time went by we learned what we truly needed and began to make them here. These are the jobs that need to be filled by the people that live here. We are still not completely independent from the outside world and may never be completely, but we have the means to buy those things that we need. All we ask is that you not take for granted how this system works and not abuse it. It is an honor system of sorts and it has worked very well since it began.

"There is so much more to Genisova. You do have the freedom to leave whenever you need, but we ask for open and honest communication about this. There are many activities for everyone here to do. We have every type of sport facility, many outdoor activities including skiing in the winter and kayaking in the summer and many, many more things to choose from. If there is something missing we are sure it can be figured out. We are serious about our process, but we all like to have fun, too. I know you have many questions and we don't have time for them all today but let's give you an opportunity to express what's on your mind."

Suzi wasted no time getting right to her point. "So how will we know what job we will be assigned? I quit my job because of an opportunity to work with some of the great minds of my field here. Is there some guarantee I will be working with them? I was personally invited by someone here who told me I would get to work with these people."

"Okay, that is a great question," began Charles. "Although I would never make a promise I can't keep and I don't like to make guarantees about anything in life, if you were asked to come here to help in a very specific field that is most likely where you will end up. However, this is not a contract agreement and there is a process to how this all works. Placement of jobs is not given for quite some time and I would only hope that your lone reason for coming here is not only for your career. I can assure you that most of the people you came here to work beside did not come here only to advance their career."

"Okay, well, I was just wondering how the placement actually worked," Suzi inquired.

"During this first year of the process there will be much discussion about what our purpose is and what we are meant to be doing. There are many people that came here thinking they would be doing something similar to what they were before, and then discovered they would much rather be doing something else. What is it that you do again, Suzi?"

"I am an astrophysicist. I was searching other star systems and galaxies for planets that could inhabit life."

"Ahh, yes, I remember now. Well, you never know, you just may find out that you were never meant to be an astrophysicist, although I do think that is pretty awesome and hope you don't change your mind about it. We actually need more people in your field around here."

A few people laughed, including Suzi. Andrew's eyes perked up when he mentioned the part about needing more astrophysicists around here. What was that supposed to mean, he wondered. Who needs more astrophysicists anywhere? Very interesting.

"The point is, we want to help everyone explore what it is they truly want to be doing, not just doing some job in a field they ended up stuck in. It is an ongoing conversation and self-discovery process. Without the concern of money, people are truly free to search for the things they are passionate about in life. Many people in life are doing things they really don't enjoy doing. We want to change that. Just think of how much more we could accomplish as a human race if everyone was doing exactly what they wanted to do and should be doing. People would be so much more productive and driven and excited about their work. It is true there are some jobs that have to be done that no one likes to do, but there is always a solution for that."

"Anyone else have something on their mind?" Charles asked.

Andrew decided to jump right in. "What are some of the rules around here we don't know about? Are there any things off limits? How often can we leave and how long can we be gone?"

"Also very good questions," replied Landau. "Yes, there are boundaries that you have to play within. Genisova is quite large, but you may not leave through any way but the main gate. There is a second gate but it is not operational yet. It will be part of the next phase of Genisova. You don't need to ask permission to leave, but we recommend you tell us you are leaving and when you are returning. The boundaries are marked on a map pretty clearly and there are warnings before you get close to the actual invisible fence. Yes, there is an invisible fence and, no, you are not dogs. This is a very advanced fence that will actually prevent you from leaving if you try. It will not hurt you, but let's just say a human could not penetrate it by herself. It also will keep people out, although we do not expect any company besides those already here. In time as we progress and get bigger and more people want to know what is going on here, we may find that some people will try to get in. We are not prepared for a mass invasion, but if there are a couple of stray intruders we can take care of that. We are a peaceful place and do not plan on creating any enemies, but we know how the crazy world operates sometimes.

"You may come and go as you please. However, it is not recommended that you abuse this policy. Especially when you first begin here, we advise staying for as long as you possibly can before leaving. Of course, there are a plethora of reasons why you may have to leave and we are just fine with that. As the process moves forward we hope that you will have the wisdom to make the proper choice for yourself. We think it will become more and more obvious as you take this journey what is best for you."

"At approximately the one-year mark you will be evaluated on your readiness for the next stage of your journey. Some people will be ready well before this and for others it may take some time before moving on. There is a council here that oversees everything that takes place. You will be getting to know all of them very well. They will be in charge of making sure you are ready to move on to the next phase."

"So, what do you mean, second phase?" asked Jonathan. "And, are we going to be graded on our performance?"

Landau paused, and then sighed a little. "I think everyone has the same concern when they get here. No, you're not going to be graded on anything. But, ultimately we are working towards something greater, something to help continue our existence once the sun has kicked us off of this planet. In order to do that there are certain standards we will have to expect of each other. It can't just be a free for all or people would not continue to work towards our end goal. This part seems difficult from the outset, but I guarantee that as we begin this process it will make more and more sense. Most of us would not be here if they were not serious about the cause. It is built into the system. The evaluation part is mostly for those people who may be confused about our purpose. That's it. If you are truly committed it will be no problem. I would tell you more, but I cannot at this point. You will just have to have some trust in what we are doing."

At this point Andrew began to feel a little sheepish about being here, but decided that he was too curious about everything at this point to quit. He was no longer scared about what was going to happen and, of course, he only just met Fiona. She's worth staying for at least a couple weeks.

Suzi became a little concerned about this statement too as she was purely there to work with the leaders in her field. Little did they both know that Landau and the council already had a firm grasp on their intentions, but had seen this before and would let it run its course as they had in the past.

"Other questions?" asked Fiona.

"What about places of worship?" asked Mohammed. "Are there any designated areas for people who want to practice their faith or beliefs?"

Charles decides to take this one. "Yes, we do have a place set aside for people to worship. It is merely a room in one of the buildings. We do not have any specific churches or synagogues or mosques to speak of at this point. It could certainly be entertained at some point on the future. We embrace diversity here and encourage people to continue being who they were before they came here. We envision the future being a modified smaller version of the outside world in many ways. Many people that already live here are spiritual in nature, but I would say not so religious. There are certainly people of all faiths already here and functioning very well. I cannot speak for any of them, but from what I see and hear from them I would say that they all believe there is not only one correct religion. People are very accepting of all walks of life. That is part of our goal here."

"What do you believe?" asked Mohammed, deciding to be very forthright.

"I believe in many things. I think we are all so different and come from so many different backgrounds and upbringings that it seems to me it would be impossible for everyone to believe the same thing. If you look at the history of religion it says a lot about the human species, but most of all it says we are not really sure what the true answers are. Of course, most will claim they have the answers, but if you study their histories you will begin to see how often they change their mind. Personally, I think that is the way it should be. It should be different for everyone. I think that the core ideas behind most religions have good intentions. When you start to get into the specifics it gets a little muddy. I don't believe it has to be that complicated. Much of the arguing and fighting in our history is because of religion. That, to me, is ironic. Peace and love have very little to do with violence. There are many parts to the religious life that I do appreciate, and I believe we are all spiritual beings. I could go on for a while but that seems like it would be more appropriate at a later time."

Mohammed had many more questions burning inside, but decided it may be better to ask at another time. "Thanks for sharing some of your thoughts."

"Are there any more questions? If not, then we would like to begin a tour around the area helping to get you familiar with everything."

Everyone was ready to get up and stretch and just walk around a bit. Their heads were spinning a little from everything they heard. Most were trying to grasp some of the ideas mentioned and deal with a whole new set of feelings they were not anticipating feeling. Not that they were bad, just different. So many things to think about. What was everything about the next phase of Genisova and what was the end goal they seem to keep talking about? What was the solution to getting off this planet? And what was that about a gate to another area they haven't begun yet?

As they all got up and start walking out, the three leaders showed the way. They began walking around the building and showing them the different rooms and what they are for. This building seemed to be designed more for just basic meetings and gatherings of different sorts. There was a very nicely furnished kitchen which could be used for preparing food, for entertaining guests and some simple dining areas. It was cozy. The next couple buildings they went into seemed to be geared towards education, with laboratories and libraries. It was starting to feel a little bit like college, however more relaxed and comfortable. No desks and hard chairs. Couches and comfy chairs, tables and lamps, small kitchens with snacks and drinks. Very casual and appealing. If they were going to be studying or learning, this was the way to do it. In an environment that didn't look like you were going to be studying or learning.

Suzi belts out, "Man, I wish my college classes were held in places like this. It would have made thing so much better." There were people spread out throughout the buildings doing what appeared to be taking classes, studying or talking with instructors about various things. Everyone seemed to be very pleasant and enjoying themselves. People would smile and make eye contact and gave a friendly 'hello' or 'how are you?'

The next couple of buildings were for eating and recreational use. A simple restaurant, a building with gym equipment for working out, with bikes, weights, treadmills, and various other exercise rooms. Most all of the areas had small kitchens with simple foods and drinks. You could tell that everything was well thought out. And, of course, everything was very keenly decorated. The person in charge of that certainly had a talent and you could sense it. The mood set by the décor matched the purpose of each building very closely. It was uncanny. There were several people busy working out and exercising. There was one room that had a yoga class going on.

Fiona had noticed that Jacob was pretty quiet during everything thus far and wondering if he was feeling uncomfortable about anything so she asked him, "What do you think about all of this so far Jacob?"

"I'm just so happy to be here. My life before was not all that spectacular and I feel lucky to be here. If everything you're saying is true I'm sure I'll be very happy here. I never had much in life, so where I am living now is already nicer than where I was. My job was not very fun so I'm a little concerned about what I'll be doing here. I don't have much education and I'm not trained in very many things."

Fiona looked at him lovingly and said, "We are so excited to have you here. We are honored that you chose to make this big change for yourself and your future. We know that together we will find a suitable place for you and your talents. Maybe you have talents you never knew you had. We are going to do some self exploration and discovery to find out what it is that is best for you. It will be an amazing journey."

Andrew was walking in the group trying his best to stay near Fiona. He was trying to think of any angle to try and strike up something interesting to say to her. Problem was, that he seemed so out of place here that he was conflicted about whether or not he should even approach her at all. He was becoming more mesmerized with her with every little thing she did. The way she talked, the way she carried herself, the way she was so confident. And this whole place was mysterious to him. He never was really one to be in touch with his spiritual side, so he was not in his comfort zone. He was in general a very outgoing and confident person. He was semi-famous as a reporter for CNC, and most people in the news world knew who he was. He lived a life different from the ordinary person, often times in the spotlight, interviewing famous or important, powerful people. He may not come across as arrogant but was definitely self-serving. He knew he would not be able to pull his famous card on Fiona, but that didn't bother him. He decided to just ask her more about herself.

"So how did you end up here, if you don't mind me asking?"

"I had met Landau years ago through my work. One of his companies consulted with our company and I was head of that particular department so I got to know him pretty well. He was very involved with his employees, similar to the way he is now with Genisova. He cared about more than the average employer would about his employees. He knew that if he could have an affect on them personally they would be better employees and make his company more successful. He did the little things and that made everything from the top down that much better with all his companies. When I heard he was leaving the corporate world to take on this new endeavor I signed up right away. He is the type of person who has such an impact on people that it was no surprise how many people followed him here. They all knew he would take care of them. He pours his heart and soul into everything he does. There is just something different about him, not like anyone else I have ever met."

"He does seem to have a different vibe about him. It's hard to explain, it's like a radiant energy that hovers around him. He demands your attention but then when he begins to talk it is not what you expect. You expect a commander-of-an-army tone, but it comes out soft and gentle but still authoritative. Hard to explain, I guess."

"You are pretty observant, I am surprised that you took all that in."

"Well, I am a reporter. We read people all day long. People are our business. You must have thought I was not paying that much attention, eh? Here just for the story, right?"

"Maybe. I'm not really sure about you yet," she said with a half smile.

Andrew left it at that. He had felt some sort of small connection but didn't want to push his luck. He was learning how perceptive all of these people were and your chances of slipping anything past any of them were slim to none.

"Well, I am going to just be open minded about the whole thing and see what happens. I really like everything that has happened thus far. It really is quite a feat that this place is still running so well. I feel like I should be waiting for the other shoe to drop, like one day it's just going to go out of business."

"I don't foresee that happening at all. There is so much to all of this that you don't know yet. It is quite amazing how it all comes together."

"I can't wait to see."

"Well, hopefully you stick around long enough to find out."

Andrew really was beginning to wonder if he would hang around long enough to find out.

The group continued to walk around the small campus of buildings in this vicinity. Some of the buildings had rooms that they did not visit. It was either that there wasn't time to go up there, or it was purposely left out of the tour. Either way, some of the group noticed that these areas were left out. It was now lunch time and they were told that they would be heading to one of the other areas to a restaurant for lunch. There were several different modes of transportation at Genisova, including bikes, hover boards with handle bars, small buses and cars. Mostly people were walking or riding bikes. The group of new arrivals were going to take one of the buses to the next area of Genisova. It seemed to be an electric powered bus, but you couldn't be sure. Charging stations were in a couple different places with some other vehicles plugged into them. It was a different looking plug so it was possibly a new type of energy supply for the vehicles at Genisova.

This was certainly an industrial area. Small factories and office buildings were spread throughout this local vicinity. There was a downtown area with some stores and restaurants but not much else. Trees lined the streets along with beautiful flowers and shrubbery. The landscape artists were attuned to what was going on here.

The bus stopped in front of the restaurant let them out and then headed over to a bus stop area where there were several people already waiting. There was what looked like a mini phone booth with a computer screen inside that was apparently where you ordered a ride to wherever you wanted to go. Landau mentioned that they may be considering making a monorail to get between the different little villages of Genisova.

They also noticed that although some people were wearing everyday normal clothing, many of the people were wearing what appeared to be a type of uniform. Everyone wasn't wearing the same thing, but you could tell that there were different types of clothes that were very similar in design and color and purpose. Very flattering and form-fitting but also comfortable looking. It turned out that these clothes were engineered and made in Genisova. They were made to be comfortable and had built in UV protection and other wicking features that made them great for many different tasks. This idea of uniforms made the ability of Genisova to make clothes much more attainable, and for the most part people loved them. If they didn't like them or wanted a change they could wear whatever they wanted. It wasn't mandatory. Most people found they were over the whole "look at me and what I'm wearing thing" because it didn't really matter to them. It actually made life easier in some ways because there was no stress over thinking about what you were going to wear or what other people think about you because of how you look. And the clothes looked cool because they were designed by a famous fashion designer who now lived there.

"How many different areas or villages are there right now?" asked Andrew.

"There are currently 10 different villages, all with different types of main functions for each area. For example, the area we just came from has the main function of education and development of most of our newest additions. There are also housing and recreation areas, but all villages have variations of those."

"So people live in all the different villages?'

"Yes, people live all over. Genisova has character just like the rest of the world. We really do want people to feel at home here and be able to express themselves. Since our beginning people have been helping build and design this world. The main areas and their purpose had been laid out ahead of time and then we let everyone else help fill in the blank spaces."

They went inside the restaurant and sat down at various tables. A waitress came out to take their order. The chef also came out to say hello. They seemed to be very excited that there were newcomers to their restaurant, like they were very eager to showcase how wonderful the food was going to be. And were they right. The food was amazing. The service was fantastic.

Suzi commented right away, "Wow, this food is amazing!"

"I agree," said Jacob.

Fiona commented, "Well, these people came to Genisova and this is where Genisova took them. It is very apparent that they are doing what they were meant to be doing. And the food mostly comes right here from our own gardens and greenhouses."

Just from taking a bus and eating at a restaurant one could see the difference in the way things were done at Genisova. Everything was well thought out and had a purpose. People were happy because they were doing something they wanted to do and enjoyed doing. It all seemed to make perfect sense so far. When lunch concluded, they were all informed that they would have the rest of the day to do whatever they wanted. Do some sightseeing, relax, get to know some of the other people, just get familiar with everything. The next day they were going to be getting a little bit more of a basic schedule of the beginning of their courses and classes.

―᎗―

The second day was a little different from the first. Each new member was assigned a guidance counselor of sorts. This person was meant to help begin guiding the new participant into creating their own schedule or curriculum for Genisova. They would be given a variety of options for certain classes, but others were for the most part mandatory. There were several different instructors on hand to help explain some of the specifics of each particular class or lesson. Some of the classes were: a brief history of civilization, religions of the world, general politics, the building blocks of science, basic math review, and classic literature. There were more but these were some of the basics.

Now some of the people were extremely educated so, for example, mathematicians were not advised to take basic math review, but the idea was to re-immerse everyone in didactic studies to begin the process of truly discovering what they liked. The classes were designed to be interesting and relevant and keep the most bored student's attention. They hit the highlights, but still had substance to them. Other areas, such as health studies and discernment and meditation or another various form of relaxation and contemplation, were more of the mandatory classes. Exercise of some form was also not optional. The idea was to get everyone in mental and physical shape. And everyone did, to some degree.

Eventually everyone began to feel better than they did before. Of course there were people who were already doing a lot of these things, but there was something about being surrounded by people all trying to accomplish a similar mindset that just created this amazing energy that you would swear was visible. Everything moved together in harmony like a well oiled machine. Most of them did not know the real reasons for why they were going through all of these mental and physical exercises, but there were reasons that eventually they would all understand.

Besides one major event, there were only minor hiccups here and there, but for the most part things would work themselves out. There were people who entered Genisova with misguided intentions and would decide at some point this was not for them. These people were pretty easy to spot and the Council had quite a firm grasp on their situations. They would eventually come around or they would split. If they came around they were given more information as to what was going on deeper inside Genisova; if they did not, they were given very little information. The longer you stayed and more trust you built, the more intel you were given. For there were some cutting edge, high security things going on in Genisova. And as it continued to grow and the number of incredible minds continued to trickle in, the capabilities of Genisova grew exponentially. And these minds were happy, content minds, and these minds were motivated minds. Motivated and inspired to find answers and solutions to save the world. What bigger motivation could one possibly need?

Landau knew the people working beside him had to be working at their top level and for the right reasons. Genisova filtered out all the corrupt and ill-motivated leaders of industries and science that sought only monetary rewards for their abilities. Everyone who has ever worked a job knows what the difference is between working under the stress and pressure to make money versus what it is like to work in a stress-free and happy environment with no worries about how much money you have to make. There was the occasional disgruntled Genisovian who was not happy with what they were doing and was sick and tired of not being able to go and do whatever it was they wanted to do whenever they wanted to do it. These people were encouraged to bring their concerns to the Council and let them sort it out.

Sometimes the people just needed a vacation from it all. Go spend a weekend or even a week and do some of the things you missed doing. Go see your family or friends you missed (however, for the most part, people were allowed to go and do this whenever they wanted). Go see a concert or to a museum or your old favorite restaurant. Most all of the people that signed up for Genisova knew going into it that things like these paled in comparison to what they were trying to accomplish, so even though they might have missed some of these things, it wasn't that big of a deal. And the knowledge that they could up and go do something if they really wanted to at any time, made it easier to swallow.

Part of the curriculum of the first year helped weed out the ones who were truly not that interested or could handle the long haul. Sitting and meditating once is not that big of a deal for most people. Sitting and meditating every other day and eventually every day for extended periods of time becomes a big deal for the person who is lukewarm on being there. It will make you or break you. And for quite a few, when some of the tasks became a little more intense it was time to bail. They would simply leave and go back to their previous life. They would tell people and even reporters of what they knew of Genisova, but it wasn't much. Most of what has been described thus far, which was not any groundbreaking news. For the most part they would say it was some weird meditation camp where they gave you a job and you didn't make any money for what you did. People would then try and ask it if was a cult or religious camp of sorts, but the people would then reply not really, because it wasn't and they knew it. They just didn't know or understand what it truly was. They knew that the end goal was to try and save humanity from the changing sun, but could only say little about that. Maybe they would build a space station or some other great technology. No one could really be sure, because they were told very little about it.

Now about that one major incident. It actually was a probe from the government that was beginning to worry about the potential, and mysteriousness, of Genisova. With this many major players becoming involved, you knew it would only be a matter of time before the government would start fishing around, or at least do their due diligence. They tried to send a couple representatives to do a little unannounced exploring to see what they could find out and they didn't make it past the gate. Then, of course, they had to go through the legal avenues of inspecting and poking and prodding around. The agent's name was Sarkovia and he had a serious way about him all the time. He looked just like one of the bad guys in a James Bond movie. The government probably hired him because of this. They set up a day to come and visit and interview members of the council and other random people. Landau told them they could talk to anyone at any time and that they would give them a brief tour of the major sites. Sarkovia replied this would be a start, and after the first visit, which was to last three days, they would decide how much more they would need to investigate into things. Landau knew that it would do more harm to try and be resistant, so he chose the passive path.

The group of three led by Sarkovia met with Landau and Charles at the Defense Center in the main village. They went into a conference room and were given a drink of choice. Landau greeted them with a pleasurable, "Hello, and how are you gentlemen today?"

"We are doing just fine, quite a bit of travel to get here," replied Sarkovia.

"So, how can I help you all out today?" Landau inquired politely.

"Well, we are here to do some investigating into what is going on at Genisova. There are starting to be several rumors going around, some from better sources than others. Enough though, that we felt we should at least see for ourselves if any of it was true. That, and then there is the part about people like you and him," he pointed at Charles, "and what you are up to here. Being that you are both pretty powerful men, shall we say, out there, in the rest of the world."

"I'm sorry, is there a problem with people like Charles and I being here?" Landau asked. "I'm not exactly sure what you are getting at." He seemed a bit perplexed, but really he wasn't too surprised with the questioning.

"Let's not play dumb here. You have to admit how it would seem quite odd what you are all up to in here. Enclosed little city, trying to seclude itself from the rest of the world. Extremely rich and powerful people like you and him and many others, apparently throwing tons of your own money at this place. And, of course, there are the rumors about the mind-controlling-jedi techniques being used here. It does all smell a little fishy, don't you think?" Sarkovia was now getting right to the point.

Landau smiled and let down his defenses a little. "I understand how this could look possibly much worse than what is truly going on here. There is no mind controlling or anything like that going on here. People are here of their free will and are free to leave at any point they desire. We do help guide people in our ways, but not much more than that."

"That may very well be true and all, but someone needs to look around and see if this really what is going on or not. I do hope that is the case, but unfortunately, there are just too many dishonest people doing all sorts of crazy stuff in the world these days. Well, I guess, since the beginning of time, people have been acting like that, but what are you gonna do?"

"I can assure you that is not going on here. You can look around and talk to whomever you want here. You can even stay and become a member if you want and then you will know for sure that it is the truth," Landau said with a sly smile.

"Um, no, that's okay. I like my life just fine and dandy out there with the rest of the crazies," Sarkovia said sarcastically.

"Well, let me know how you would like to do this. Would you like a tour of all the facilities? That would take quite some time to see, but I can provide you with a map and then you can figure out how you would like to go about this."

"Let's start by just walking around and getting our bearings a little bit. How big is this place actually?"

"It is pretty big. There are actually ten villages, if you will, spread throughout the property." Landau stopped for a second and then had an idea. "You know, now that I think about it, there is one thing that we have been working on here that I would like you to have a look at. I think you may be very interested in this particular field we have made strides in."

"Oh, really. What could we both possibly have the same interest in?" Sarkovia asked.

"You will just have to wait and see," Landau replied.

"Fair enough. Is there some sort of fence that goes all the way around the perimeter? I noticed the odd shaped pods spread apart every 30 feet or so. Are you trying to keep people out, or...in?"

"Out" Landau replied.

"What for?"

"Once you understand a little better what we are trying to do here, it will make more sense. I hope that answer is good enough for now."

Sarkovia seemed to not like this response. He wanted a direct answer and instead received a vague response that told him very little. It definitely made him more interested in finding out why they were trying to keep people out.

"That doesn't really help me much, but I can now see that I am going to have to dig deep to find some of the answers I am looking for."

"You may dig as deep as you want. I guess, one may reply, why does anyone put up a fence around their yard to keep people out? It is a free country last I checked," Landau replied.

"Well, let's get started here. We plan on looking around for a couple days and checking out as much as we can before we report back on what you guys are up to here."

"Sounds great, we look forward to working with you in any way we can help."

This all took place halfway through the second year of Genisova. There was much infrastructure already built, but there was still quite a bit of new construction in the making. Landau told them up front what the purpose was, to try and create a place where people could come and put a dedicated team effort into researching, designing, and ultimately building a solution to the Earth's inevitable problem of the changing sun. There were no light sabers or droids to showcase—yet—and so there was not really much to show them. Basic facilities and buildings designed more for the future of this place. Not much of anything was going on at that point. Mostly it was still trying to get what they called Phase 1 up and functioning well. This basic setup would be the foundation for the next phase, which would be research and development of their solution, whatever it may be.

The officers there to ask questions were a little concerned about what these solutions may be and how they would affect national safety. Landau agreed to let them have limited access, but still some access to what was going on now and in the foreseeable future. To help appease their curiosity, they did give them a sneak preview of the one area of common interest. Surprisingly, Sarkovia did show some interest, and concern, for what they were working on.

Landau knew that if they were going to get off this planet the government was going to have to know what was going on and that would probably be the only way. He was not opposed to the government getting involved, but he did not have to let them control how he was going to go about doing it. He knew that there would be a time when the government may step in and say that something was going to be an issue. But he wasn't doing anything at this point that would warrant them stepping in. The question would be, if in the future, they did go into space, what are the guidelines? Who owns space? Who is to say what you can and can't do once you leave the atmosphere? Time would likely tell.

Suzi tried her hardest to avoid having to meditate or take any religious classes of any sorts. Her advisor, Cedric, was gentle with her and let her start slowly with anything she was adamantly opposed to. He informed her that eventually she would have to try the meditation but only when she was ready. Anything to do with religion could wait for now, too.

"Why are you so opposed to these type of classes?" he asked.

"I don't believe in any of that stuff. I'm really surprised so many of you do. There's nothing there," Suzi replied casually.

"Oh, really. How can you be so sure?"

"Scientific evidence. That is, it is lacking any proof. Something I can measure, witness, anything."

"I see. Let me ask you a question."

"Okay."

"Would you say that you loved your parents and that they loved you in return?"

"Yes, I would have to say yes, why?"

"Can you prove it?"

She just stared back at him, not knowing what to say. "Love is just a feeling, an emotion. It's subjective. It doesn't prove there is a God. It is just word to describe an emotion, which is a chemical reaction inside the body"

"I hear you, but what if our way of looking at spirituality and God was wrong all this time and what we needed was a shift in the way we thought about it?"

"Meaning?"

"Okay, what happens in science when everyone in the field is stuck on a problem? Something no one can solve and has no idea where to begin?" Cedric inquired.

"I don't know. Try something different I guess. What's your point?"

"Exactly. All the great scientific discoveries were made by someone changing the way they thought about the problem. Of course, no one had thought of it before because they never changed their view of looking at it. Will we ever be able to combine quantum physics with general relativity? My guess is it will only occur someday when some brilliant mind completely thinks outside the box and sees something no one ever thought about before."

"And this is how you find God?" came her sarcastic reply. She was having none of it.

"Once upon a time people thought the world was flat, the earth was the middle of the universe and had no idea that gravity even existed. People would have never made these discoveries if they hadn't thought outside the box, from a different perspective.

Maybe this thought process has to be applied to finding a higher power. People can feel things in their heart but there is still a disconnect between the heart and mind. Can the two be connected? I think there are some things going on here that will arouse your curiosity, at least a little bit."

"Like what?" Suzi sounded partially interested.

"Oh, no. I'm not going to give it to you that easily. You think the only things we are working on here are looking for planets and trying to fly space ships?"

"That's why I'm here, to see what you are all up to," she said with a smile.

"That's great. We are very excited to have you here and can't wait to see what you are going to do. You never know what else you may discover on the way."

—⁂—

Mohammed was pretty excited to get started with his program to see where he was going to get placed and what he would be doing. Of course, he was also waiting for the "looks" from anyone but hadn't noticed any yet. People seemed to be generally nice and too concerned about the task at hand. Jonathan and Theresa were fitting in just fine. They were loving every aspect of this whole process. Their big concern was their children, who were having their own problems. Nothing changes the fact that kids will be kids. As enlightened as all the adults strived to be, children could have cared less about things of this matter. An eight year olds primary concern in life is, where is the fun? What I am I going to play with next? Let's play games, let's play sports, let's play video games. Where are the Legos? But also, who are going to be my friends? And this part was a bit tricky here. Kids don't always understand the unwritten code that adults sometimes abide by. They can be mean even when they don't intend to be, and this was already happening for them here. Chase seemed to care less about what the other kids were thinking, but Beau was quite a bit more sensitive to these things.

School had not officially begun, but there was instead an improvised day care where all the children went throughout the day. The existing members that were teachers were essentially in charge of the children year around. Except they were not in class right now. It was pretty much unorganized playing, with an occasional organized camp-like activity. The best part was that all the children's parents were around the corner all the time and could usually break away from their job to come spend time with their kids. Jonathan was eager to get involved with whatever department they wanted him in. The Council was hoping that his transition would go smoothly because they had desires to fast track him. His skills were much needed to help design many different things they were planning.

All the new members found that their transition into Genisova went fairly smoothly, but they all knew there was quite a bit more to it then what was being revealed. Beneath it all was an underlying feeling that there was quite a bit more to come. And their suspicions were right. This format was built into the process. All new members were eased into the whole thing and then were being discreetly evaluated by not only by the Council but also by other members, in particular their instructors. The leaders had a good handle on all the members before they even started. Jacob, Jonathan, Theresa, and Mohammed were all less of a concern to the Council, while Suzi and Andrew were being scrutinized more closely. This is how it went here. There was a lot at stake and even though their gates were open to anyone, there was a code that was meant to be understood by everyone. The end goal was not going to be an easy task and not exactly for the lighthearted or lukewarm volunteer.

Suzi was someone for whom they saw great potential. Her knowledge of space was highly sought after here and her help would be greatly needed. However, there was more to it than that. The founders of Genisova wanted more than just science, because that is what they believed. Not a belief in a religion, but an acknowledgment that there is more to all of this than what we can comprehend at this point in time. The world as we know it was not functioning very well and the current belief systems were insufficient. It was agreed upon at the beginning of Genisova that what all religions sought was something valid, but the way in which they went about getting there was not working. Too many different opinions and too many people that thought their way was the one and only way, and you had to believe it or else you were wrong. Well, just like science is still looking for a theory of everything, so was religion. If there is a God, then they wanted to believe it would be for all religions. If it was the God for all religions than there had to be a theory that worked for everyone. Many people who believe in some sort of a higher power agree with this. Every different religion's idea of God should not be exclusive. To the people of Genisova, this idea to be inclusive was imperative.

The more we learn about space and the rest of the universe, the more we know the probability of another star having a system of planets capable of life. This also makes the idea of a God being exclusive for just Christians or Muslims or Buddhists silly. Is it realistic to think that if there was life on another planet that they would have to believe in Jesus to get to heaven? We have already discovered water on moons in our own solar system, thus exponentially increasing the probability that there is water on other planets or moons somewhere out there. There are billions of stars, just in our galaxy alone. There are billions of other galaxies out there beyond ours and probably, most likely, even more out there that we haven't discovered yet. Billions. BILLIONS! Not a hundred or even a million. That's billions of galaxies with billions of stars each with probably many planets. We have eight planets in our solar system, some with up to 60 moons, some capable of harboring life. It was time to expand the human idea of God. And so Genisova did.

They realized that the possibilities were beyond comprehension and they wanted to expand their horizons. Science alone did not have all the answers. Even if you don't believe in some higher power there still is no answer for what came before the beginning of the universe. Genisova believed that, once again, the answers to questions like these were in the means of the thought process. Time is relative and this alone makes everything a bit hard to understand. If you move faster, then time slows down. How is this possible, and why? Maybe someday it will make more sense as we are able to travel at faster speeds more regularly.

Gravity is thought to be the central force throughout the universe, and we really have no idea what causes it. Yes, the sun pulls on the earth and other planets keeping them in orbit, but why? What causes gravity to happen? Just because something has mass means it has to pull on another object? Why? How come? Because God made it that way? It appears so, because we don't have another explanation. What lies beyond the edge of the expanding universe? Nothing? Nothing what? Just nothing? How can there be nothing? There has to be something, right? Once again, it must be our way of thinking that cannot grasp these concepts. This Genisova realized and was ready to try new concepts in the thought process.

The truth is that the generation of people entering into Genisova had already gained a more extensive understanding of the universe we live in just by going to school. The things taught now were the basics of education and no longer cutting edge information, like they were 20 years ago. They were much more advanced with science and math and computers than people merely 20 years before them. The evolution of the intelligence of humanity was ripe for taking a huge step forward into another level of thinking. There was a list of things that the Council of Genisova came up with early in its formation stages. This list was of things that would push the boundaries of technology and science to enable them to accomplish things that were not possible before and allow them to reach their goals of saving humanity, one way or another. This list was top level security knowledge only and even though people slowly began to realize what these things were, they knew that these types of things could change the rest of the world, too. If this knowledge was made known to everyone, people would be after this information and probably would go to great lengths to get it. People entering Genisova were vetted pretty heavily and even though they let everyone one in, there were levels of advancement that kept the information in check to some degree. Landau knew that eventually he would have to tell the government what they were up to and would even have to share the information, but the Council was going to be in control of it.

—∞—

As the first few weeks went on, the new group of members began to feel more and more comfortable with their surroundings. There was an unmistakable energy about the place and one could not deny it. We all know that feeling when you walk into a room with a certain type of people and there is just a great energy about it. It is so hard to put your finger on just what it is, but it is there nonetheless. You may think back and then try to deny it, but it won't change the feeling you had, the energy you felt. Well, here is a little secret about reality: it is all based on energy. On a molecular level we are all just particles moving about with energy. This energy can actually be measured and some people do this. Why is it, and we would all agree that there is a certain feeling we have about the 'energy' around some people or places. We all experience this, but then we just move on to the next thing and kind of forget about it. We tell ourselves, that was cool, but, now back to reality. Back to normal, boring or 'low level' energy. Why? Why do we all turn a blind eye to this nearly magical thing that happens? Are they supposed to be just fleeting moments? Not approachable, not touchable? Why can't we look more closely at this and try to see what is really there? That energy was being created and harnessed at Genisova, and it was undeniable.

Andrew, who was merely there for a story and nothing more, maybe some more fame, was getting sucked into to it, too. At first, he thought it was just adrenaline or something like that making him feel this slight high all the time. He felt better, slept better, ate better, had a light mood about him and seemed to be just happier. He kind of forgot about his job and making money and the next story. He was getting a little carried away. And, of course, he couldn't wait to run into Fiona whenever he got the chance. He wasn't exactly sure what she did and he would go days without seeing even a hint of her, and then, there she was, out of the blue, just in time to make his day. But he wasn't anxious about not seeing her. He was very busy completing all the tasks and taking classes and doing yoga and meditating and learning how to cook and so many different things. Things he would never have done on his own. It gave him a new feeling of confidence. Not the type of confidence you have after you leave a job interview and you're pretty sure you got the job. The type of confidence you have when you finish building something by yourself you never thought you would be able to do, or you cook yourself a meal that you never thought you would be able to make. Whatever it was that was going on, he liked it. He still had a skepticism about everything and also a greater curiosity about what else was going on here, but he was content just living day to day and listening and learning and seeing what they had in store for him next.

Suzi, on the other hand, was growing impatient already and wanted to cut to the chase. She was extremely intelligent and highly educated and was not impressed by many of the silly classes she had to take. Especially anything to do with this spirituality nonsense they all felt so strongly about. She was trying to grin and bear it, but it was getting harder. She saw very little purpose in most of it and just wanted to start working again. She was ready to go. She wanted to see the research facilities and what all the hullabaloo was about. She knew there were state of the art labs and equipment hiding somewhere on this campus of craziness. She had been asking lots of questions about this; in fact, it was all she pretty much asked about. She was told that there were quite a few other areas, each with their own concentration of study or purpose.

There was a medical research area with a hospital, and quite a few other facilities. There was an agriculture area where pretty much all of the food came from. There were areas for most all of the different fields of study or commerce that are available in the outside world. And, of course, there was an astrophysics department in the space and exploration village. This is what she was waiting to discover. She was told that she could go and visit this village but would not be allowed into any of the buildings. It was one of the more higher security areas at Genisova. This excited her even more and made it that much harder to be patient. But, this also made her resolve to get through everything they were making her do so she could find out what was so secretive.

Jacob was getting along just fine as he began his journey. In most all ways his life here was either as good or better than it had been before, so he truly had a feeling of gratitude about everything. Although there was a simplicity to life here, he felt the essence of everything had a purpose, making it all feel special. The food tasted better, people were happier, everything was clean and aesthetic, even the water tasted better and the air seemed cleaner. He was so excited to get an opportunity to find a new purpose in life, not only in his job here, but in helping the cause save the future of mankind. He really couldn't understand why anyone wouldn't want to be here. From his vantage point beforehand, this was a complete improvement on all aspects of life. He questioned nothing and went to all his classes and exercises with eager anticipation, wanting to get as much out of them as he could. He loved learning how to cook better, how to eat healthier, how to relax his mind and spirit through meditation. It made him feel sharper at everything he did. His mind seemed clearer and everything in life just seemed to make sense. His lack of knowledge and worldly experiences going into this whole thing had turned out to only benefit him even more than most others. The only problem that confronted him in life was that he was sort of overwhelmed by some of it and was thinking that maybe there were quite a few different things he may want to do. A good problem to have.

Jonathan was an engineer that specialized in aerodynamics and design. He was also someone they were eager to get into the system so they could utilize his talents. He had graduated top of his class from a leading university in his field, so his presence was pretty exciting. Theresa was ready to help out wherever they needed help. She was obviously hoping she could teach, but would be willing to do whatever they needed. Their kids were an extra handful to deal with as are all children of their age and they took their parenting seriously. They were hopeful the other parents at Genisova would be similar to them to help ease their mind about bringing the children into this atypical environment. As all parents, know getting help watching children is wonderful and it turned out that most all of the other parents felt the same way and were more than willing to return the favor of watching the kids when need be.

―⁓―

Landau was happy with the progress of Genisova and there had been few roadblocks to the growth and development thus far. An occasional minor issue here and there, like someone wanting to go back home too often or the occasional reporter trying to dig for more information on the workings of everything. He knew the government would have to get involved at some point so he tried to think of this with every move they made (This was part of the reason he began to introduce one piece of information to Sarkovia). They had calculated how many people they needed to run the basic survival departments and how many people they would need to start concentrating more heavily on their long term goals. This being a self-sustaining space station big enough to support a city's worth of people. This was all groundbreaking work because no one had ever done this before. There were no test samples to look at to see what worked and what didn't. Now the earth may someday become uninhabitable, but the space station would most likely need resources from earth for some considerable time until the next home planet or moon could be found. Also, what other options were there for everyone else stuck on earth because not everyone would fit in a space station.

The data suggested that the earth would not only continue to climb in temperature, but also the UV rays would become drastically more dangerous. So while humans could adapt and migrate further north into colder climates, which would become warmer, the UV rays would still an issue. Landau and the Council had thought about this already and had purchased a large plot of land further north in an ideal area very similar to the current one. This was to be the future location of Genisova once the climate had changed so much that the current Genisova location would not be livable. The UV issue was something they definitely wanted to address, and this is what they proposed: To create an invisible dome that would shelter the entire community from the UV rays. How would this work? Was it even possible? That is why they wanted to attract the greatest minds of the world and give them the resources they needed to create a working model. Basically a giant, invisible umbrella to allow humans to walk around and continue to live without the threat of the sun's harmful rays. This was a solution that would allow humans to continue to live on earth, but you could not leave the umbrella and the majority of the earth's population would have to move toward the poles and rebuild the human civilization. This would still only be a temporary fix as the temperature would continue to rise and eventually even the polar regions would be too hot to live in.

At that point humans would have to primarily live indoors indefinitely. In order to go outside they would have to wear special suits. However, the ramifications of the earth's temperature rising would also include things like the inability to effectively farm food, thus making life even more difficult. Not to mention the difficulties that would present themselves for people not being able to interact with other people for all the things they need to survive. There would be geological and biological changes that would affect all plant and animal life. There would be a need to create a new way to sustain life. This is why Genisova was beginning to work on these things now. There was no time to waste because they didn't know how long it would take to create the solutions and they didn't know how much time they actually had. Time was of the essence, and once the Genisovians understood this and bought into what was going on, they were told how urgent what they were doing was. This did create some stress for many people, but all the mental, physical and spiritual strengthening they were doing in the meantime helped them to cope with it. It was important that they were well balanced people who would be able to work and concentrate at their highest level whenever needed.

There was an advanced research and development campus which was typically where all the brilliant minds went. This was a play land for almost all of these people and they were overjoyed to be able to have at their fingertips the means to do whatever they wanted to develop solutions to these problems. The facilities here were state of the art and diversified to adapt to many different areas of research. You could walk into one building and find people working on developing a rocket ship that was capable of easily exiting and re-entering the earth's atmosphere and that could land back on earth making travel to and from a space station very easy. The next building you walked into people were designing a new type of energy source for short and long range space ship excursions. The next building was working on a new type of security system for protecting the people of Genisova. There were amazing things going on here and it was of the highest level of security. The people who worked here loved their work and would not trade their position for anything.

A growing concern of the council was how to fund everything going on at Genisova. Many of the founders of Genisova had devoted their careers to the cause, but had not given up their corporations in the outside world. The money they made from their companies would sufficiently fund Genisova indefinitely, but their aspirations to grow and move into space and all that would come with this enormous project would require considerably more funding. For even though they could create and sustain the most basics things needed for survival, much of what they needed in the end would come from outside Genisova. The materials needed for many of their projects could not possibly all come from within their own territory. Things could be assembled and created, but the raw materials would need to come from all over the world. For this the council kept on good terms with many different companies near and far who they believed were fair and just companies. People they knew they could work without too much trouble and would probably even support their cause to some extent.

One of the major breakthroughs that Genisova made was in medicine. Long has the world searched for cures to different diseases, but none more than cancer. The doctors and scientists at Genisova had developed a cure for most all types of cancers. This was, of course, a huge development in the world of medicine and in all of the world. However, when this discovery was being made the Council decided to try and detract the attention they knew it would bring them. They had a very good relationship with one pharmaceutical company in particular and had made a deal with them before releasing this highly profitable information. They would give them the ability to sell these drugs and let them take credit for this discovery, but they wanted the majority of the profits. They would also let them have the same deal with any other drug they developed in the future.

Finding a cure for cancer was the mystery that had eluded so many for so long and a small fraction of the profits of its earnings would far outweigh any other drug any company had ever produced. Curing cancer was also a multifaceted problem because many of the different types of cancer were essentially different diseases because of they way they affected human cells.

Basically, the cure had to be for each of the different type of cancer, not just cancer in general. On top of that it was understood that even cancer cells affecting one organ in a person's body could come in several different shapes and forms. This was a seemingly insurmountable task. The researchers at Genisova essentially used an advanced nanotechnology to help solve this riddle. Along with creating an improved early detection device which helped prevent the disease from ever spreading. New discoveries in all fields were occurring at an astounding rate here. There was something going on at Genisova that could not happen anywhere else on earth because it required a new level of concentration and cooperation among the people working on tasks. With the breakthrough discoveries in medicine and the profits from these achievements, Genisova would be able to thrive and keep moving toward its goals. As they made breakthrough discoveries in other fields, they would use a similar process of outsourcing this product into the world and these would all continue to help funding Genisova.

It wasn't long before Sarkovia and friends made another unannounced visit. Too many things were not adding up to the people in Washington. Too many rumors of such a wide variety of things going on at Genisova that were not making sense. There was quite a bit of interest in some of those whispers because, the government could think of many useful ways that they could employ some of these technologies for their own benefit. For the purpose of helping the common people, that is, of course.

The investigators, let by Sarkovia, arrived at the gates one day out of the blue and asked for a meeting with Landau and his Council as soon as possible. The security guards were aware of who this group was was and told them they could wait in the defense center for the time being until they could try and find a time he could meet. The security guard led them into a comfy conference room and told them to make themselves at home. It could be a while before they were able to locate Landau, let alone, find time for him to break away from what he was doing.

It turned out that Landau was with some scientists that were working on the material to be used for the structure of the space station and the space planes. He answered his phone and told them it would be an hour before he could actually meet with them. He also told them to get the researchers in charge of the parastun project ready for an impromptu visit.

An hour and a half later, Landau arrived at the defense center. "Sorry to keep you waiting, just not enough time in the day as it is."

"That's quite alright, Mr. Landau," answered Sarkovia. "We're ready now to have another look around. I have been informed by my superiors that I need to bring back more information this time or else I may get into some trouble, so I hope you can help me stay out of trouble." He had a grin that matched his words.

"Well, I think we can be of some assistance, but no guarantees as to the extent of how far we can take things," Landau replied.

They took the closest shuttle to the research and development center and went inside of the parastun facility to get a closer look at what was going on. As Landau had requested, the team of researchers were ready for their visitors. They were pretty excited to get to play show and tell a little bit about what they were working on. So much of what these people were all doing was kept secret and there was little to no praise for their accomplishments. It was all part of what they signed up for, but it still didn't change the fact that they were human and wanted some 'love' for what they were doing.

Sarkovia seemed to be a little excited himself to get a sneak preview at some of the secret work going on at this bizarre place where so many intelligent minds were stealing away to. Landau led them into the research room, which was somewhat like an indoor shooting range. There were targets and a bunch of sensors and screens that the team was looking at.

"So what exactly is going on here?" Sarkovia asked.

"One of the main goals of Genisova is a peaceful way of life for all. We don't need to look too far outside our borders to find violence of many types. Who would argue that guns have not become a problem of epidemic proportions in our world today? What is the purpose of guns to begin with? To kill, of course. But why? Because we hate people so much? Or, because there are no other options for people looking to harm others. That may seem like a ludicrous question to ask for people trying to find a peaceful solution. But! But, if you look at it from another perspective, you could maybe see that if a criminal could commit their crime without killing another person, maybe they would. Maybe."

Sarkovia seemed confused like the rest of his group of officials, "So, you are trying to invent another means for criminals to commit their crimes? I'm not sure I follow you so clearly."

"Yes."

"Okay, explain."

"You see, if we have the means to develop a 'gun' that doesn't kill someone but has the same desired affects, that is to essentially make someone incapable of moving, what are we waiting for?"

"I see sort of where you are going, but many people that want to kill someone else, want them dead for good. Not able to get up an hour later and keep living."

"I understand, but I would argue that there are many, maybe most, situations, where just getting the affects of killling, without killing, actually would suffice. For example, the police. Why do the police need to kill someone when trying to apprehend them? It has clearly been a major issue in our society for quite some time now. Why not give the police the means to essentially disable someone without killing them."

"Okay, I'm still listening," Sarkovia said.

"If we begin by replacing all police guns with a gun that gets the same affect without killing someone, then we can start to reduce the number of guns in the world. People may begin to see that maybe they don't need to kill their enemy in order to get what it is they want. How many people in prison for murder maybe could have committed whatever their crime was without killing another innocent human? I wonder if you asked them now, now that they are serving their sentence for their crime, if they were to do it over again, would they use a gun that wouldn't have killed their victim?"

"So what actually is this new gun you claim will replace all guns in the world?"

"Well, it is still a work in progress, but right now we call it the parastun. It essentially works by shooting a tiny bullet, more like a small glass marble, that once it hits its target, within seconds, paralyzes them for a short period of time. It utilizes a new technology where the pellet carries a special type of electrical charge plus a trace amount of a neurotoxin that affects the nervous system and renders the victim unable to move. They can still breathe but are unable to move."

"Why do you think this will work?"

"We think police would embrace this idea because it essentially wipes all the blood from their hands when there is blame pointed in their direction. The victim can be fired at just as though an officer was going to apprehend them and once they are disabled they can restrain them. Win-win. The other reason for our development of this technology is because guns are not really a great idea for a space station. One stray bullet and game over. Holes in the wall of a space station spells catastrophe."

The look on Sarkovia's face changed suddenly to full attention. "So it is true you are planning on building a space station. If that is the case we have all sorts of concerns about what is going on here. And it seems you have multiple intentions for this new weapon, some of those your own."

"We have created it for our own intentions but feel others could benefit from its purpose. We also would like to use it here at Genisova, on Earth, for defense purposes. And yes, we are not waiting around for the government to save us from the sun."

"Well, creating a new weapon of any type needs to be cleared by multiple authorities and we will need to be in the loop on all of this going on here."

Landau doubted it needed clearance from anyone, really. Sarkovia clearly had many concerns about all of this but could not argue too much at this point because at least they were telling him about some of the things going on. He couldn't help but wonder why they were telling him this seemingly secret information. He was clearly set on keeping the pressure on Landau until he knew everything that this unlikely group of people were up to. Why were all these brilliant minds contributing to this seemingly pointless mission? Did these people know they were being led down a blind path to disappointment? Something wasn't adding up.

After months of waiting, today was the day Lucina was finally leaving for Genisova. Much contemplation and soul searching had helped her decide that everyone she dated after Landau had left her with some feeling of emptiness. She at least had the insight to look inside and recognize that feeling. She could never get him completely out of her mind and maybe we never get people we fall in love with completely out of our mind, but she felt this was different. If you are a loving, compassionate and optimistic person you probably will always have feelings of some sort for those you loved once upon a time. She may have loved things of this world, but she also had a deep understanding of human nature. To her, this was somewhat of an experiment. She would show up and perform her test. That is, she would make herself known to him and view his reaction and make a decision to stay or leave. If she felt there was still any sort of connection, she would stay and give it more time. If there was nothing left between them, there is no way she would be able to remain there.

She had finally convinced Charles to sneak her in and so today was her first day at Genisova. He had to get every single Council members permission so that when Landau found out, he could say they were all okay with it and really felt there was no harm in having her there. Landau had recently been very preoccupied with a new breakthrough in research and development, so he was somewhat distracted and easy to slip past at this point in time. Charles had told Lu to wait until a time like this presented itself so it would be easier to get her settled in. He went and picked her up late the night before and had just entered her information into the system a few days earlier so Landau did not likely pick up on it. Now, it was time for the new members introductory class. She was extremely nervous about this and was trying to control her emotions. She thought, I've come this far, what else is there to lose at this point? She went to the building for the class without Landau noticing her. She sat in the back of class and waited anxiously for it to begin.

Landau walked into the room and Charles said to him, "Here is the list of the incoming group. There was a very last minute addition so I though you might want to review."

"Oh, okay, I guess I just realized I never looked closely at the list recently. Is it someone who should be on my radar for something?"

"Just look at the list."

He glanced down the list and his face went pale and the expectant look on his face dropped to one of confusion. He slowly looked up and saw her sitting in the back looking down and reviewing something on the tablet sitting in her lap. His heart began to race and the blood rushed to his head making him feel a dizzy. Part of her hair fell on her face and her beauty hit him like a shockwave all at once. Then, suddenly, he thought, was this some kind of joke? How did she get into the group without him knowing about it. He suddenly was angry at Charles and the entire Council for he knew they must have approved this without him.

"Is this for real? Is this just some silly prank or is she actually coming to stay at Genisova?" There was a bit of anger in his voice.

"She is planning on staying. She asked me privately as a favor to not tell you because she knew it might present a problem. She said she wanted it to be something that she decided on her own without any persuasion from you." As Charles was saying this, Lucina looked up at Landau, and their eyes met. She did not look away from him, but held his glance and stared deep into his eyes trying to speak without saying a word. He did not know what to feel. What was she doing here? Why was she here? Clearly not to try and help save the world. For him? It didn't make sense.

Fiona began the class by welcoming everyone. She, too, noticed the awkward energy in the room and wanted to break it up into something different. Interestingly enough, Fiona herself, once had had some feelings for Landau. When they first met he was already dating Lu, but after that she had considered approaching him about it. They had gotten to know each other well over the years and now she had figured if there was something meant to happen between them, it would have happened by now. This was some of the reason why she was still single, but not all of it. She was very eager to see how this new situation would present itself to him and what he would make of it. None of the other new members knew who Lucina was, so to them there was no problem. She was just another candidate. Little did they know.

After Landau had composed himself a little bit he was trying to decide what he should do next. Should he interrupt the class and pull her aside or wait until there was a break and then approach her. He was very frazzled on the inside but held himself together for the rest of the new members. He gave his little speech about himself and why he began Genisova and then quickly turned it back over to Charles. He decided to just wait it out. When the question part arrived he held his breath to see what she might say. Lucina raised her hand to ask a question and Landau began to sweat.

"How much communication is allowed with the outside world from within Genisova?" she asked.

Charles felt like he should take this one, "We allow as much communication as you would like".

"Aren't you concerned that people are going to video tape images from in here and let the rest of the world know what is going on?"

"There really is nothing too spectacular to show going on here. Anything that is of any special importance definitely has higher security around it. You can video tape any of the general common areas all you want. It looks just like anywhere else on this planet. We have not really had too many issues with it. There are videos on our website showing the grounds. Was there something in particular you were inquiring about?"

"Not really, just wondering what some of the boundaries are," she replied.

"Most people that come here are not too concerned about what is going on out there. I don't mean that in a condescending way, but more that they are just more focused on being here. I think the people that come are not here to sabotage what is going on here."

"I got it. Thanks."

There are a few more questions and then there was finally a break. Lucina got up and walked towards Landau. He waited for her to get to him and then he leaned over and gave her a half hug. He then motioned for her to come out away from the crowd. They walked out into a hallway and then outside. Landau had a confused and angry look on his face.

He stopped and started talking quickly, "I don't even know where to begin. I have to admit I was pretty surprised when I heard you called but I never expected this. What are you doing here? Are you just here to talk to me? I didn't even know you wanted to see me. This is all very confusing to me."

"Well, you know me, I haven't changed a bit. Still just 'go for it' Lu!" she said with an awkward smile. "One of my weaknesses, or maybe strengths, is that I don't think about it too much, I just do it. I don't know how to explain my life, my situation, but it has led me here. I never lost track of you and where you were and what you were doing. It was always there, in the background, even when I was on the verge of marrying someone else. And I really did love him, but something was off. I couldn't go through with it."

"Something was off with me too, remember? How is this any different?"

"You were always different," she said with a touch of sadness.

"So, you're here to tell me you're still in love with me and want to get back together?"

"No, I would never come here with those expectations. I came here because I had to see you and talk to you to make sure that this feeling I have that won't go away..." she paused for a moment and looked down at her feet, "Life is too short and I want to make sure that I haven't made a terrible mistake."

Landau relaxed a bit and said, "Of course, I will always love you in some way, shape or form, but why now? It's been so long. This must really be important."

"Something happened to me." She stopped. "And all I could think about was you and how you always lived like everything happens for a reason. It was like the universe was trying to tell me something, and I do not usually pay attention to things like that, as you know, but I did, and it has brought me here."

"You realize where you are at and what is involved with being here, right?"

"I think so. As you know, this sort of thing is outside of my comfort zone. But, I figure, all I can do is try. If there ever was some remote chance that there is anything left between you and me, I realized that this is something I would have to do. I don't really know how to look within like you do. I know how to love and that has to be worth something. I just thought most people are like me and don't worry so much about finding a greater purpose in life."

"That may be true, but once you begin down that path it is virtually impossible to turn back around. When you get a glimpse of what is possible, the universe just keeps pulling you in and won't let you go. Maybe the universe is finally calling to you. But it cannot happen unless you initiate it. You have to take the first step, and sometimes the first step is simply just listening to the world around you."

"Tell me more about this place. Not the generic version you tell everyone."

"Where to begin? There is so much going on here. Just like I am telling you to listen, I listened and then I had a vision and I followed it. The sign was from the sun this time and it could not be ignored. Our own star, the source of all life on Earth, is now making us seek alternate methods for survival. We need the sun as a source of energy, but we have to change how we get that energy from it. The future of life depends on us figuring out a new way to survive. Unfortunately, humanity has not reached a point yet where it has the knowledge or technology to adapt enough to survive. But, we think we have found a way to accelerate our capabilities."

"How do you know all this? Are you sure there is no hope here on earth?"

"We don't know exactly what is going to happen, but the long term outlook is not good. However, if we sit around and wait to find out, it may be too late. Things of this nature take a long time to develop and come to fruition. You don't just up and build a space station or colonize another planet in the blink of an eye. It may take a long time and there will be many obstacles along the way. Many people may risk their lives so others will have a future. There are just so many question marks as to how this is all going to go, but what else can we do? We can't sit around waiting for the government to do something. Half the people in Washington don't even believe in these scientific projections. They will only begin to do something when its too late."

"How are you going to accelerate the process? What is the secret you know that no one else does?"

"Synergy."

"Synergy?" she sort of giggled, "That's it? The secret to the universe?"

"Maybe. We are all just simply energy. The entire galaxy, universe, is just energy. Teeny-tiny particles, vibrating and moving around. Even rocks. Have you ever been on a trampoline when everyone is jumping up and down at their own pace? It makes it hard to even jump at all, sometimes knocking you down. But if everyone starts jumping at the exact same time, then you all can suddenly jump super high together. That is what could happen if we all worked together instead of against each other."

"I get your point, but what does that have to do with saving humankind?"

"There is so much more to us than we know. We are capable of so much more, but it has to be accomplished together. We think the way to fully harness our potential is synergy. There are so many more layers to us and we have to dig deep to get at them. It takes time and practice and patience. The rest of it is hard to explain."

"What exactly are you talking about? I don't really understand what you mean? Potential and layers and synergy. Can you be a little more straightforward?"

"Probably not. When you sit in silence and just let your consciousness be, eventually, you reach a higher level or go to another dimension of sorts. Does that make sense?"

"So by meditating you can make some form of transformation?"

"Yes, but there is more to it than that. We are creating another level of that consciousness here together as a community living together, working together, and doing everything together in harmony with the same intent and purpose. It may sound hokey and far fetched, but if you stay here long enough you will see it and feel it. Ask anyone here. You will feel it when they talk about it. It really isn't something that can just be explained in a single conversation, but this is the idea in a nutshell."

"It sounds amazing, but I really don't fully understand. Guess I will just have to stick around and see what it's all about, eh?"

"I still don't know the potential of all of it, but we are making some unbelievable progress in areas that no one else has ever been able to before. It is startling what we can all accomplish together instead of in competition or divided. I would love for you to experience all of this, but I don't want you to do it for the wrong reasons. If you are truly here to see what my life is now all about, then you have my blessing to be here. If you let go and and just immerse yourself into all of it, good things will happen."

"Okay. I think I may." She looked down with a smile on her face.

"Let's get back with the group and join in the tour."

"Why do I have to go to this meditation class?" Suzi was beginning to sound like a broken record. Her instructor, Perjuna, laughed and smiled at her. "Why not?", he replied.

"You have something better to do?"

"Something better then sitting in a room and doing absolutely nothing? I really don't feel like I need to answer that question. I don't see the purpose of any of it."

"You will."

"When?"

"When you are ready."

"I'm ready. Let's get on with this. I know that I am not going to get anywhere of importance here until I get past this."

"How do you 'get past this'?" Perjuna inquired. "Do you think this is a test of some sort?"

"Well, isn't it? Once I pass this part of the process I can move on to the next part, right?"

Perjuna smiled again and laughed as though he knew a secret and she did not.

Even though he was not trying to upset her by doing this. He could see she was frustrated.

He began, "Why do you resist this so much? Why not just let your defenses down and give it a try for real? Don't fight it. Just let go. Just try to sit and not think about anything. Don't be angry that you are here and not in a lab somewhere. That will happen in time, but right now, you are supposed to be here."

"Okay, I will do whatever you want me to do. I have already done this several times and nothing magical has happened yet. Just me sitting in a room and my random thoughts running wild about nothing. It is very frustrating and I don't feel like there is any measurable progress."

"It will, in time. Don't worry."

"Oh, I'm sure it will," she said with a trace of doubt. Suzi went into the meditation room and began to go through the motions they expected from her. She figured there had to be a limit as to how many times they would make her sit through these sessions. At least she hoped there would be. Maybe there wasn't. Maybe they were expecting her to have some great epiphany after she walked out of there. Should she fake it and just make something up? What did they want from her? She had already sat in this silly room and followed the instructions for the guided meditation. She could see how people would be attracted to this exercise to calm your mind. But to calm your soul and hear things from some higher level was just craziness. She walked in and grabbed a couple of pillows and sat on the floor with the others in the group. They all seemed pretty excited to sit here and do nothing. She turned to a man sitting next to her and said, "Are you getting anything out of this?"

"Yes, you could say that," the man replied.

"Like what?" she asked.

"Clarity, calmness, relaxation, happiness."

"Really? How? What do you do?"

"I just sit and be quiet and open my mind to the possibilities of the infinity."

"Infinity? How so? What does that mean?"

"I'm not exactly sure how to explain it, but I feel like it opens a realm of possibilities that are endless. I can see things and feel things I can't feel in the normal world of reality."

"The normal world? What else is there? You really believe all that?"

"Sure. It feels real to me. And if it feels real to me what else is there? You see things and feel things in your life, right? It's really just your brain perceiving the world as you see and feel it, correct? What's the difference? It's all really how the mind receives its information."

"I'm not sure I follow you. I feel like there is a large difference between the real world I experience and the dream world you are telling me about, or my own dreams for that matter."

"But, are you sure? What is your proof? You seem like someone who knows what evidence is. Have you never had a dream that felt real? Maybe one that woke you up in the night? Isn't that the brain perceiving something and it having an affect on you? Listen, I know what you are getting at, but maybe, just maybe, you get a little of what I'm getting at."

"Maybe...maybe."

"Hey that's a start. What is it that you do anyways?"

"Astrophysics."

"Really? Me too!"

At first Suzi thought he was joking with her, but then came to the sudden realization that he wasn't.

"Yeah? What's your name? I haven't seen you around here much."

"Kristopher Andersen."

Suzi's mouth started to hang open as she realized who she was talking to. How did she not recognize him? She was suddenly having very mixed feelings about a lot of things.

"I haven't been over here to this class in quite a while and I thought I needed a refresher. I enjoyed this particular session so much. It was quite wonderful. Do you enjoy it?"

Suzi was retracing in her mind their conversation and wondering what she should say next. "Well, I am pretty new at this type of thing. Not really my forte, meditating. Any suggestions for helping me find some meaning in this?"

"I wouldn't necessarily look for any meaning here. My advice would be to not try and control any of it. Just try to not do anything, including thinking any thoughts. Seems like it would be the easiest thing in the world and, well, it turns out it is quite the opposite, nearly impossible. Why is it so hard for our brains to slow down and do nothing? It's a crazy world out there and our minds reflect that appropriately. Chaos."

"So, do nothing? That's it?" Suzi said reluctantly.

"Once you master doing nothing, thinking nothing, you will be truly surprised—truly, as to what you will find. I will simply leave it at that."

"Okay, I guess, if the advice is to do nothing, I won't argue with you about it. I will see how good I can be at doing nothing," she let out a big sigh and smiled lightly.

Kristopher smiled back at her and closed his eyes.

The class was beginning and they had to end their conversation. Of course, once Suzi had found out who she was talking to there was no way she would have any chance of sitting quietly and having no thoughts. She thought she knew what he looked like but for some odd reason he looked different. She couldn't put her finger on it. Anyway, she listened to the guided meditation and tried her hardest to put all of the wild thoughts out of her mind, but it was pointless. She would have to wait until next time to make any progress.

After the class ended, Kristopher came over to her and told her he was very excited to get to know her better and eventually work beside her. He couldn't wait to hear her advice on the work he was doing currently. She tried to get him to tell her what it was, but he laughed and said, soon enough, soon enough. What was it with all these, so-called enlightened people smiling and laughing all the time and then saying nothing? It was driving her mad.

After her class, she went back to her place and called Darius. They had not seen each other in quite a while now. She had been to visit him once, after the second week she had been there, but not since. She had started off missing him quite a bit, but had found that it had subsided lately. Sometimes she actually would forget about him for days and then call him out of guilt. They had a nice visit, but she had been thinking about their relationship more and more since she left. She wondered whether or not they would make it in the end, and she was slowly realizing what it was she truly wanted to happen.

Mohammed had continued to become more accustomed to the way of life at Genisova. He enjoyed many of the classes and exercises he participated in. He definitely gravitated towards the religious and spiritual type classes. Pretty much the opposite of Suzi. He was interested in discovering the other religions they discussed and whether or not there were other people of faith here at Genisova. The instructor of A Brief History of Religion was a woman named Angeline. She was very interesting. She had been a professor of religion at a small university and he wondered if she practiced any particular faith. She had been raised Jewish, which was the faith of her mother, but her father was Catholic and from Brazil. He had many fascinating conversations with her and was pleasantly surprised at how well she knew the Islamic faith and its history. He had not wanted to pry too much but had worked up the courage finally to ask her what her own personal beliefs were, especially having studied so many different religions. They were talking about the similarities between the three monotheistic faiths of Judaism, Christianity and Islam.

"What was it like being raised in a family with parents of two different faiths?"

"It was not that bad, actually. We practiced a lot of tolerance because we had to," she replied.

"And now, what do you think after everything you know? Have you resolved their differences?"

"Well, no, not really. I believe that there are many valid declarations made by all of them. The world is in perfect design, the way I see it. One may say, we don't need religion because they can't all be right, and I would respond, I wonder where the world would be without all of the religions. It is quite possible that if there was only one religion and the rest of the world had none, that the one religion would not have survived. Once upon a time the world was a very barbaric place. Imagine the majority of the world godless and barbaric. I wonder what they would have done to the other part that believed in God? In many ways the world needs all the different religions."

"So, you don't believe there is one and only one correct religion? How can they all be right or only some be right and others wrong? Many religions claim they are the only way to God?"

"First of all, I think that religion is meant to be a personal thing, not a group thing, if you know what I mean. Not to say that people shouldn't interact amongst other people of religion, but more that you have to decide for yourself what you believe. Like I said, perfect design. Religion, to me, is a path to God. God is sitting at the top of the mountain, but there are many paths to the top of that mountain. The question is, who, or what is God?"

"Well, I think that God is the creator of the universe and the one who is in control of all of our fates. God is the perfection we strive for. The reason we try to live good, honest lives. Who do you think God is?"

"I can't be quite certain that God is a someone. I think that God is beyond our comprehension, but at the same time we know it quite well. It is tricky. In some ways outside our reach, but certainly within all of us. Just the concept of God alone is something that our mind has a difficult time coming to grasp with. Like infinity. We know it's out there at the very end, but at the same time, it's not. The idea of God is definitely something we all struggle with when we try too hard to think about. Thinking about life and how we are supposed to live our lives is actually much easier. Probably why we focus so much on that instead of trying to figure out who God is. I have studied most all religions and most believe that God is infinite in all ways. For how could God have any shortcomings, and if God did, what would they be? And, if God is infinite in all ways, that would mean there are no limitations to God in any ways. Which in turn means God is everywhere, for how could you contain God in one particular area? And, if God is everywhere, then God is in you and me and everyone. God wouldn't just be part of me and part of you, that wouldn't make sense, so God is all of you and all of me. The problem is that most all people of religion struggle with this idea, because that would mean they are God and that is blasphemy or something like that. But, the logical mind would say different."

Mohammed paused and took all this in, pondering the significance of these ideas. He couldn't really argue with the facts presented before him. He also believed that God was more or less infinite in all ways. It had never occurred to him to think that if he believed God was infinite in all ways then God could not be "limited" to a certain location or time. It was beginning to dawn upon him that he was personifying his version of God and giving him human-like limitations.

"Do you believe some of the things different religions teach are wrong then? They can't all be right."

"I still believe the universe is in perfect design. Good and bad, right and wrong, yin and yang. How else could the universe be designed, only good, only right, only hot, only up, only one side of everything? What would be the point? There has to be a duality of sorts to everything. Without it we are robots and free will has no purpose. But there is more to it than just free will and although there is a form of perfection in the duality of nature, I do believe we have a propensity for goodness. We want to love and be loved. It is very simple. Most all religions teach that at their core and I want to believe it is true."

"If only it was that simple. Why are we learning about all the different religions here at Genisova? Is it just for general knowledge or appreciation of them? Or is there an underlying message that is trying to be hinted at here? I don't feel a push in any particular direction from you, but one can't help but wonder, what it is all for."

"We are not trying to convince anyone of anything. Except maybe tolerance. There is so much to be learned from all the different religions. Yes, some are more appealing to the masses, but some are geared for other more particular people. All the religions of the world really have been trying to teach a similar version of the same message. Doesn't that mean something to most everyone? The one problem that I do have with many religions is the fear that they teach—and I don't think that is what was truly meant to be taught. Nobody should be coerced into being a good person. Any religion that makes you feel like their way is better or the 'one and only way' seems to me pretty arrogant actually, not holy. Jesus did not seem to me arrogant. Looking at all the religions together should make a thoughtful and open minded person wonder about some things."

"So you think that I am wrong for believing in Islam? I don't feel like it is wrong. But I don't worry so much about other people and their beliefs."

"No, I would never tell anyone what they believe is wrong, because it is not. I can't stress enough how it is an individual decision a person has to make about their faith. It's personal and it should be. If everyone only worried about themselves we would have a lot less problems in the world. I think you will find that almost all the people here think this way. If they didn't before they arrived they probably do now."

"Are there not any people here who are religious? If they are I don't see any places of worship."

"There are quite a few actually, but no on has made an effort to build something like that. Is that something you would like to do here?"

"I don't know, maybe. It seems to me that at the very least most people here are spiritual. Maybe a place of worship would be a benefit for everyone, not just those of religious background."

"I think that would be welcomed openly."

—⁂—

Weeks turned into months and the new members were beginning to get a sense of what they would be doing in the future at Genisova. Every now and then, each member would have a meeting with the Council. This was more or less a sit-down talk to see how things were going in general, although one couldn't help but feel like they were being evaluated. The Council would ask questions like, "How are you liking it here?" and "What do you think about this whole process?" Lots of open-ended questions to see how they would respond and get a sense of where they were at in their mission. This was a normal procedure at Genisova and most everyone didn't make a big deal about it.

It was understood that no one was getting "kicked out," but that this was merely to check on progress and how close they were to going to the next phase. That phase being the next level of trust and the beginning of their work there. People like Andrew and Suzi were a little more up tight at first and tended to ask more questions inquiring what this interrogation was all about. To them, it was a test as to whether or not they could stay, or if they would be made to sit in limbo forever. Andrew gradually became more relaxed because he really was enjoying himself, but deep down knew his original intention of being there was not altruistic.

At Suzi's second meeting with them, she just blurted out, "So when do I get to actually do some work here?"

The Council was all there and Fiona just simply replied, "When you are ready."

"And when exactly is that? Can't I at least start doing something? Something little, one teeny, tiny thing? Anything?" Several members laughed mildly.

"You are doing something," Fiona said. "You are working on a different part of who you are, even though you may not believe it. You have to begin to have some trust in the process. Don't you see everyone around you and the affect it has on them? You must admit things here must seem a little bit different than other places you have lived or worked."

"Like how different? I see people who look to me like they are going through the motions of what you want them to do."

"Maybe that is where you should start. Maybe start noticing others around you and see if anything seems different."

"I will admit I was totally surprised when I found out that Kristopher Andersen was here, and it appears he has been here for some time. That caught me off guard."

"So if you respect him for the work that he has done, do you now have a different perspective of him because he is already a Genisovian?"

"I'm not sure. I haven't really thought about it."

"What do you think about?"

"Really all I think about is getting an opportunity to work beside some of these brilliant minds and find out what they are up to. I guess I am starting to wonder more about what they are actually up to. Are they doing their own work or are they only doing what you are making them do?"

"No one is being forced to do anything they don't want to do here. Once the people understand what the end goals are, they just begin to apply what it is they know towards getting to those goals. You already know what the dilemma is that mankind is facing. Have you ever thought about how what you know could contribute to the solution? It must have crossed your mind at some point."

"Well, not really. I just feel like a pig locked up in a cage waiting to be let out and then I will begin to think about what ever it is we need to do."

"Okay, well, think about it now, what can you come up with on the spot?"

"Now?"

"Yes."

"Okay, I guess the main problem is trying to either get off the planet or figure out a way to stay. I know mostly about things in space, not so much here on earth, so I certainly could help in calculating many of the necessary conditions for living on another planet or moon. This would certainly be my area of expertise."

"So let those thoughts simmer around inside and see where they go. Let them start the chain of thoughts that lead you in a new direction. Maybe your new train of thoughts to solving this problem will bring the rest of you to a new understanding of why you are here."

"I can see how one could become consumed with those thoughts. Is that what they are working on here? There has already been tons of research on all the planets and their moons in this solar system and the level of habitability of them."

"This is true. Most of that work has been done. But the minute details of carrying out these scenarios has not been figured out. There are also many existing problems with most all of these potential scenarios. Improvements have to be made with materials, computers, energy sources, space travel and the ability to transport people and materials. We are still quite a ways out from making anything happen. Many new and exciting ideas are in embryonic form as we speak. It is extremely exciting stuff awaiting new fresh minds—like yours."

"You're just teasing me now."

"Maybe. Maybe not!"

This got Suzi all worked up and her brain spinning in a frenzy. They were beginning to sense something with her that made them divulge more information than they ever had. This made her happy. This also made her more anxious and compelled to try and jump through their hoops faster.

Jonathan and Theresa continued to cruise along seamlessly with the already existing members of Genisova. As each day went by they became more and more confident they had made the right decision. It was not an easy decision and making it for four people instead of one was much more consequential. Jonathan was pretty eager to find out where he would be helping out and it would come sooner than he expected. They had now been there for almost half a year and because of their patience and progress some people from the research and development department approached him about something they were working on. The head of this particular project's name was Ian. He was an industrial and chemical engineer and specialized in plastics and design. He had been watching Jonathan closely and had asked the council if it was okay to begin the transition to his work position. Although they had not given him the full go ahead he did feel like it would be okay to get his input on this material they were working on. They agreed to give him a partial graduation into phase two. He approached Jonathan while he was reviewing work for one of his classes in one of the public lounge areas.

"Hey Jonathan. My name is Ian. How are you today? "

"I'm good. Very good. Just loving life right now," he replied.

"I work in one of our research and development departments and we have been watching your progress very closely. We are very impressed thus far. Do you think you would be interested in giving some input on something we have been working on? It is a little bit higher level security, so we would actually have to first go to the security center to get clearance and enter your information into another system. This would be the beginning of your clearance into a new branch of intelligence. You will have to fill out some paperwork and sign a privacy agreement stating you will agree to not share this information with anyone."

"I didn't realize that this would ever be necessary here. I thought it was all built on an honor system of sorts."

"Well, yes and no. We technically can't keep you from leaving and giving the information to anyone, but we are not really too worried about it. Especially in your situation where you have a family to consider. We may be taking a risk, but we feel strongly and trust anyone who is truly behind what we are doing here. It is the reason why virtually nobody has ever left after reaching a higher level of research."

"I understand, this is just catching me off guard a little bit. I mean, I am super excited about the opportunity and your trust in me, don't get me wrong."

"We are glad you are part of our mission. People like you are the reason it has been so successful thus far."

"Okay, let's do it."

They took a transit over to the security center where a team of people greeted them and began their execution of a procedure they had done countless times. This alone revealed a side to Genisova Jonathan had never seen before. The technology he witnessed in the next few minutes made him realize he was in a whole new world. He walked through a whole body scanner in a special room that was all glass that you could see into but not out of. Voice, eye, finger and hand print, hair samples, saliva and anything else you could imagine was being recognized and displayed in a genetic code on a screen floating in the air. It was not done in a secretive fashion and he was being told about everything they were doing as it was happening. He was not sure what all of it was for, but it sure was impressive and a bit overwhelming. He was not afraid, but suddenly felt that he should be sharing what was going on with Theresa.

"Should I be telling Theresa about all this?" he asked.

"Do you want us to have someone contact her? We will not be able to tell her everything about why we are doing it," replied Ian.

"I just feel like it is a much bigger deal than I had anticipated."

"We take all of our highest level information very seriously. You are about to be informed about something only a few people here know about. It is something that could change many things for many people."

"I get it. I will tell her when I get home. She will understand. I am not worried about it."

"So what is it that is so secret?"

"As you may know, the main goal here at Genisova is to build a space station, and someday multiple space stations that will provide a safe haven from earth as it becomes more dangerous. There are many challenges to creating something of this magnitude. One of the main obstacles is a type of material to not only build the station from, but also the space ships that will be carrying people. This substance must be not only strong and light, but it must also be able to block the harmful radiation from space and the sun. We think we have developed a new blended composite that is stronger than anything else and is so light it would make travel and building much more efficient. It uses would be countless and its production would be fairly inexpensive compared to similar substances. This would become the building block of future space travel and colonization of other worlds. To make this material requires a special process that we have not yet perfected, but when it is, it will make Genisova the only place with the ability to make it. There are many other space programs, private and otherwise, that would certainly love to have this information. Thus the high level of security."

"Wow, that is something I would have never even thought of. I could see how this would make all of the missions that much easier. How do you need me? I'm not a chemist."

"We actually are in the design phase of building the shuttles, cargo carriers, and the actual space station. We will need a larger ship for carrying all the materials for building the space station and this is where the weight and strength factors really come into play. There are already many suitable materials for completing our mission, but the weight issue slows down the process, doubling even tripling the time it will take to complete everything. Everything from the cost of liftoff to the amount of energy and fuel needing to get from point A to B adds up. This material is not necessary but will reduce costs and time and make everything much more efficient.

This is just one of several integral parts we are working on to make the entire process better. We want you to look at the designs we have for the ships and even the station and get your input."

"That is very exciting. I can't wait to see it." Jonathan was getting this warm fuzzy feeling inside, like he was being let in on the biggest secret in the world.

"We will get your clearance issued asap so you will be able to get into some of the areas of the design department. Tomorrow morning I want you to meet me out front of the transport station that goes to the space and exploration village. Your information will be entered into the system and you will be able to enter into some of the restricted areas you could not before. I will begin to show you some of the details we are working on and you can at least begin thinking about these preliminary designs and how to improve them. You will still have limited access and will need to continue to participate and progress in phase one of Genisova. There are still areas you need to work on but the timing of this particular issue is of a greater need. And, because of your wonderful progress thus far combined with your exceptional knowledge in this arena, we do make some minor exceptions in cases like this. The trust part you have gained and you have the knowledge we so dearly need. You only need to keep working on the rest of you and soon you will be there."

"Well, I am excited and honored that you feel like you can trust me. I want nothing more than to help the cause and get us all to the end goal. Thank you and I will see you in the morning."

He left the security center and walked back to his house and began to tell Theresa the news. She was not at all surprised and was very happy for him. She knew he was a special man and had highly sought after intelligence. Before coming to Genisova, he was recruited by many high level organizations desiring the knowledge of his amazing mind. She asked him what it was that was so secret and he said wasn't sure how much he could tell her yet, so he should probably wait until he knew for sure. She understood and was not at all upset about this. She fully trusted in the process. She could tell Jonathan was elated about all that had just happened.

—⚋—

Andrew had decided it was time to take a short leave from Genisova. Somehow, he had actually stayed all this time and never left once. There were a couple of occasions when he had planned on going, but then ended up changing his mind and stayed. He knew that his boss was going to be expecting a big report at this time and had been trying to get information from him to find out how it was going. Andrew had just responded by saying he was still working on his basic training so to speak and they were not giving him much of anything yet. He had learned quite a bit actually since he had been there, but, even though he couldn't explain why, he felt like not giving away too much information just yet.

He actually was enjoying his stay there. He was making quite a few new friends and to his pleasant surprise, they were all very genuine, happy people. There was a completely different vibe or energy to this place and although he didn't want to admit it, it was true. And, of course, there was the fascination with the mysterious and beautiful Fiona. He understood that she was very high up here and that there was no way she would give him the time of day unless he actually showed that he cared about this place. It was a bit of a motivating factor for his actions, but it wasn't the lone factor.

Until he arrived here Andrew had never really thought much about more than his career or his status among his peers and friends. It was just a code he thought everyone lived by. He never really knew anyone that looked at life the way the people here did. He was never spiritual and was not raised with any semblance of religion in his life. Even though the people here were not by any means what he would consider religious, they certainly had a different perspective on life. They all seemed to have purpose and felt like there was something greater in charge of their actions. They were all very loving and compassionate people but were not preachy and didn't try to make anyone else act a certain way. They did not judge him, even the ones who maybe knew why he was there, and they always made him feel comfortable.

He liked going to his classes and was even giving the meditation a real effort. He had not had any epiphanies yet, but it was helping him clear his mind and relax more. He spent more time reflecting upon deeper questions he had never pondered before. He had heard before about the concerns over the sun and its impending doom, but it hadn't really had any affect on him. It was just another story, like all the other apocalyptic claims people would always try to make. Global warming, greenhouse effect, etc..they never actually began to have any real consequences for most people so they were never taken seriously. Occasionally people did make changes in their lives and governments did slowly make larger institutional changes, but not much ever came of it.

Since he had arrived at Genisova, he had a different perspective on things. He listened when they informed all of their members about the reality of what was happening. They taught them and showed them the actual science behind the claims. It was real. There was no denying it. And it all made sense—the reason for everyone being here, the ideas of trying to do something—anything to try and save people from the rays of the sun. He still had many questions, but was content learning what they made available to him and waiting until he was ready to learn more.

He had already learned that there were 10 different villages or towns spread throughout Genisova. From what he gathered, the main village, as it was called, was essentially the gateway into Genisova. There were many administrative and business centers here as well as all the security and defense buildings. There were various housing establishments spread throughout the village. There was a main industrial area that was where all of the major manufacturing was done. This was centrally located so all the different villages could communicate easily with it for production of whatever it was they needed to be fabricated.

There was a main health and medical center where people were not only treated for any type of ailment or disease or injury, but it was also a highly advanced research facility. There was an education and development village, which was pretty much like a small college campus. There was an agricultural village where food was grown and processed, and there was also a research center here, mainly concerned with the advancement of food. There was an engineering village, computer and technology village, and an arts and design village. These were all self explanatory. The last two were the science and research village and the space and exploration village. Needless to say the last two were more focused on the future goals of space travel and space stations, but they all had their place and importance for the existence of Genisova.

It took Andrew quite a bit of time to gather all this information. Although it would make for a great story, he was genuinely interested in all of it. It was fascinating. How did this mini world function so well and without much need from the rest of the world? At first he thought it was just crazy that all these people would not want anything to do with the rest of the world and all the amazing things in it, but then he slowly realized that this wasn't the case. The people did miss things from the outside world, but Genisova was just more important to them. If people really needed to go do something outside, then they just went and did it. He knew a group of people that would go to see their favorite orchestra every now and then. They would take a couple of the cars from the onsite transportation lot, drive to the airport and fly out to the city they were going to. They would have a wonderful dinner at an excellent restaurant, go the show and then hang out in the city for a couple days. They got their fix and then flew back and got back to work. It really wasn't a big deal.

Now he was getting ready to make his first trip out for a quick weekend. He was planning on seeing some family and, of course, reporting back to his boss about what he was up to. He was just having a tough time trying to figure out how to tell him what he really wanted to say. He was afraid that he was falling for this place and he was concerned about how Evan and company would react. His life was so different than it was before. He never thought he could actually thrive in a place where there was no money. And that was another thing that he sort of forgot about—money. How had he gone six months without even thinking about it that much? Its kind of like going on a long vacation and you are having so much fun that you kind of forget about your real life and job and bills and most all of reality. When he got on that plane, he had that feeling like he was coming back from the Caribbean after sitting on a beach for 10 days.

But how could that be? He wasn't on vacation. This was no tropical paradise. But the money part was gone. No job, no bills, no stress. Genius. Too good to be true. But he knew that eventually the free ride would end and he would be expected to contribute. And in a weird way, after basically eating, sleeping, doing everything for free, he felt like he was looking forward to working. He felt almost obligated to pay them back for his stay. He did wonder what exactly he would do there, since his interviewing skills were of no use to them. He wanted to contribute in some way. He was actually developing a little sense of pride about living here. All his cynicism was gone and it was all just pure curiosity at this point. He had seen Fiona the week before and asked her opinion about leaving for the weekend.

"Hey Fiona, have any advice for leaving for a short weekend and how to go about doing that?"

She paused for a second and asked, "I'm not exactly sure what you mean. Why? Is there a problem? Where are you headed?"

"Just back home for a bit. See some friends and family."

"And your boss? Is that the problem you are referring to?" she snuck in with a smile.

"Yes, probably so."

"What are you going to say to him?"

"Most likely the truth."

"And what exactly is that?"

"That this place is quite different than what I had expected. I came here pretty pessimistic and ready for as short of a stay as possible. Here I am almost a half year later and I can't believe I haven't left or even missed my previous life that much. I guess, maybe, I just lived a dull, boring and superficial life for the most part."

"That can't be true, but you must not believe that completely. Your work as a journalist is a very important job. Just think how much more crooked the world would be without people like you keeping them honest."

"Yeah, I guess so. But most of the job was much ado about nothing. The people I often interviewed were considered important by society, and I half believed it, but now I am not sure why. The people here are who I now consider important. People like you. Aren't you one of the members of the Council of Genisova? At first, I thought smoke and mirrors, but, now, now that I see all that is being done here, it is just amazing."

"Wow, I would have never imagined you would have been so insightful. I underestimated you and your depth."

"What can I say? I am impressed. It is one thing to come into a situation with low expectations, it's another to have those expectations blown away in a fashion you never thought possible. I really had no idea what to expect about this place when I arrived. It has changed my perspective on so many things, and surprisingly it is mostly internal stuff. I had never paused and looked around and just took it all in, ever, in my life. Its like I was walking around like a zombie, asleep or something, unaware of so many things. I think back to everyone I know and I feel like snapping my fingers in front of them and saying, Hey! Wake Up! You're missing out on what life is really about!"

"Maybe you should go back home and start letting everyone know how you feel. What do you think they will say when you tell them this news you have?"

"I don't know. They will all think I'm crazy and acting weird."

"Why do you think that is? I mean, I pretty much think the same thing would happen."

"I don't know. Why do people live like they do? Caught up in all their worldly problems, chasing each other in the rat race of life. I did it pretty blindly, going on and on unaware that there is another side to life. It is only by mere chance that I ended up coming here in the first place."

"Now that you have been here a while and thinking a little differently about life, do you really believe it was mere chance that you ended up here? Have you ever stopped and thought about all the events in your life and how they all played a role in getting you to where you are today?"

"Standing here in front of you?" he said with a smirk.

"Exactly." She hesitated and gave him a half smile back.

"So you think there is a divine guidance to everything that happens in life?" Andrew asked.

"Do you really think it is all random?"

"I'm not really sure. There are times in life when it seems like everything just falls in place and is happening for a reason, then there is everything else, which just seems like pretty random events happening. And am I to believe that all the bad things that happen to me are supposed to happen and are part of the big master plan?"

"Yes."

"Really? How so?" He was not buying it.

"Actually, we learn most from the hardest parts of life. Think about your life and many of the difficulties you have had to overcome. Were these not the parts of life that you actually learned the most from? Not only that, the harder you struggled and worked through something the more rewarding it was in the end. Do you think it is more fulfilling to run one mile in a race or 26? Do you think there is a difference in the sense of satisfaction after someone completes a marathon than for someone who goes for a one mile jog? Just about anyone can up and run or jog a mile. A marathon takes months and months, even years, of running and preparing just to be able to finish the race. It is a journey of sorts. You get it?"

"I see what you are getting at, and I guess when you put it that way, things do make a little more sense."

"Don't get me wrong, there are some horrible atrocities that happen to people in life and these things can be very, very challenging to overcome and find meaning in. But I believe life is in perfect order and we are all playing our role in the master plan, as you call it. Some people actually sit up and pay attention, most others just ramble on through their lives, not really caring too much about these greater meanings. It is still okay. There are always lessons to be learned from life. Some understand this, others don't. Eventually they will, it just may take a long, long time."

"And you feel like this place, this plan to move on to the next frontier, is part of the master plan?"

"I think this universe is so old and so big and so mysterious, that this is just the tip of the iceberg in our history. It's just that our time here on Earth is almost up, so it's time to get ready to move on. We are capable of great things, much greater than we have accomplished thus far. We are only beginning to understand our capabilities. But it will never happen if humans continue on as they are, disconnected and fighting and consuming and just being selfish. It will happen only if we harness the combined abilities of all our intellects and ambitions. This place here is working on doing just that. That energy you feel, and I now know you feel it and are starting to understand it, is not a coincidence. It is happening because all of our energies are singing together in harmony. Imagine just for a second what this world could be if everyone, not just the people of Genisova, came together and worked together for the same cause with peace and love in their hearts."

"It really does make you stop and wonder. So, what was your advice for going home again?" He said with a laugh.

"Say whatever comes from your heart. You can't make people change. They have to come to it themselves. It's part of their journey, their marathon. Try to enjoy your time away. Make some observations about how you feel out there compared to in here. I can't wait to talk to you when you get back."

"Is that a date?"

Fiona gave him a sharp look of surprise.

"I'm just kidding. But, I have to ask, how come you are not married or dating anyone? I mean, you are amazing and beautiful and intelligent, should I go on?"

She blushed a little. "I was almost married once, but it just wasn't right so it didn't happen. And how do you know I'm not dating anyone right now? And, what do you care? Aren't you just going back to your life as you knew it before?"

Even though he did not want to confront this question before him, he knew sooner or later he would have to deal with his emotions about this. He just continued to assume he would be going back, but he would be lying if he didn't actually have some sort of attraction to this life and weird, crazy and splendid place he was living in right now. Finally, after much hesitation and clear confusion about his answer, he replied, "I guess so."

Fiona takes him by the hand in a platonic way, clearly feeling bad for him and what was written on his face. "You don't have to leave. We all love having you hear. You have much convincing to do before you would have move on to phase two, but it is assumed that everyone that comes here is going to stay, even though that may not be true."

"I have really been avoiding my thoughts on this whole thing. I have just been enjoying myself and trying to not think too much about anything, especially the life I left behind."

"Well, there's no rush to make any decision. Go home this weekend and see how it feels and maybe that will help with your ultimate decision."

"Okay, thanks. I really appreciate your concern for my situation. I know me coming here in the first place goes against all that you are about here. It really was an innocent decision that turned into something I never thought it would. But in a good way, and I am glad I'm here."

As she walked away, Andrew couldn't help but be overwhelmed with emotions. He felt like he was connecting with Fiona in some small way, at least, and now he had a real decision to make about what he is doing with the rest of his life. He hadn't been thinking too much about what he would do if he stayed here. He just assumed he was going back. This place was just a job, a temporary gig. It wasn't supposed to be much more than a story, maybe a big one that would further his career. And, wow, what a story he could tell about this place. The world would love to hear more details about Genisova. But, would anyone believe him? And, truthfully, he didn't actually know too many details about what they are up to besides the obvious stuff. He would need to stay for probably much, much longer in order to gain their trust and be placed in an area with any greater knowledge of what else was going on at Genisova. His feelings betrayed him as he thought that if he did stay that long, it would become even more difficult to leave. And now, Fiona was actually giving him the time of day. What in the world was he going to say to his boss?

—⋙—

Things definitely began to change for Landau after Lu's arrival at Genisova. But he resolved to stay focused on the tasks at hand. The Council had been continuously looking for new innovative ways to speed up the process of all of their endeavors. One of the most challenging projects, but the one with the ability to have the most widespread affect on all other research, was beginning to have some new and interesting developments. This was the project that Landau had been watching the closest and waiting for any signs of hope.

There was also more heat from Sarkovia and friends. He had called several times inquiring to speak with Landau, trying to get any type of information that might be of benefit to the government. Each time the Council would try to appease them by giving them some tidbits of information about some new developments but nothing in too much depth. He was slightly interested in the parastun and was eager to see how effective it would ultimately be.

The team working on this project had finally reached a point of development that they could actually safely do a demonstration for Sarkovia, so they did. One of the key researchers was so confident in the device that he volunteered to be shot with the parastun to prove that it was safe and effective. He stood at the end of the indoor shooting range and took the bullet to the torso and fell down instantly. Sarkovia and his team rushed over to him and examined him to see if he truly was incapable of moving and still alive. To their satisfaction, he was. This was unbelievable. This could be a huge breakthrough. Now, was the Council willing to turn over their knowledge of how it worked? Not yet. Sarkovia was not happy.

Mohammed was now beginning his next step of integration into Genisova. He had approached the council some time ago about building a place of worship for people of all faiths and religions. There were many talented architects and design specialists at Genisova and they were more than wiling to help in making this structure a work of art. It was simple, yet calm and relaxing. It blended all different major religions and, at the same time, was not offensive to anyone. It was a blend between modern and classical architecture, somehow reflecting various religious traditions in its appearance. It was unique. Mohammed loved it and it was very well received by everyone at Genisova. It made it very clear that all were truly welcome and there were no labels placed on anyone who entered into it.

He was being assigned into a new technology sector and he was very excited about its subject—artificial intelligence, or

AI. In the last 20 years there had been many advances in this field, but it still had not been brought to a level that could be considered dangerous. It is widely thought to be the final downfall of man, as computers will eventually become more intelligent and capable than humans and take over. However, without the ability of original thought or creative thinking they were still struggling to advance past a certain level. But at Genisova they believed there was still great promise for AI.

They were just beginning to get the movements of droids mastered. This was an incredibly difficult challenge to overcome. There are so many tiny details that happen with every step a human takes, details that become instinctive and autonomic, making them virtually impossible to replicate. Where Genisovians really wanted to use droids was in outer space. A droid could function in space without needing to breathe air or eat or all the other things humans cannot do in space. A droid could work around the clock, needing only to be charged occasionally. Their goal was to create a droid that could function in outer space while being given basic directions by a human either on earth or in a space station. They were even exploring making the droid mimic the motions of a human, like an interconnected body double. Almost like a virtual reality video game where you controlled a droid, except it was real. Having these droids do the bulk of the work in space eliminated many challenging issues for efficiently building a space station. Because the droids would have a basic AI, they would be able to interact with the person controlling them, giving feedback and suggestions on how to go about solving dilemmas. These were exciting new developments they were working on and making some pretty great progress.

—∽∽—

Theresa had now taken a position as a full time teacher for the elementary school and was on the advisory board of education. She and Jonathan had a different set of priorities than most members of Genisova as they had children to raise all the while they were helping the cause. But, their first priority was their children. It was extremely important to them that they had a close hand in everything their children did. Before the kids were in school full time, Theresa had made the decision to stay home and be with their children. They felt very strongly about this and felt like it was a priority over their careers. It had become almost normal for both parents to work full time in the world, and the children would spend a large amount of time in daycare or grandparents or other family members. The world had become difficult to live in with only one parent working so most people practically had to work to make ends meet.

At Genisova most of the other parents also placed a high priority on their kids. This fact set their mind at ease about the entire transition they were going through. The kids were settling in at school and finding their own way. The school was glad to have Theresa there to add another person with an education background to the mix. There were only a handful of other teachers and so there were many in-training, learning as they went along. This meant, those with education degrees were not only instructing the children, but the adults too. Luckily there were enough educated people in all the different fields willing to pitch in with the job of teaching these children. For example, it was set up so that a scientist in a certain field, lets say biology, could spend several hours a week teaching the children biology. And so on and so forth with all the varying subjects that they needed help in.

Theresa was an elementary teacher, which they desperately needed, so she had a position waiting for her pretty much from day one. This also made their kids feel more comfortable in their new surroundings. Because these kids were not getting to experience that much of the outside world, there were quite a few field trips set up going to various places. It was pretty easy to get the parents to participate so they were able to go to some fairly cool places, like Washington DC, Chicago, New York and even some national parks. This was also made possible because of the small numbers at the school. It was very manageable. It was turning into an amazing educational experience unlike most anywhere else. They also spent a good deal of time at all the various villages learning about the medical sciences, agriculture, and all the other fields on site. For the most part all of the children loved it and were so busy with all the extra-curricular activities that there was little time to worry about not being in a conventional school.

—⟨⟩—

Suzi was now thinking about a different approach to everything going on here. She still was not convinced that there was any divine power up above, but now she was open to seeing if any of their exercises could actually benefit her. She could see how meditating could help clear your mind and relieve stress and, of course, exercising and eating better were easy to do. It seemed as though the main thing they were looking for was the person to let down their guard and just let the whole process work its magic. At least that's what she thought. Little did she know that there was no exact protocol that they were looking for. Just time and then an intuition that the person was ready to move on to the next phase.

They were hoping that the individual person would begin to see the benefits of this way of life and let it become a part of their life. If the person felt like they were being coerced into doing these things then it wasn't going to work. Most people that entered Genisova were aware of the basics that were expected of everyone. Those that came in unaware or in hopes of having it their own way, were in for a slight surprise. The process doesn't work with someone who is set against it. For someone like Suzi, who wants some of what Genisova has to offer but not other parts it is a bit of a challenge to complete the process. As smart as Suzi was she was figuring out that in order to get to the next phase, she was going to need to give them what they wanted. Except, the problem was, this was not something you could fake.

She had now had five different meetings with the Council and was not sure she was getting anywhere yet. She kept asking about her eventual position and they kept deferring to other things. She had also been dealing with her indifference as to what to do with her fiancé. They had taken a turn for the worse and had not seen each other in quite some time. It had now been nearly a year since she arrived. He had tried to make a case for her leaving, but there wasn't enough motivation for her to leave, just yet. Even though she was frustrated by part of Genisova, she was extremely curious as to what the possibilities may be in the end. He thought he could wait it out, but had lost his patience right away and had actually been seeing another female friend from work more and more. Part of him was considering getting more serious with her, but part of him would rather be with Suzi. But, he was a man, and most men are fairly easily persuaded by a woman who knows how to be persuasive. In other words, she was attractive, he was lonely, and his fiancé had no arrival date any time soon. Suzi could sense it. She hated to admit it but she was more in touch with something inside of her. Her relationship with him became more and more clear to her as she was surrounded by the people of Genisova, who were thoughtful and caring, and just different in so many ways.

She was starting to look forward to her conversations with Perjuna. He was subtle but effective apparently. She still had a scientific approach to everything she did.

"How are you today my lovely Suzi!" Perjuna beamed at her.

She had to admit his perpetual happiness did kind of start to wear off on you.

"I'm very good, thanks!" she replied trying to match his enthusiasm.

"How are you doing with your decision you have been struggling with?"

"It is funny how things have become more clear to me since I have been here."

"How so?" he led her on.

"It is hard to explain, other than I just know things to be true, like the fact that Darius and I do not belong together. It has never been more clear to me."

"Why is it hard to explain?"

"Well, before, I was very conflicted about what I wanted and why I wanted things. His absence and being around all the people here has made it very clear to me that he is not right for me. It wasn't that we didn't have much in common. However, I feel different now. I don't like to admit that I have changed, but I have."

"There is nothing wrong with having a clear idea as to what you want in life. I think something else is guiding you," he said with a smile and a wink.

"Oh no, here we go again. Some magical power from above, divine providence guiding my way."

"There are different labels used for different entities, but could it be we are all talking about the same thing? If there was a divine power guiding all of us, how could anyone truly have an accurate label for what it is? Have you ever felt like certain events in life just seemed to be too much of a coincidence to be true?"

"Such as?"

"You can't tell me that you have never felt a greater connection with someone or something in life. You love looking out at the stars, isn't there any sense of wonderment there, a feeling that you cannot possibly understand its magnitude?

She was relentless, "Define wonderment."

"Has there ever been a series of events that have led you to the place you were supposed to be at? I don't know, perhaps you wanted a job and it turned out that you knew someone who knew someone, and all these things just fell into place to make it all happen? This happens all the time to people all around the world and it is one the reasons people believe that there is something more to all of this. It's just too good to be true and so people have to explain it somehow because they don't understand it."

She paused and thought about this for a moment. "Okay, I would have to admit there have been times in my life when things seemed to line up in just the right order for me to accomplish things. Like this one time my old partner and I were looking for this planet in this certain galaxy and we just couldn't find it, even though we knew it was there. I was up late one night going over my data and I fell asleep. My computer was still processing these equations I had entered and I suddenly woke up out of my sleep and there it was. I couldn't believe it! If I hadn't woken up just then I would have never found it."

"That is it! You see it! That was the universe trying to get your attention. Do you still think that was just a coincidence?"

"I don't know, but what other evidence is there for God besides coincidences? I need more. I just think most people believe in God because of fear or guilt or because they just don't have any of the answers, so they give it a label—God."

"Fear and guilt because of love. Their intentions are good even if they don't fully understand. Or maybe they lack the knowledge to comprehend what they read or hear. There are many things in life that no one can understand, even you."

"I read the Bible, its full of silly contradictions. The people who wrote the Bible were making up the stories to fit their goals and to make people act a certain way. Nobody was around to take notes on all the specific events that happened, and then the people who actually wrote it down hundreds of years later took the liberties to fill in the blanks any way they wanted. That is, to make sure the story was convincing and the people would feel as though they would have to believe—and they would have to behave—or else they would go the hell. That's what I think."

"Perhaps. Perhaps not. Mabye other people are not as perceptive as you are. It is not realistic to think everyone has the abilities to comprehend as well as others may. The Bible was written with good intentions, not evil, corrupt intentions of controlling the people. But people know love, and people know right from wrong. In essence, all the holy books are simply about love. Remember, they are just words. Words are just letters put together, and letters are just sounds, and sounds are just vocal cords vibrating air, and the air and vocal cords are just molecules vibrating. I thought you might appreciate a scientific approach to the words of the holy books."

"So what you're saying is not to dwell too much on the specifics of the words?"

"We scrutinize so much of what was said and written by the prophets that formed all the religions. Not that we shouldn't heed the messages conveyed, but to over analyze the words can lead to trouble. And the message is the same. It is universal. Once we get past the semantics of it we can then go deeper."

"And you guys want me to go deeper. That is not an easy task to do from the outset, especially for someone like me."

"I am not saying you need to do anything. We just want you to explore the possibilities of there being more to this realm than what you commonly see and feel with your basic senses. That's it."

"Just explore, eh?"

"And you are doing it. Everyone moves at their own pace and that pace is perfect for each person. There is no race to the finish line. We hope that you begin to feel what most all of us feel sooner or later here at Genisova."

"Now it's a feeling I'm looking for?"

"You said yourself that you are different. How are you different? Do you feel different?"

Suzi shrugged and put her head down, "You caught me with my words, didn't you?"

Perjuna began to laugh and then smiled at her. "We are not trying to change anyone here, just help you see your potential. A professional athlete does all sorts of things to get themselves prepared to perform the best they possibly can. We feel like life is a sport here and we want to prepare everyone for life the best that they can. We think a sound mind, body, and soul are necessary to reach the human potential, but most people don't have any idea how to do this. And even if they do, life gets in the way. Too busy with their job, their relationship, chasing kids, their social life... oh, their social life. Here people are committed to focusing on improving all areas of their life. It's not for everyone, but for those who make the choice, we think it is beneficial."

"I see your motivation, but how do you know that your way is the best way to improve people's lives? Seems like quite a big assumption to make about how people live."

Perjuna smiled again and paused for a long moment. "If you are quiet and listen long enough, the instructions are there for the taking," he almost whispered.

She just stared at him. He truly believed this was the secret to life. Something happened at that very moment. She was caught in a daze for a second and suddenly felt lightheaded. She then began to feel as though she was trapped in some sort of time warp. Her body felt like it was floating in the air, although she was still standing on firm ground. She felt like she could see forward and backwards in time all at once. Faces and places and stars and galaxies all spun around in her mind. She felt almost nauseous, then a tear slowly ran down her face.

Andrew did finally report back to his boss, but it was not the story they wanted. He told them enough to give them a story, but he also told them that he was not coming back, and that was the real story. They were startled and, then, really wanted more details. His reply was simply, "You will just have to see for yourself." In the end, the network decided to do a shorter story. They did tell the world that their own reporter had began undercover to explore what was happening at Genisova and had decided to quit his job and join Genisova full time. The story began to gain some momentum and to the network's surprise people all over began to call and inquire more about this man who left for this mysterious place. It also began a bit of an uproar with some fanatics who said he was being brainwashed and that they should go and rescue him. Some people said he was being blackmailed into staying and that they should investigate what was really going on inside this crazy city of lunatics. Right wing Christians called it a work of the devil and that it should be shut down. They warned people not to be persuaded by temptation and that the devil worked in sly, evil ways.

The story did say that the government had already investigated Genisova and had reported that nothing of any danger was going on there. They also said the government did have an open relationship with the leaders there and that although there was nothing to worry about, the information of their doings was private and did not need to be disclosed. The larger details were also revealed because at this point it was general knowledge that they were planning on building a space station and that they believed that the sun was certainly going to cause major problems with all of planet earth. They did not believe that the space station was a permanent fix and that they realized it would be impossible for everyone to live on space stations, but that this was just a stepping stone into advancing our abilities to move off from earth.

They were also working on ways to protect people on earth from the changing sun. There were no details, but some pretty good guesses as to what this would entail. This little story caused not only a stir with fanatics, but also with most average people who were just too busy to stop and realize what was actually happening with the earth. People began to petition that the government should also do something for the rest of the public. If this group of people were preparing for end times, then shouldn't the government be doing something, too? Were they making plans to build a space station? Was the information about the sun correct? There began to be bit of a panic.

Needless to say, Sarkovia was immediately on the phone with Landau and the rest of the Council. Things really got crazy when congressmen from two different states resigned their positions and left for Genisova. There was also a famous actress, two famous singers, and a professional baseball player who all gave up their lucrative careers to join Genisova (this is another story for another time). The buzz began to take over social media and, really, all of the media. People began to drive up to and camp around Genisova. There began to be a waiting list to get in and there were a couple of instances where people actually tried to break into Genisova.

They, unfortunately, had to up the security measures. They were not sure if these people were wanting to join, just curious, or wanted to attack Genisova. Helicopters, planes and drones began to fly over top of the property, but there was very little they could do besides take photos. One helicopter actually landed and people got out, but there really wasn't much for them to see. They were then prosecuted for trespassing. It was revealed that there were also two neighboring areas that bordered the original territory. There was a secluded area with several modern, industrial buildings up in the nearby mountains. It was difficult to see from too far away. There appeared to be no road to this area. It was suggested that there may be a tunnel or hidden transportation system to this little section. The other area was now in construction. It was what appeared to be an airport runway area. It was connected by a visible gate with a road through the far back side of Genisova. This was clearly going to be mission control, and the launch and landing area for the space crafts.

Not only did this news stir up the people of the U.S., but it also began to make the rest of the world take notice. There was now a set meeting at the United Nations to try and deal with the potential backlash from the people of their individual nations. The US decided not to make any decisions about what they would do until after this meeting. There were all sorts of things to consider. If they did decide that there was an issue with the sun, then it could send parts of the world into a major panic, which could have devastating consequences. This would have to be handled delicately. The White House was already aware of what was going on at Genisova and had been monitoring them fairly closely. It was clear that they needed to get even more involved now. They had not expected the sudden uproar from the news story and how quickly things would ramp up over this.

Landau was also getting a little concerned about how things had taken such a sudden turn and was worried about what might become of it. Washington had decided that they would need to now have a constant presence at Genisova and they were desiring to have more control over what was happening there. Enter Sarkovia and company. Sarkovia and his crew of investigators jumped all over this opportunity to get inside Genisova. However, this is where the Council drew the line and it would become the first major conflict at Genisova. Some other countries in the world were now making plans to build their own space station and try to possibly beat Genisova to the sky. China, Russia, Japan and five European countries were in the process of making plans to build their own version of this space station. Genisova thought this was great, actually, and wondered how they would go about this.

There were suddenly many phone calls to the Council from several of these countries desiring tours of their facilities. China and Russia also called but only to make some inquiries. China, in an effort to seem powerful, actually declared that they would be launching a mission to colonize a planet and a moon. They apparently had already been working on this to some degree, and they had the wealth to throw at it. Now they were ramping up their efforts. There had been attempts in the past to send a crew to Mars, but, ultimately they all fell through. There was just not enough solid research and evidence to risk sending anyone there yet. The closest of these was a droid that was supposed to be sent to Mars in a year or two. This was going to be a test mission to try and see how things would go. But, even though the droids kept improving, the mission kept getting delayed to wait for more of these improvements. Genisova was also working on improving their droids and its AI. Their main goal was to improve its mobility and ability to receive commands quickly and smoothly.

Great Britain showed the most interest in Genisova. They wanted to come and tour the facility and get a better understanding of the technology they were working on. They were very open minded and wanted to collaborate as much as Genivosa would be willing to with them. The Council now had some big decisions to make. The ideals of the city they had created were now being inquired about. There would be scrutiny and the desire to share information. This did not settle well with the Council. They were now under pressure to make some impactful decisions about the future of their mission. If they shared some vital information they risked it being leaked to the world and as much as they wished goodwill upon everyone, they felt like there was a right and wrong way to go about doing this.

In the end they decided they would give anyone that inquired some basic information about the way the things operated at Genisova but no specific details of anything of higher intelligence. After about a month of the media's continuous coverage it began to die down, as nothing too exciting ever happened. Like all things in the busy world of today, nothing keeps anyone's attention for too long. Eventually people go back to their busy lives and their old worries and forget about the news of yesterday. The curiosity of Genisova had increased the number of people wanting to become members, but they did not have the means to handle too many people at once. They took in the maximum number of people they could handle and tried their best to keep all the same program in place. They were also beginning to move on to the next phase of Genisova.

—∞—

It was true that there was an area adjacent to the existing villages of Genisova that was accessible only from one gate on the far southwest side of the property. This was, of course, the staging area for the space travel. There would need to be all of the existing infrastructure for building the space rockets and also the actual space station and a place to launch everything. The plan was to build larger pay loaders that would be able to bring large quantities of materials into space to build the station. The amount of ships and the amount of flights that would be necessary to build a space station of this magnitude was enormous. The plans would need to be fully developed ahead of time before the first flight even began. How big would the station be? How long would it take to build? These were questions that they were wanting to know as soon as possible, but they were waiting on the technology to improve in some areas to help reduce the amount of time and energy necessary.

There was so much planning involved with building a city in space. Of course, if you do it the right way, you build part of the structure first and then make it livable. Once it can sustain life, then you keep adding on to it. The main thing they were waiting on was a new fuel source with even better propulsion to lift the materials in to space. The problem with most fuels was the weight of the actual fuel. The creative way of thinking said you should not carry the fuel source at all, but instead, use the elements floating around the space craft and create the fuel.

This was why the concept of a new building material was so crucial to the entire project. The science behind this new material was under the highest level of security. What they found was that the secret lay in the way the atoms of any particular material were shaped on a molecular level to give it strength. Once they developed the technology to arrange the atoms in a certain way, they could control its properties better. By knowing this they were able to continue to try different geometric shapes with many different materials until they were able to find what they were looking for.

They also were looking for a material that was relatively common and thus less expensive. Making a strong and light material out of diamonds was not going to be of much help. It needed to be made out of a common and basic element. Lastly, this material needed to protect the people inside from harmful radiation and UV rays. They believed they had finally found the answer to this key piece to their plans. These two pieces of the puzzle—the composite material and the fuel—were nearly to completion and so the plans for Phase 2 were in the making. This created a whole new area of research and development and would require much more manpower. Good thing Andrew's story had brought some much needed new help to the fold.

—∞—

Andrew on the other hand, now had a newfound fame, but one of which he was not sure he desired. He had made the decision to stay long before he went and gave the network his final story. He could have just left and not returned, but he felt obligated to do something. He did have a final meeting with the Council before he did this and they gave their recommendations on how to handle it. He took their advice and then went home and made final arrangements for moving back to Genisova. He did not schedule a meeting with his boss and decided to just show up one day and catch him off guard. He met with his secretary and asked if he had any moments in his busy day to chat. She said she would inquire and see what he wanted to do. He waited for about a half hour and then was told he would have about 10 minutes.

"Great, that's all I'll need."

"How is your report coming Andrew?" the secretary asked.

"It's done!"

"Wow. Are you here to set up that appointment?"

"Nope. This is it."

"Oh. Really? Is something wrong?"

"No, everything is absolutely perfect," he said matter of factly.

"Ok, well, he is ready for you now."

Evan opened his office door and said, "The prodigal son returns at last!"

"Something like that," Andrew said as he got up and walked into his boss's office and sat down.

"So, it must be good since you just showed up so impromptu like this."

"It is good, but maybe not in the way you may like."

"How so?" Evan now seemed a little concerned.

Andrew paused and looked down, and then let out a big sigh.

"I don't know how to say this, but, I'm leaving my position here and am going to join Genisova full time."

"What? Are you serious?" The look of shock was all over his face.

"Yes. Completely and assuredly."

"How can this be? I think it is in your contract that you have to finish this story. I have to say, I am very disappointed in this decision."

"Well, I had a feeling nobody would take this well. Please, just sit and listen to me for five minutes, if you have them, and try to understand what I have to say."

"Okay, shoot."

"I left here with no intentions of ever staying there. Honestly. I didn't even hardly know what this place was about. I was so caught up in living my life here and trying to further my career that I was hardly aware of anything else going on. This place and the people took me by complete and total surprise. I am the story here. Like it or not. I can't say enough about everything that I experienced. If I thought it was for everyone, I would tell them to drop what they are doing right now and go and sign up. But, it's not, so I won't, but I think about it."

"What was so great about this place? You have my attention for a moment here."

"This is going to seem kind of corny but there was an energy there that I have never felt before. Wait, let me rephrase that, I have felt the energy before, but only for fleeting moments. It was nearly a constant while I was there. It is hard to explain and really you almost have to go see for yourself to understand what I am talking about. There are some extremely intelligent people there, not to mention the people that created this place. They can't all be crazy. I was very pessimistic when I began, but was so surprised by the people I found there. I generalized and judged before I even set foot in the door. Now I have the utmost respect for the people there and what their mission is, both in their greater mission and what their individual mission is for each person that comes in there."

"You seemed to have fallen under their spell over there. Are you sure this is what you want to do? Seems to me like a bunch of weirdo quacks. We are going to do a story and now I am starting to think you may be the focal point, for better or worse. The public may laugh and joke about you doing this. Or maybe even more than that."

"I know this seems like a ludicrous decision, but believe it or not, I have spent a lot of time thinking about it. The truth is I began considering it shorty after I arrived. Trust me, I am the last person I thought would be feeling this way. It has taken me completely by surprise."

"What are you going to do there? Do they need journalists? What about all your friends and family?"

"There are actually quite a few different things I could do. Turns out I actually have several different interests in life. But, there, it doesn't matter what I do. I just need to contribute to their society and help the cause. My family and friends will understand. I never really had any great friends in life, which I realized more and more the longer I was there."

"It sounds like you've got it all figured out. Aren't you going to miss anything about the world we live in? This place makes it seem like we live in a version of hell out here."

"Of course there are many great things about the world that I will miss, but not as much as thought I would."

"How so? And, how do you know?"

"Well, for starters, it is not prison. They have fine foods and some of the nicer things in life, but just not in excess. The process, we'll call it, that you go through here helps you to realize what is truly important in life, and it's not money or the things it can buy. If I really want to go have a fancy dinner at an expensive restaurant, I can. But you know what, when you do that, and then go back there, it's just different. The lavish lifestyle loses its allure, somehow. When you see things clearly, you have a greater understanding of what is truly important in life, and it's not a $200 bottle of wine."

"Somehow you do seem changed. Not sure if it is for the better, but you even are talking different. What I really want to know is, what are you giving me for the story?"

"Everything that I am telling you."

"That's not a story! I need some footage, interviews, something solid here. You have to have something sneaky in there."

"Actually, what I am giving you is all I have. I still have not been given phase 2 clearance. I was called out on the very first day I arrived as to what I was up to. But it didn't matter to them. They still treated me the same. They just fed me into the process like everyone else. Sinner or saint, rocket scientist or grocery teller. It doesn't matter. They knew exactly what I was trying to do and it changed nothing. But I have not gained their complete trust and most likely never will until I do what I am doing right now, which is resigning."

"Hmph. I can't believe this. Weren't you being paid while you were doing this?"

"I don't know if I was. I don't care. I don't want it because I don't need it. You can keep it and if they already paid me, I will give it back."

"Wow, giving your money back? That's unheard of! Are they coercing you into doing something you don't want to?"

"What? Are you serious? Do I look like someone being forced into doing something? Listen, I'm okay. I'm going to be just fine. The network is going to be just fine, and so are you. What you should be doing the story on, is the crisis that planet earth is going to be in in about 100 years."

"Its kind of hard to get the general public excited about something that is going to happen in 100 years."

"I get it, it's a tough sell, but these people know it is real and they are actually doing something about it because in 100 years, it will be too late. So long Evan. It really was great working with you. If you ever get tired of this rat race, give us a call."

He walked out of the office, smiled at the secretary and looked around one last time with a sense of wonderment. Once upon a time, this place was his future dream and now it seemed like a distant dream. How things can change in the blink of an eye.

—⁂—

Speaking of changing, his life back in Genisova was also changing. Now that there was such a buzz about this story, people began to take notice of Andrew. He was now a hero of sorts because of what he did. Of course, people here didn't treat him too different, but in a way they did. They would say things like, "That was pretty cool, what you did with your old job" and "We are so glad you chose this life over that life, we think you made the right choice." They all had made the same choice at some point in their life, but his choice was now becoming "the" story that the rest of the country was talking about. All the other leading scientists that came to Genisova were essentially just taking a new job, but because his job was so glorified and created such a stir in the national news, he was being made out to be the first person of interest to do this. And, there was something about the way it all happened.

All the other people for the most part were actively seeking out Genisova because it was a good fit with their lifestyle and intentions. Andrew came into it blindly and naive about what was going on, practically an opponent of Genisova. Then, out of his own discretion made the decision to renounce his life from before and join the cause. This is what made him such a celebrity on the inside and such a huge controversy on the outside. It was debatable in many circles as to whether or not he had made the right decision. Some said he was crazy or being blackmailed, and others said he was audacious and bold. One way or another, everyone had an opinion about Andrew. Even though he had loved the limelight on the outside, he was starting to relish the quiet life a little bit more at Genisova. The Council applauded his decision and the way he handled it. It reflected their qualities beautifully and was more or less a great advertisement for what was going on at Genisova. And with the good comes the bad. And the bad were starting to show up at Genisova.

They thought they were pretty well prepared for the individual who was trying to cause problems at Genisova, but not as well for a large group. After you passed the first gate, there was now a second gate, which was pretty much like going through the sensors at any airport, except with new advanced technology. It was virtually impossible to get anything through this gate that was a weapon of any sort. Of course, people were getting crafty at building weapons and explosives at this time and it could be challenging to catch some items. Although they tried to minimize the amount of shipments of all items in and out of Genisova, there was still quite a bit of material that had to be imported.

They realized this would be the likely place for anyone to try and sneak something into Genisova. This is how the first major problem occurred at Genisova. It began when a current member, named Anton, had been acting very odd lately. When this began happening, the Council was informed and were watching him closely. You see, Anton, had come from the outside with an attitude that he was going to try and destroy as many members of Genisova as he could. Why? Because he did not have a life worth living and felt like someone had to pay for his miserable life. This reason made no sense at all, but is this not the reason why any madman tries to do something heinous? Who can understand anyone that does something like this.

All members were not allowed to have any type of weapon in their home. The only weapons in the entire property were the parastuns used by security guards. They did not believe in violence but they did still need to protect themselves in worst case scenarios. These weapons were meant to be a message of commitment to peace and non-violence.

Anton had studied quietly the workings of certain aspects of Genisova and had discovered a possible area to sneak in a weapon or steal a weapon from a guard who was not alert. He had wandered one day into the loading dock area in one of the buildings in the industrial village, and was out of place enough so that one of the loaders had enough sense to inquire who he was. He was then questioned by the Council on what he was up to, but he just said that he was curious and didn't know it was a crime to wander around some of the buildings. He then took leave for about a week without much warning and when he returned seemed even more distressed.

He began to show up at odd places and not show up at his classes. The Council had never had to remove a member of Genisova but were considering putting him on high watch. He was certainly up to something and they knew it, but there wasn't much they could do besides be vigilant. The only good thing was that there was rarely a large group of people together. Anton was trying to decide what was going to be his best chance for causing the most destruction. His attempt was foiled as he was caught in the loading dock once again, but the workers there had been alerted to him and so they tried to apprehend him. There were two men unloading a truck and one went for help and the other confronted him.

He had taken a knife out of the kitchen of one of the restaurants and tried to attack the worker. He stabbed him a couple of times before help arrived and was chased down and hit with a parastun. The victim was rushed to the hospital and although injured pretty badly, did not die. However, this whole scenario brought a whole new problem to the Council.

They truly felt this was an isolated incident but had to prepare for the worst. The attack now raised some new issues with the residents of Genisova and there was growing concern. Maybe Andrew and his story was not such a good thing for their greater cause. People began to inquire about how it happened and what they should do to be prepared. They really did not want to bring weapons into Genisova at all if possible, but this was definitely the time to introduce the parastun. They had a general meeting for everyone to attend so they could discuss this in an open forum. The consensus was that although they were worried about something like this happening again, they still did not want to increase security and guards policing around the property. The use of the parastun would be used only if necessary but everyone was glad that a new technology had been developed that would not be lethal. They decided that there would be more security cameras installed around the property and that everyone would agree to wear a watch or wristband or one of any other devices that would help security keep track of suspicious people. For now, this was the end of this dilemma.

Landau was eagerly watching the development of some key research projects, several of which had been nearing completion. They were close enough that development of the next phase of Genivosa began, which was an area designated to be the launch site and mission control. Another area of concern for the Council was the reality of living in space indefinitely. There were many potential issues that were associated with human beings living in space. The major space flight contenders had been working on many of these issues for years. They had resolved long ago that the human body was not very well designed to be in zero gravity. It wreaked havoc on many body systems including the brain and vision. Not to mention that the harmful rays in space, if not blocked properly, would be detrimental and could cause cancer. Even with a cure for cancer, if you continue to expose yourself to the cause, you would eventually die.

They had solved many of the issues or at least reduced many of the effects space had on the body. Genisova was not completely sure of some of the potential issues of living in space, so this would be an experiment of sorts. There were now a couple small space stations in operation orbiting earth and humans had lived on these for up to three years without coming back to earth. These stations were only large enough for a handful of people, usually scientists doing research. Every time these people came back they had fewer and fewer symptoms, and the ones they had were being resolved as quickly as possible. It was likely that the first humans on a Genisova space station would need to come back to earth for various intervals until all the different kinks were worked out.

The fact was, no one had ever lived permanently in space and what this would do to humans over time was unknown. But we would never find out until we tried. They knew this project was going to take a long time to perfect and there would be problems along the way. One of the main problems, zero gravity, could be reduced by creating a revolving space station which would create artificial gravity, thus minimizing its affects. The design of the space station was up for debate, but some things were for certain and this was one of them. They were actually designing four space stations, with intentions of making the latter ones more advanced as they went. This helped solve some of the debates going on, as one would just remind them that they could use their ideas on the next one. There were so many things to work on for this immense project. The details were endless and exhausting. From designing the space station to the transportation rocket ships to solving all the issue of living long term in space. The Council and Landau had a lot on their minds.

In the meantime, some other developments they had been working on were also getting closer to working stage. The next big development that was almost ready for prototype was the UV reflector shield. There was no guarantee that the space station was going to be successful or how long it would take to develop, and it would be impossible for everyone to live there. The next best thing would be to try and develop something to allow humans to live on earth for as long as possible. The invisible umbrella, as it was nicknamed, was that last hope. This would allow for humans to walk around under the sun as if they were wearing enough UV protection from a space suit. How would this work? Was it possible?

The scientists at Genisova had been working hard at this dilemma for the entire time of its existence. They believe they had come up with an answer. It would involve building towers around the area they wanted to be protected. These towers would communicate with each other, sending out an invisible force field that would deflect some of the UV rays and thus protecting the people below. This force field was essentially trying to imitate the magnetic field that protects the earth from the sun. They had developed a way to enhance this effect and connect it between the towers. There were some limitations to this process and they had not tested it over a long period of time, but it had shown signs of being successful. There was also the problem of protecting the space station from UV rays. This could be solved by shielding the walls with a new material they had designed especially for this purpose. The design of the space station would hopefully allow for much sunlight to enter as it would likely need to grow vegetation for food. There was just so much to plan for on this space station and the rest of planet earth's survival.

Maybe most importantly on Landau's mind was Lucina and her journey through Genisova. He tried to not show any favoritism towards her and limited his contact with her at first. He wanted to see how serious she was about it and get an unbiased experience there. When, after a couple weeks, she decided that she wanted to leave for a weekend, it was very difficult for him not to pry and find out why. It turned out that she really had not planned for this to happen like it was. She thought that maybe Landau would give her a week or so and then intervene and let her hang out with him for a while. After it became apparent that she was going to get no "special treatment" she began to get impatient and frustrated.

She fully participated in the curriculum and actually was enjoying it more than she expected, but in the back of her mind she had different plans. She just wanted to see if there was still any connection left between them, but this was getting her nowhere. She had decided she would play a little game and leave for a while and see if it registered on his radar or not. She went back home and went out with her friends and visited with family. She went to see a new musical that was the hottest ticket in town, after having an amazing dinner at her favorite fusion sushi restaurant. She spent a day at the art museum and just enjoyed some other things that were not available in Genisova. After a couple days away she realized it was going to be hard to go back and give up her life on the outside. She left on a Friday and stayed until about Wednesday the next week when she began to feel a pull to go back and see if Landau would even notice she was gone. She decided to wait until Friday and then she would go back.

Landau, on the other hand, was very busy with so many other things that the time did fly by. He would like to think that he didn't miss her when she was gone, but the truth was, his mind kept wandering back to her. He was frustrated that he couldn't control his thoughts. After Tuesday he checked to see if she was back yet. When she wasn't he actually felt a little pain inside and lost his appetite. This feeling shocked him, because it was a distant memory that he couldn't remember experiencing for a long time. He then grew angry, surprisingly, and told himself to forget about her. When he found out a week or so later that she had returned, he found himself confused and happy simultaneously. He decided that he would go and meet with her and find out what was going on. She was alone in her room one evening and he simply showed up and knocked on her door.

She opened the door and acted a little shocked to see him, "Oh, hi, how are you?"

"I'm good, how about you?" he replied.

"I'm fine. Just back for another go at this place." She invited him in and they both went and sat down on the couch.

"I see. You sound a little unsure about yourself. Is this really where you want to be?"

"Yes, and, no. I'm still trying to figure out what I want. Going back home made coming back here pretty challenging. The life here is not as exciting as my life was back there, I'm not going to lie to you."

"Then why did you come back?"

"Why do you think, Landau?"

He knew the answer to this question and began to blush a little, but then quickly responded, "Would you like to go on a little adventure with me?"

She livened up quickly and replied excitedly, "Yes!"

"I would like to show you something, something I really should not be showing you."

Lucina felt like responding modestly and saying, "Well, you don't have to break the rules or get in trouble or anything." But she also knew that then she may well be waiting for another month or so before she would get any real close contact with him. This was her chance, so she said, "I promise not to tell anyone whatever it is that you are going to show me. Where are we going?"

"There is another part of Genisova that very few know about. It is where the most secretive work takes place at Genisova. You would have to get clearance to go there, but I can handle that. Meet me tomorrow at the security center and we can get you added to the clearance list."

"Landau, why are you doing this? Is there something you would like to talk about? I feel like there is something you are not telling me or that you want to tell me but are not sure what to say."

Landau paused for a second and then started, "Lu, you know that I care for you very much, in a way unlike maybe anyone else I have ever met. It has bothered me that we were unable to reconcile our differences before, but it is not like there was any animosity between us. Just two people taking separate paths in life. The part I am not sure about is what to do with those feelings that still lie deep inside me."

"I think it is very clear that I would not be here if I did not still have very similar feelings and, I too, do not know what to do with them. The love that we shared was intense and passionate and magical. Something like that does not leave anyone's soul quickly, if at all. The problem is that I don't think that I ever wanted it to leave me. I felt like it was a gift given to me, that so many people never get the chance to experience. It has stayed with me and left me with an empty feeling inside ever since we separated. Remind me again why it is that we left each other, both feeling this way? It is almost a riddle to me that I cannot solve."

Landau just sat there, not knowing what to say. He looked down and she reached over and touched him gently on the face, pulling his eyes up to meet hers. They locked eyes and the rest of the world began to fade away into a blur. Slowly they leaned in to each other and kissed softly. It was the first time he had kissed a woman in years. He actually couldn't remember if he had kissed anyone else since they last kissed. He wanted to kiss her more, but he knew that it would be unwise and that if there was to be more of anything between them it would have a chance to develop in time.

"What is happening?" he quietly asked with a half dazed voice.

"I don't know what you call it here at Genisova, but I think it is something like synergy," she said with a devilish grin.

He laughed at her little sarcastic stab and got up to go.

"I am not actually sure why I even came over here tonight, but I am starting to understand a little more now. Sleep well and meet me tomorrow at the center. I think this may help you understand me more than anything else I could possibly tell you."

"Landau, I really did miss you."

He left and she closed the door. She was overcome with joy and eagerness to spend more time with him. It was like when they first started dating so many years ago. She also was left with a wonderment of where he was going to take her and why he was virtually breaking all the rules for her just to bring her there. It was going to be difficult to get any sleep at all.

Landau went home and found himself breaking into an uncontrollable smile about every other minute or so. Home for Landau was where he was going to be bringing Lu tomorrow. For he lived in the mountains in an area that was secluded from the rest of Genisova. It was only accessible through an underground tunnel that was beneath one of the research and development buildings, and only certain people were allowed up there. There were a couple other Council members that lived in this area, but it was also an area of the highest level of security.

Lu really wanted to impress him in the morning, but things were different here at Genisova. People didn't care as much about appearances and most people dressed similarly through the day. She wanted to stand out, but did not want to make too much out of it. She decided at the last minute to not worry about what she was wearing and just focus on being attentive and genuine with him. She knew that he didn't care so much about physical things like this, but this was a hard thing for her to let go of.

She had made her way in the world through looking a certain way and wearing certain clothes. She was very attractive and these types of things actually took her far in so many ways that she began to question why it worked so well for her. Her vanity in the outside world had helped her charm so many other people, but here her good looks were worthless. No one cared what she was wearing or that she was beautiful. The people here cared about making a difference in the cause and contributing to the society. They cared about their health, their mind, their soul, and about reaching their potential. This she had learned in the brief time she was there. It was making her question her motives in her other life.

She left to meet Landau and they went in to the Security center together. He had her sit in a room and went to talk with the chief of security. He was gone for about ten minutes and then came back with a disheartened look on his face.

"It appears that they know me too well here. They had already alerted the chief that it may be possible that I would try to do something like this," he said sheepishly.

She broke into a smile. "So you're saying that they actually know you better than you know yourself? It is kind of funny, really. They were planning on you trying to sneak me into your secret place and they were one step ahead of you. Ha! I love it. What are you going to do now that they know what you are up to?"

"Well, it seems as though I need to sit down with all of them and have a little chat about my intentions."

"And what are your intentions, Landau?" She was certainly loving this attention she was getting and apparently already had garnered from the rest of his friends here.

"I guess, our little adventure is going to have to wait for another day. Is that okay? How about we get some breakfast?"

"Is that a date?"

"I guess so, if you want to call it that. Let's just say we can sit down and get reacquainted, how's that?"

"I would love that."

Their secret mission would have to wait. But that was okay. Instead, they took a walk through one of the villages toward Landau's favorite places.

"Let's go to this cozy little place I know, they have the best coffee. You know how much I love a good cup of strong dark roast. I have had little to do with any of the agriculture here, but I have specially requested this blend. Wait 'til you try this."

The sun was barely up and its rays gently touched the trees and flowers surrounding them. As they walked, they could feel the energy between them flowing, creating a bond, connecting them on a higher level. If you have ever fallen in love for the first time, then you know this energy, this connection. It doesn't need to be described because you already know what it is. This invisible force was the thing Genisovians were focused on. Little did Landau know he would be experiencing this like he was at this moment.

They reached their destination and ordered some yummy breakfast. Landau loved the bacon and avocado omelette and Lu tried the eggs Benedict. It was fantastic. The conversation flowed easily back and forth as they picked up where they once left off.

The happiness inside both of them ironically made them a little sad that they had both been so selfish about their relationship before. They had lost out on all this time together, however, this was the path the universe took them on. Before they noticed, it was already noon. Landau suddenly realized he had to get some stuff done. They got up to leave and were not sure exactly how to say goodbye. They wanted to embrace and kiss, but realized this may not be the best idea in a public place just yet. Instead they fell into each others arms and hugged like two long lost friends.

All the pieces were falling into place at Genisova. They had reached a point where they felt like they could begin designs on the rocket ships or rather, space planes, that would be carrying people and the building blocks of the space station into space. Jonathan was heavily involved in this process and was thrilled to be a part of it. The droids had also reached a point where they could be sent on the missions to begin building the space station. The first station and those that would follow were going to be placed in one of the 5 Lagrange points, which were locations in space around the earth that were in a equal balance of gravity between the sun, earth and moon. These areas allowed the station to orbit without much concern of gravity pulling them out of position. The design of the future space stations were proposed to grow in size and capabilities.

They would be able to dock and load space ships more easily and become future ports for future travel around the solar system. As you could imagine, this was a designers dream to be able to actually have a say in things that once upon a time were just science fiction in movies like Star Wars or Star Trek. This was becoming a reality. It would be a very slow process, but it was going to happen. Space ships or planes had become more commonplace in the world and building them was not that difficult a task, but making them have more advanced features and with new responsibilities was the challenge.

The new material, which they called Staralene, had been perfected and was now being used to make the rockets. It was being incorporated into the design of all the future space stations and was making the estimated time for completion shorter. The plan was to send as few people as possible at first into space and as many droids as they could handle. The droids had been designed to be able to make basic motions necessary for building the space station. They had a very basic Artificial Intelligence that could process simple commands and carry them out. Each droid would need to have a commander on earth to control them and give the correct orders for building the station.

The first station was going to be fairly simple in design and smaller in size so as to function as a sort of prototype where they could study how well the design functions in space. They also would only allow limited people at first live on the station as they began to work out the problems as they arose. It was believed that all of the potential health problems were resolved for the most part, but there could be things that they had not accounted for. After several months, designs for everything had begun and the attention of all Genisovians had shifted in this direction. It was all that anyone talked about. They had poured their lives into this project and were now seeing it come to fruition. It was an amazing accomplishment to get this far, even though there was a long way to go and many potential roadblocks on the way.

One of these roadblocks was the ever-present Sarkovia and friends. They continued to ramp up the pressure for the Council to give them more details and information. At this point they had discerned there was assuredly more secretive events happening in the secluded area up in the mountains. They had figured out how to access this area and were requesting a tour. Fortunately, the security to access this area made it virtually impossible to do on your own. One had to pass their protocol and until you were entered into their system, you were not getting in.

Suzi had begun to embrace some of the ideas of Genisova that she initially had rejected. She did not all of a sudden believe in God or become super religious, but she began to recognize the feelings inside that were certainly changing who she was and helping her become a more conscious person. She could not necessarily come up with a valid reason for why she felt changed, but no longer fought the feelings and emotions she had inside that were inexplicable. She was more aware of her surroundings. She was calmer, more relaxed, and did not feel stressed about achieving as much as she possibly could in her field. She took things as they came and was okay with the outcome.

She began to believe that life was happening exactly the way it was supposed to. She began to think about how she had spent all of her career searching for planets in our galaxy and others looking for potential areas for life to exist. This was an amazing thing to behold. What if we did find life on another planet or moon? What would this mean for mankind? How would it change people's perspective on the universe? These thoughts began to have a different affect on her than before. She used to just look at it all as just data and a puzzle to solve. Now there was more to it. It had more weight. She couldn't explain it, but it did. She was in awe of the immensity and mysteriousness of the universe. She also noticed now that she was back to doing what she loved that it came to her much easier.

Creative thoughts and ideas just flowed from her and it was like a new high. She was in love with living her life. She began to see how all of her colleagues were happy most all of the time and everything was always positive about them. They were always encouraging and never seemed to lose hope. The environment was contagious. She was amazed at the breakthrough discoveries that were made there on a regular basis. However, she was not surprised for some odd reason. Little did she know that there was a reason why these discoveries were happening at an unprecedented rate.

Her task was to focus more on where we as humans would go to once we figured out how to live in outer space and then travel further distances. Would we learn how to hibernate? There was a team working on this. Would we learn how to travel at speeds much faster than we already do? There were teams working on this. Would we be able to open wormholes and bend the fabric of space time to get to distant galaxies? Yup, they were working on this. Could we someday learn how to "beam me up Scotty". Working on that too. These all seemed like things of science fiction and impossible to our minds of present day. However, once upon a time humans flying in a plane or talking through FaceTime on a handheld phone would have been considered miracles.

The human mind has so much potential and that was the main thing Genisova was working on—the human potential. They knew there would be answers to all these questions that had evaded humanity since we were able to ask. It was only a matter of time. Their goal was to accelerate that time. Dr. Andersen was one of the leaders of her field and was fascinating to watch in action. There was something about him that was different than most of the others in their department. Suzi couldn't quite put her finger on it, but she knew something was up.

—⁂—

Mohammed had entered the next phase in his work life but had also become a sort of leader for the place of worship he had helped build. This building had become a center for spirituality of all sorts. People from many different backgrounds had shown interest in the idea of the building and once it was completed it was a definite newsworthy item to the Genisovians. People who had not been from any religion were curious about it and people who were more on the religious side were excited to have a place to worship. There were no clergymen or religious leaders in Genisova so there could be no formal ceremony for any of the different religions; instead there were different times of the day set aside for different services.

Some small groups formed to listen to different readings from the various different books and the rest of the time was for discussion, some singing or chanting or silent prayer and meditation. Besides these various requested times for certain religions the rest of the time was more or less an open format. People came and went as they pleased and used the place of worship as they saw fit. Often there would be conversations and discussions that broke out between the people there. It was often found that there was a strong source of religion in many of the inhabitants of Genisova, but very few of them were extremely strict of their faith. Many of them had been brought up in a certain religion and then, as they became adults and were left to practice on their own, their devotion dwindled. Not necessarily because they wanted to, but because it was not as urgent to them in their life. They maybe no longer felt the guilt associated with most religions if you are not practicing it as the strict doctrines recommended.

The world was slowly becoming a more tolerant and open minded place. Every new generation was born into a world where parents raised their children more aware of all the different religions of the world and that maybe their own religious beliefs were not the only way to god. It only makes sense to think that if you were born into a family that believed in Hinduism and everyone around you believed in Hinduism, and had for centuries, that you would believe in Hinduism too. You wouldn't just up and decide to be a Christian one day even if you had heard the Bible. Unfortunately there are people of all religions that think there is not room for another belief and that all those other people are wrong and they are right. Pretty arrogant actually. But it is human nature to want to be right and believe that what you believe is right. Who really wants to practice a religion that you think is wrong? Of course, you think it is right, or else you wouldn't be doing it. (Unless you did it out of guilt.)

By and large the people who were in Genisova were of an open mindset. They appreciated that all religions have some value and are a medium to get to God or whatever label you want to give it. They recognized that there was more to us than just what we see with our five senses. They may not be able to explain this higher power, but to leave space in their consciousness for that belief was enough. What people did understand were the feelings associated with prayer and meditation and in communion with others. There was an undoubted connection between humans and it was on a heightened level when these types of the things were part of the equation. There is power in prayer, as they say. Whether you believe that there is a God sitting up in heaven answering the bell or if there is a higher level of energy that is connected together when this happens, there is something there. In fact, the people at Genisova took it to another level. They understood this on a deeper level and dedicated an entire team of people to research this.

Some research showed that when people were prayed for while they were sick, their chance of recovery was greater than when not prayed for. There was some subjectivity to this, but the fact they were even researching this showed there was potentially something worth looking into. The team was dedicated to science and finding the connection between the two. What was the science behind prayer? They felt that the answers were hiding in a place that no one could see. Of course, no one could see it, but they could sense it. If they could see it then everyone would know it was there. But most people don't. So they began to look for mysteries in science with no explanations and go after these areas. One in particular that seemed to keep coming up as a possibility was what science referred to as quantum entanglement. This is an area of quantum physics that found that two separated particles on a molecular level would show an unknown form of communication between them even when separated by large distances. The communication between these particles would happen instantaneously, making this seemingly impossible communication at a speed faster than the speed of light. How is this possible? What could make them instantly know what the other particle was doing? It is as though there is an invisible energy that connects these two separated particles and allows them to magically talk to each other.

This was discovered long ago by Einstein, but even he would not believe it was true because it did not make sense. This is exactly what the team was looking for. Something that was beyond us, but still measurable and right in front of us. It would seem as though there was another dimension at hand here. That or a form of energy or maybe consciousness at play. Something that was above all that humans were trained to measure in a conventional way so it was time for humans to start thinking differently about it. They knew they were on to something. Just like we all know that even though we have a brain and it does our thinking, there is something behind even that that we cannot explain. The source of our original thought.

Mohammed had embraced his role and tried to expand upon the events happening at this place of worship. He had developed a wonderful relationship with Angeline, his religion instructor. They had continued to have deep thought-provoking conversations about the great mysteries of life and how humans have gone about trying to solve them. He began to have a much deeper appreciation for all other religions.

He began to see the validity to the other religions, yet he still maintained passion for his own. Most of the people that he had conversations with had no problems with other belief systems. In fact, most of the people had pretty much a unique version of their faith. For all religions, despite their claims to have clear cut solutions to the mysteries of life, they clearly reach a point of the unknown. There is no possible way to know what happens before birth and after death. It is, as they say, a matter of faith. But so much is left up to interpretation, which is why most all religions have so many divisions amongst them, all claiming to have the correct interpretation. The basis of all religions is faith and most certainly faith in the unknown. But still faith in something.

This is what all these people that Mohammed talked to said. They told him that they believed in something more than what they could explain, and they were pretty confident in that faith. It was the common denominator amongst all these people. They no longer felt the guilt of not practicing their particular religion, but found that this connection to the divine could be found anywhere and mostly in other people. The point of religion trying to make you feel like a God was upstairs in the clouds keeping track with a clipboard was absurd. In fact, if you asked even the most devout of any religion they would all probably agree with this statement. So where do you draw the line? Are any of the religions clear cut in their answers to the big questions? Most of the people of Genisova felt that there was much gray area in trying to answer questions like what happens when you die? If God is completely good why is there what appears to be evil in the world? Who created the universe? Who created God? These types of questions were part of the reason all of these people were at Genisova. And because they could not necessarily find the answers in religion.

Andrew had finally graduated from the first phase and was now enjoying his new job in the Human Resources department. He helped mostly with the acceptance department that worked with new members. He also helped coordinate communications with much of the outside world. Many of the new members that were interested in learning more about Genisova actually got to talk with Andrew. His ability to talk with others combined with his particular experience helped many new members agree to sign up. His story helped set people at ease about making such a big decision. He continued to try and spend time with Fiona, but found it was fairly difficult. He had wanted to ask her out, but was not sure how it would be if she flat out said no. It had actually been about a month or so since he had run into her.

She was very busy on the Council and there had a been a lot of changes going on, especially with the launch of Phase 2. Not only had they begun creating the new arena for building and launching the space vehicles, but there was quite a bit of craziness going on in the world concerning Genisova and the future of planet earth. Some of the other countries of the world had made the decision to also build a space station in case the predictions about the sun did come true. When they began the process they also began to realize how underprepared they were and how expensive it was going to be. None of the new players in the game set a timetable for when they would begin building a space station and had no idea how long it may be. Needless to say there were many inquiries from all of these countries and even from many others who were considering if they should do something or not.

They needed to increase security, especially since all these different countries were beginning to realize that Genisova may very well be more advanced with their technology for dealing with the sun. Fiona was very involved in all of these processes along with continuing to run the existing population of Genisova. The Council had to begin to delegate some of their responsibilities to new members who they had decided were capable of helping them out. This was a big help in freeing up time for Fiona. It came to be that there were a group of people from Japan that had decided to move to Genisova and Fiona had taken some interest in them because of Japan's interest in Genisova. She was tasked to watch over this group and find out their true intentions of coming to stay here. Were they genuine or were they seeking information? She knew that Andrew had contacted them before they came for their initial visit. She wanted to look into it further so she dropped by Andrew at his work to see what she could find out. Andrew was going about his regular day when she walked up and said hello. Andrew was caught off guard and immediately began to think about what he looked like.

"Oh, hi there! How are you? It's been a while," he began.

"Yes it has," she replied.

"It's been too long, if you ask me. Are you avoiding me?" he joked.

"Well, you know, since you have become a bit of a minor celebrity around here, I didn't know if you would remember me," she shot back at him, chuckling.

"Yeah, it has been a bit of a roller coaster ride since I made the move to do that. I had no idea how it would all go down, really. I was kind of hoping the whole story would just fade away and I could quietly sneak back in here without much commotion."

"It was a bold thing that you did and I think you handled it beautifully. You continue to surprise me."

"I have always wanted to thank you for your personal support of me. I also wanted to tell you something that I am not sure how to tell you."

"Oh yeah? What's that?" she responded with a bit of curiosity.

"Well, when I first came here and met you, I was very taken aback by you because you were not at all what I thought I would find here. In fact, I had a crush on you from the moment I saw you, which I am sure you could tell because you are so, well, so you. For a while, the thought of being around you is what helped keep me here. That is to say, on the days when I thought I could take no more and wanted to get out of here, I would say to myself, well, then, it's goodbye to Fiona. And I would talk myself into staying for a little while longer. Then as time went by and I experienced more of this place I slowly fell in love with this place. I didn't need the thought of you to make me want to stay. So, for that, I thank you. Indirectly you changed the course of my life."

"Wow. That is a lot to take in. So, are you saying you had a crush on me and you no longer do?" she said with a grin.

"Well, it's different now. I'm not going to lie, you are very attractive and what guy wouldn't think you were amazing and beautiful and all those things. But, after I decided I wanted to stay here, I realized that if I told you how I felt and you said, "No thanks," then it could change my comfort level of staying here. For that matter, I have noticed that dating inside Genisova is not talked about very much. I know that there are many people that have met here and have begun dating and even some that have gotten married. But, there is not much drama surrounding it and I felt like I needed to respect that."

"Okay, wow again! Andrew you are hitting me with a lot of stuff all at once here. I appreciate that you respect all of that. It is indeed a bit of a tightrope walk in here. I am not sure what to say in reply because I am so caught off guard."

"I am actually okay with whatever response you give me. I am not trying to imply anything at all. I don't even know if Council members can even date measly commoners like me."

"Don't be ridiculous. We are all just people here. Some have greater responsibilities but we are all still equals."

"I feel like I am just a beginner student learning the basics still and you are a zen master who looks at me as the little child learning his way. The more I understood the ways of life here, the more I realized, not that you were out of my league, but more that I wasn't in a place that was ready to date someone like you. I knew I needed to put the time into just being this new person and being okay with who I was. Learning as much as I could and making changes in my life. I hope this is all making sense and not sounding crazy. I am now more comfortable with all my feelings and it is easier to express my thoughts."

"You are so cute. And silly. I never look at anyone that way. I do understand how you feel, but I would never approach someone that way. That is, look down upon them like I am better than them. I am not going to lie either, when I first met you I was watching you very closely, not because I thought of you like that, but because none of us knew if we could trust you. I really didn't begin to take you too seriously until you had been here for quite some time. We are so busy on the Council, there really is not much time for much extracurricular activities, let alone trying to date someone. Now that you have changed so much and I see you for who you are, I can say that you are potentially someone that I could get to know a little better in that way."

"That is a funny way of saying what I think you are saying. Are you saying what I think you are saying? I mean, I am okay either way, really."

"Yes, I am saying we could get to know each other a little better and see if there is even a remote change of anything more happening between us."

Andrew could not believe his ears. His heart began to beat really fast and his palms grew a little sweaty. He felt a little flush in the face.

"So, you will go on a date with me?"

"You know, I actually had a completely different reason for coming to see you here today. Business that is. We are so far off track now. Yes, let's have lunch or dinner sometime and get to know each other a little better before we get too crazy."

"That is so awesome! I can't believe it. So, what were you coming to see me for?"

"I believe you did the acceptance work on the four Japanese newcomers, correct?"

"Yes, why? Is there a problem?"

"No, but what can you tell me about them? Besides the obvious stuff. Do you believe their motives are true?"

"It is really quite difficult to say. Their English is not the greatest, but I understood enough of them. They seem pretty harmless. What are your concerns with them?"

"Well, as you know, there has been quite a bit of interest around the world in what is going on here in Genisova. We feel as though there is some interest in finding out more information on any or all of our cutting edge technology we have developed here. The Japanese were one of the more interested parties out there. Who knows how far people are willing to go to acquire information."

"I can give you all the information I have on them. They will still have to go through the same protocol as everyone else that comes through here."

"You are probably right about it, but we always keep our eyes and ears open to any suspicious behavior. Like you, for example, when you first started here," she teased.

"Ha, ha. Well I will keep you posted as they get started here. Now, about our dinner plans."

"Okay, okay. Let's meet at the new restaurant in the medical village. How about seven?"

"Sounds fantastic." Andrew was trying to be cool and not show too much excitement, but it was nearly impossible. Just one more thing falling into place in his life.

—⋘—

Jonathan, Theresa and their kids were also very excited about the next phase of Genisova. Jonathan in particular was having an extraordinary experience. He was getting to help out with design of both the space planes and station. The rockets are being called planes because that is more so what they were, planes. They were able solve the issues of flying a space ship that leaves a runway and then is able to create enough speed and momentum to leave the atmosphere without the aid of a rocket booster. Eventually they designed a plane that could convert into a "rocket" in the air which would allow it to leave the atmosphere. This also relied heavily upon the new source of fuel and the way the engine burned this for energy.

Of course, at Genisova they took existing ideas and made them even better. Now they could take off and land on a runway without having to deal with a gas fuselage that needed to separate and be dropped in the ocean. Also, the development of the new building material made this even more efficient. The kids were asking all sorts of questions about the future and what it holds for them. Would they able to go and live on the space station? What would life be like there? Would they still have to go to school? And most importantly, would their be a playground? They were both excited and anxious about what lied ahead for all of them. Theresa continued to be very involved in the school. They had developed a core of good friends that also had children and were in a very similar situation with their families.

—⟋⟋⟋—

Lucina had waited patiently while Landau gathered up the courage, and a reason, to let her into the mountain village. Most Genisovians knew it was where something went on that was very top secret. There was much speculation about what went on there, but very few really knew for sure, or at least the people who did know were not telling. There were some hints given, such as, it will change all that we know about learning or it will be a breakthrough in communication. People began to speculate what it could be. It was also known that it was not a secret weapon or piece of technology like a new computer or droid. There was talk that it was a form of Artificial Intelligence but most people said that it was not.

Landau had to make a decision about Lu in order to get her inside but he needed to have a conversation with her about it. This was about a week or so after they met at the security center.

"So, there is something I need to explain to you before we talk about taking you in to the mountains."

"And what is that?" she replied.

"There are several different ways I can go about getting you in there, but probably the best way would be to be honest with the Council about everything. I really don't want to have to convince them with some half true reason for taking you there. The real reason I would want to bring you there is so that you could see something that you have never seen before and that would explain to you much of who I am."

"And this reason is not good enough for the Council?"

"I think that they would not allow me to bring just anyone back there. And for good reasons."

"Well, I'm not just anyone. They all know who I am."

"Yes, they know who you are, but who are you to me is the question they are going to ask."

"I think I am starting to see where you are going with this."

"I really do want to bring you up there, but if you and I are, well, if things don't go so smoothly, then where are we? And if things happen like they did before, then we will go our separate ways, and then I could have made a mistake?"

"What is it that is going on in there? It's starting to drive me mad."

"I wish I could tell you. I want to show you. I want to show the world, but the world is not ready. Not yet. But, soon, I hope."

"So what do we do?"

"I think we need some more time alone out here together. Let's see where things are going to go, and then I will feel more confident going to the Council and saying who you are to me and why it is so important to show you everything. Then, I believe, they would understand."

"Sounds like we are going to be spending some quality time together, eh? How is that going to happen with how busy you are?"

"I guess we will just have to create the time. I can make it happen and I want it to."

"Well, finally, something to look forward to."

The Chinese and European groups had both decided to go forward with a space station but neither gave any timeline. They had also created divisions devoted to solving the problem of existing on earth as the sun gets worse. There was some open communication between all nations in the scientific world and this future crisis seemed to be breaking down the barriers even more. There was a sense of urgency around the world over how to approach the problems confronting us as a species. People were beginning to truly wonder what would happen to them if the sun did begin to become more and more harmful. The basic facts were that even if we did create several space stations, there would not be enough room for 10 billion people on them. Simply put, not everyone could go. In fact, most everyone would have to stay.

There was good chance that people could continue to survive on earth for a certain amount of time, but we would have to adapt. Many people would die here on earth. Not only would the suns radiation be damaging directly to humans, but it would have many effects on everything else from animals to vegetation to water to soil. Humans and animals would be way more susceptible to melanoma, the ground would become infertile, and plants would wither and die in the heat. Life in a space station would probably not be a better option for quite a while, but eventually it would become the safer option. The Council of Genisova was betting on this becoming a reality, but also were realizing that this transition could take quite a long time to become a stable living environment.

The leaders of the world had decided to create a new department for dealing with future space travel and colonization. They all began to realize that, as more and more countries decided to take to the sky and build space stations or build colonies on planets or moons, then there would need to be some order and general agreements about how they should go about doing it. Some sort of cooperation would be beneficial to everyone. Let's just say that there was a particular area on a particular moon that was the best place known to build a colony and more than one country was interested in that area, then who would get to go there? In other words, who owns what in space? Just because the thought of building colonies on the moon seems so remotely impossible now, doesn't mean it will be in the future.

As more and more countries began to see the future possibilities it was a common agreement that there should be some semblance of a space government of sorts. So the United Nations Space Agreement Division was created to help direct everyone in some general direction. This was a big deal because it meant a couple things. First, Genisova would need to have a representative from the U.S. at the table speaking for them. Two, the fact they were creating this group at all gave the problem of the sun some real weight. It gave it some credibility and this meant to many people that it was real. There was a huge spike in crime, drugs, depression and suicide throughout the world. Many people who were dealing with difficult situations in their life just decided to not care any more. What was the point of it? Who cares anymore? We were all going to die anyway. There was no hope for these people anymore.

Additionally, talk about there being limited space on the space station made this reality even worse, because people with a lower income realized their chances were slim to none of getting chosen to live there. Other people handled it differently. People of the religious right vowed that this was the end of the world predicted in the Bible. Christianity had a spike in new followers as they begged for people to repent and accept Christ as their personal savior or else they would burn in hell. There was also a large group of people who decided that there was still hope and that the only way to solve the problem at hand was to work harder and work together.

Whatever your personal situation was this news affected you. It was talked about more and more in the news and social media. High profile people began to take notice and ask the government what their plan was. Genisova was also getting quite a bit of interest from these people of extreme wealth. However, most of them were not interested in the process they would need to go through to get a seat in the sky. Many of these affluent individuals would try to make an extravagant offer of money to the council and buy a seat on the future station. Much to their chagrin, they were all quickly denied. Nobody could buy a place in Genisova no matter what the offer. One offer was said to be for $20 million. When it was found out that this was shot down, most of the others with these intentions decided to look elsewhere for solutions. This was through either other private ventures or through our government or other countries' projects.

Things began to get sticky in these arenas, as most politics do. Money was being thrown around by the wealthy trying to have as much influence on their best possible chance of getting into the sky—with the least amount of work. The US government had created its own division in NASA to work on this project. There was already much in place to build something like this as they had already conquered space flight and smaller space stations. The problem with this entity was how big to build the space station and, most importantly, the cost.

So many people now wanted a say in everything from how big it was going to be to what was going to be on the space station to who was going to get to go live up there someday. It was a big mess because nothing ever could get started due to all the disagreeing upon what to build. Not only that, they had not developed the technology that Genisova had, so they kept having to start their plans over, designing it with different materials. The Genisovians had spent years of concentrated effort trying to solve these specific problems and had not shared many of their secrets about design and materials.

The government, with Sarkovia leading the charge, now had decided that they were going to try and seize as much information as possible from Genisova in order help build their own space station and space ships. They were calling it a matter of national security and were not going to take no for an answer. This began to be a hot national debate as people of all different types had a say in who was right in this decision. Many people believed that, if Genisova had developed some technology that would help solve the future crisis and would enable our country be the front runner in building space stations, then Genisova should gladly hand over all that information- ASAP. Others felt like, if the government could simply walk in and force a company to give over the fruits of years of labor and highly sensitive information, that it was a major invasion of privacy. This meant nobody was safe from the government. It could be the first domino to fall in citizens truly losing their rights. This worried many people and left them not sure which side to take on this argument.

People began to worry more and more about the issue with the sun and wondered what else could be done to solve the problem. Was there a viable solution for people to remain on earth if the sun's condition worsened? There was a lot of unknown in this predicament. Scientists around the world would have to guess as to what the conditions would be like. Creating a sheltered city of sorts would create a solution of some sorts. But how would this be done and how big would it have to be? It was true that something would have to be done for the people remaining on earth. As more and more people came to this realization it became evident that there was much work to be done in coming up with a solution.

Existing companies that already worked in a field that could be of use began to change their work direction towards developing solutions to help protect humans from the sun. This turned out to be a very lucrative decision amidst much upheaval in the economy and stock markets. These people looked at this problem as real and potentially threatening and used it for their advantage. Some large investors decided to get together and purchase large quantities of property in the far northern and southern regions of the earth. These areas which were currently colder climates would become warmer as time went on. They, of course, were following what Genisova had already done. A whole new work force was created by trying to figure out how to remain on earth for the next several generations to come. Meanwhile, Genisova was way ahead of the game.

—⚋—

Despite all the other crazy things going on at Genisova and around the world, Landau and Lu had continued to spend more and more time together. Lu was slowly getting used to living in the giant hamster cage, as she lovingly called it. She would still jet out of town every now and then to indulge in some of the things she missed the most, but over time she did this less and less. It was in direct correlation to how much she would miss Landau when she was gone. The more she missed him the less she wanted to be away. She continued to go through the process of the first year and she actually admitted to slowly feeling different and more centered, as she would say. In the past, she would have never called herself anything remotely spiritual. She had the advantage of having Landau's ear all the time and could ask him questions about whatever she wanted. Landau wanted to know if she felt like there was any purpose behind what they all went through as they entered Genisova. He had carved some time out of his schedule and they were hanging out at her place. She had been content not to rush learning about the secretive work going on in the mountains, but still was wondering when she would be able to visit it.

"So how are you feeling about all of this? Do you see any value in it?" Landau asked.

"There are parts of it that I feel are more beneficial than others. I think it is probably different for everyone. What was the real reason for creating this process?"

"In the beginning we came to an agreement that if this place was ever going to work that we would need to weed out those who were here for the wrong reasons. It became apparent to us all that the purpose would be twofold. One, to discourage people who came seeking something else, and, two, we knew it would benefit the people here and prepare them for what was to come. Just look now at all the people who want to try and buy their way into here."

"Okay, but when you say, prepare them for what is to come, are you talking about the space station in the sky, or something else?"

Landau's face went from serious to one of pure delight.

"I'm so glad you caught that. It is to help prepare them for the physical things to come in the future, like going into space or surviving here on earth, but, yes, you are right, it is to help prepare them for something else. There is more to this place than just what you see here. All of this is working towards something that is beyond what anyone has ever experienced."

"You are making me feel as though you cannot live up to the expectations of what you are promising."

"Well, it has already been happening and it is going to change the way we all look at reality. You see, humans are more than just a bunch of particles put together to take that shape we see every day with our eyes and hear with our ears and feel with our body. There is more to us, and most all of us already know that, but no one has been able to really demonstrate what that more is. There is another dimension, shall we say, that is hidden to pretty much everyone. For thousands of years we have been unable to tap into this hidden part of us. At first, as humans were evolving, we were too busy trying to figure out just how to survive. Then, once we figured out how to do that fairly easily, we have spent most of our time trying to live our lives to the fullest extremes in a physical way. We try to master the system that we created in order to make money that will buy us all sorts of pleasures and experiences that we think make our lives fulfilled and well lived. And that has been just fine and dandy to this point. I, myself, have taken advantage of this system and utilized it to my own benefit, probably to an extent that most others have not. You have lived a life fully with all sorts of physical pleasures that most others try to attain. The goal of trying to live this type of life has consumed the lives of most everyone, but there is more. And it cannot be found in the physical realm, so to speak."

"And, how does one achieve this elusive state of utopia you seem to have found?" Lu replied doubtingly.

"That's the thing, one cannot do it alone."

She looked at him surprised and unsure of what to think. "How did you discover this?"

"It has taken years to unlock this secret. Have you wondered yet why there have been so many new groundbreaking discoveries made here at Genisova? It is not a coincidence. Are you aware that the true source of the cure for cancer came from Genisova?"

"What do you mean? It was discovered here?"

"Yes, it was all figured out ahead of time how to keep its true origin hidden from the rest of the world."

"But, why? What is the purpose of hiding something like this?"

"We did not want to attract any attention to what we were doing here. We knew that this discovery was too significant to withhold from the rest of the world, so we figured out a way to share it, but not disclose where it came from. Its discovery was also key to our plan here at Genisova. In order to survive in space, where cosmic radiation is intensified, a cure for cancer would enable humans to survive longer. Genisova actually is reimbursed by the pharmaceutical company that sells the cure. We just didn't want the publicity to interfere with our end goal here."

Lucina was pretty well speechless at this point. She was not sure what to think. They only wanted the money from this discovery, but not the notoriety from it. What were they doing that was so secretive that they didn't want the world to know who cured cancer?

"It does seem somewhat peculiar that there have been so many amazing discoveries, now that you mention it. What is the connection?" Lu inquired.

"That is what I want to show you."

Now more than ever Lucina wanted to know what was going on up in the mountains, hidden away from the rest of Genisova and the rest of the world.

—∞—

Since she had arrived at Genisova, Suzi had very few conversations with Landau. She had met with the Council several times before she had graduated to the next level but besides that she had actually tried to avoid members from the Council. She had now been working closely with the other scientists in her field and was thriving, as most others did. She loved working purely for the work itself and not having to worry about making money and the pressure of performing well in order to keep her job. Her team was assigned to work on future phases of Genisova, once they had established space stations and were ready to move onto the next frontier. She had specialized in looking for planets in other solar systems that could potentially harbor life, particularly humans. The problem was, how would we ever get there?

The universe is so big that our minds can barely comprehend it. The nearest star in our galaxy is four light years away, which means that moving at the speed of light, which we cannot do, it would still take us four years to get to. With the top speeds at which we can travel today, it would take humans 81,000 years to get there. In other words, we are not getting to another star system until we figure out how to go faster. This, of course, was something that Genisova was working on. It was one of the allures to many young scientists searching for an arena to put their talents to good use.

Suzi was now looking closer at the existing planets they had already discovered to be suitable. They had discovered ways to analyze these far-off planets with greater detail and were now looking even more seriously at which planet could be a future home for humans. If you are going to travel to another star you might as well be pretty certain there is a good reason for doing it. Suzi was narrowing these planets down to about 5 and then critically analyzing them further. It was an exciting task and she couldn't get enough of it. Landau had been visiting her department and had been inquiring about who would be a suitable person for the project he was working on. He had known about Suzi's path to getting where she is now and how she was very resistant to many of Genisova's methods. He decided to approach her and ask her a few questions.

"So how are you liking Genisova now?" he inquired.

Suzi was not sure he was talking to her. She was a little nervous with him walking around, seeming to be observing everyone pretty closely.

"Oh, I wasn't sure you were talking to me. Yes, I am enjoying it very much, quite more than I expected."

"I hear excellent things about your work and what you are accomplishing here. We weren't sure you were going to stick around and make it to this point."

"It's funny how life turns out sometimes. Two years ago I would have never guessed in a million years that I would be here, doing this, living this life. It is quite surreal."

"Do you feel like you have found your purpose here? What do you see as your goals now that you are here?"

"You know, when I get up every day, all I think about is getting over here and getting to work. I just can't describe how thankful I am for having found this place to do what I love. It is a dream for me. But there is more to it. I walked blindly through life before, in a way. I was doing what I thought everyone else was doing and what everyone else thought was the right way to do things. Even my personal relationship was on auto pilot, so to speak. Now, I see things so differently. It is like a veil was lifted and I can see what I could not see before. It was there all along, but I could not see it because I did not know what to look for."

"You seem like a completely different person to me than when you first came here. We watched you fairly closely and were hoping that you would be patient and give the process some time to help you see your path. It is a true joy to see you today, happy and content as can be."

"My perspective now is changed. I used to think that life was random and there was nothing more to it than that. Some people, maybe most people, have a big event happen in their life and then they credit it to some divine order or something. I can see now how every little thing you do in life is in perfect design. It can be hard to see at times, but eventually it all makes sense. I have realized this is not an easy thing to do. You have to be really focused and not distracted by the normal chaos in our lives to see life from this perspective."

"I couldn't agree more. I can't explain how impressed I am that you have reached this point already."

"Well, like I said, I am just as surprised as you are. But, really, once your perspective changes you really can't go back to the way you were before. I think it would be impossible, and who would want to?"

"So do you think you would want to live up in space at some point? What do you think about the divine order of the sun becoming such a problem for us?"

"Once again, this is a tricky thing to see. I have thought about this. Why would the universe be telling us our time is up on earth? Is it to force us to try harder to search for other alternatives, or is it more about bringing us all together once and for all to try and solve the solution. I think, quite frankly it is a little bit of both. There will be difficult times for the people of earth and there are going to be many casualties when it is all said and done. Hopefully we can see the big picture and come together despite all our differences. Otherwise, it will be survival of the strongest, and then pray they can prevail against all the odds."

Landau could see that she had changed irrevocably and that she was now laser focused on the tasks at hand. He was not convinced just yet that she was ready for his project, but would maybe consider her in the near future.

―᠎ɷɷ―

The new space planes had been designed and production had begun. The designs for the first space station were also completed and the building in which it was to be built was also completed. This would be where all the actual parts to the station would be built and then loaded onto the space planes. While the space planes were being completed and tested for flight the space station was being built inside the new warehouse. The rest of the world had still not even begun designing a new space station that could harbor large quantities of people. There were all sorts of new companies trying to build future communities with houses interconnected in mini cities that would be resistant to the sun if it were ever to get worse. The problem was that nobody was willing to sell their life away just yet, because the sun had not become a problem—yet. And, they were either located closer to where people live now, which will be incredible hot, or in the colder region that no one wanted to move to yet.

It was clear to Sarkovia what was going on at Genisova by this point. What he didn't know was the details. He understood the plans for the station, the space planes, the new materials and fuels. The Council had a plan in place to deal with his pleads for information. They just simply would only give him a little bit of information at a time. Bit by bit they fed him the details of Staralene. Until he had all the information there really wasn't much that could be down with it. The government was so busy dealing with so many other urgent issues, Genisova was becoming less and less of a priority.

Landau was nearly ready to take Lucina into the mountains and see what is was they had been hiding so carefully from the rest of the world. He would have to go before the Council and plead his case about why it was okay to bring her in to the research facility up there. It was not really much of a problem for the Council, for they new it was really up to him to make the right decision about it. They were more of a checks and balance system to make sure his emotions were not clouding his judgment in doing this. It had now been nearly 9 months since Lu had arrived and she felt comfortable about living there. She had not left Genisova for nearly two months and really did not miss much of her former life. Her friends and family were extremely surprised that she just disappeared from her previous life and now apparently was not coming back any time soon. They did, however, realize that ultimately it was all about Landau. If they truly knew Lucina then they knew she would do whatever was needed for the sake of finding love. Of course, being with Landau now helped alleviate most of Lu's desires to go back home.

The Council asked Landau his reasons for bringing Lu up there and he replied, "I feel I have spent enough time with her and she has spent enough time reflecting about all of this. I am convinced that this is the direction life is pointing us to now. Even if we do not end up being together, she will understand what our goals here are and she will not try to ruin us. This I am sure of and will deal with the consequences if I am wrong." They were all happy for him and Lu and, deep inside, hoped things would work out between them for they knew this was a void in his life, even though he would probably never admit it.

—⟇—

Lu was unusually nervous on the morning of her trip to the mountains. She was sitting in her house having a cup of coffee and waiting for Landau to pick her up. She reflected upon all of her life and everything that had brought her to this moment. What was the point of everything? She thought about her life before she came here. She thought about the world of materialism that she had surrounded herself with. She was able to access most things that money could buy, she had dated virtually anyone she ever wanted and almost married into a life that would have assured that she would never want for anything material ever again. Now that she was reflecting upon her life it was really just a series of wanting things and buying things. Going on expensive vacations and living in over-the-top luxurious houses and driving ridiculously expensive cars. But after she would get the next 'thing' she wanted, there was always something more-the next thing and then the next thing, without end. Did these things make her any happier? Was she really ever content? It was always temporary. It never lasted.

Quite honestly, now that she looked back at her life, she wondered how happy she truly may have been. Not having true love. Her family was living the same type of life and was caught in the same dilemma. What is the real point of living? How does one achieve pure happiness? She would never have even considered these questions before because she was so caught up in trying to live this extravagant life chasing after the next 'thing' to make her feel good inside. Trying to make everyone else feel like she was living this incredible life. But, against what she would consider all odds, she turned it all away and chased after this person who had made her feel unlike anyone else she had ever met. He was handsome, intelligent, kind, (and wealthy) but had something else about him that she had never encountered before in all her life. For a while she began to take it for granted, but their time apart made it more apparent than ever.

There was something mysterious and almost magical about Landau. He had a love and appreciation for all the little things in life that most people took for granted. He saw the world differently, and believed in something greater for all of humankind. But, although there have been people throughout history who have cared for humans in this way, he was able to put himself in a position to actually do something about it. He had poured billions of dollars into this project to do something no one would ever have dreamed of doing. He had already turned away from the life that money could buy and resolved to search for something higher. Had he married earlier in life and had a family, maybe his perspective on life would have been different. If they had ended up together earlier, all of this may have not happened. There are so many things that could have turned out differently.

I could have chosen to marry someone else, but didn't, she thought to herself. She laughed quietly and smiled a bright smile. She was beaming. Landau walked in to pick her up. He held her hand and looked at her and asked her what she was thinking about. "Just about how glad I am that I came here to be with you. Whatever happens, I am just happy and thankful for the chance to be by your side."

"Of course, I am so glad you are here with me. I am beginning to wonder what life would have been like without you."

"Well, I can vouch for that. I remember all too well. Coming here to Genisova makes it even more obvious to me that we are supposed to be together. I would never have imagined a place like this could ever exist let alone, be created by you. You truly are magnificent. Whatever happens in the end, you should be proud of your effort to do something for everyone. Who knows what will become of the rest of the world with the powers that be running everything."

"They have turned to us for advice, but our solution is too slow and methodical for the rest of the world. They don't have the patience to do things like this. The people in charge are under the pressure of people with money demanding that things be done as soon as possible."

"That doesn't surprise me in the least. Two years ago I would have probably been one of those people demanding that someone do something right now."

"We will persevere, but what I am about to show you will be what truly helps humanity forge into the future. You see, the future of humanity lies with us delving deeper into our capabilities and using them to the fullest of our potential."

Landau had picked her up at her place and drove her around the grounds of Genisova. They toured all the different villages and made their way to the research and development village. They entered one of the main buildings and went into a restricted area where she was granted clearance. This must have been what all the fuss was about. They took some steps down to another level that had a look of a modern looking subway tunnel. Everything looked like out of the future. Clean, white, glass everywhere, sunlight coming down from a clear ceiling. The train was already stationed there and waiting for them. They approached the doors and they opened automatically. As they entered the car a female voice began to speak.

"Hello Lucina. Welcome. How are you today?"

Lucina peered at Landau with a surprised look of "what am I supposed to say?" She laughed and answered, "Very well, thank you. And how are you today?"

The voice paused for a minute and then replied, "Well, I am good. It has been a busy day of taking people back and forth to Andromeda One already. We are excited to have you here."

She smiled and said to Landau, "She seems nice Has she been expecting me?"

"She has a fairly advanced intelligence compared to most others, but she has been informed of your clearance and to be expecting you. Really she is linked to the defense department, so once we cleared you she automatically knew."

"It's a nice touch."

"I guess."

"I'm glad you like me," the voice interrupted.

The train began to take off slowly. It was not on tracks but seemed to be hovering over a different type of track. The tunnel went all around them and was made mostly of glass above so you could see out.

"Is this the only way to Andromeda One?" Lu inquired.

"There is another road that can be accessed by the appropriate vehicles, and there is a helicopter pad there for landing all sorts of different vehicles. There is a one and two-seat drone that people can take to and from if necessary. They are used occasionally if someone is in a hurry or if the train is being unloaded or loaded with anything. Most all of the construction building materials were transported with the train."

As the train began to gain speed it moved with complete quiet and smoothness. It traveled underground for a what seemed to be about half a mile and then began its ascent up above the ground. It advanced slowly up through the mountains and the view became spectacular within seconds. The sun was out sparkling with a bright blue backdrop to the jagged edges of the mountains climbing up into the sky.

"How far away is it?" Lucina asked. She couldn't help be overcome with awe. She thought about how this could be the transportation of the future.

"Several miles. Not really that far. It's hard to buy too much property in the mountains. But just far enough away to make it somewhat isolated and challenging to get to. The only true access is from the property on Genisova. Not many people know about it. People have flown overhead, obviously, but we have never had anyone try to reach it on their own. It would be very difficult to reach with out taking the train or flying. And, really because not many people know about it, there is little reason for people to try and break into it."

"What would they be looking for?"

"Information."

"Could you be any more vague?"

"You'll see. Maybe what you see wouldn't even interest most people."

The train took a couple of sharper turns as it continued its climb into mountains. Suddenly as the train straightened out, a small complex of futuristic looking glass and cement buildings came into view. Flat roofs made of shiny metal mixed with satin looking concrete walls. Varying shaped windows and unconventional angles to the structures helped to blend them into the mountainside they were nestled within. The train began to slow down and they went inside a tunnel into another glimmering subway station. The voice came on again and said, "You have arrived at your destination, Andromeda One."

The train came to a stop and the doors slowly opened. Lu looked around with eager anticipation of what she would see next. They walked into the reception area and up a few sets of stairs into another room with sealed doors for security. They walked up to the doors and the voice came on again saying, "Now scanning for entry." It took about five seconds and the doors opened.

"What exactly is she scanning?" asked Lu.

Landau looked at her and said, "A lot. This is a very high security area and the technology is very advanced. She knows more about you than you do."

They walked through a couple of halls and there was a door leading out into a small courtyard area. It had a little pool with a fountain and some modern looking chairs and benches.

"What's this little area for?" she asked.

"It's a quiet area for reflection or thinking or just enjoying some fresh air."

"It's nice. I could see you sitting out here dreaming of a place far, far away," she said with a smile.

"I can't say that hasn't happened on several different occasions. I'm glad you like it."

They walked through another door and into the entryway of what was apparently someone's living quarters.

"Where are we?"

"Home."

She looked at him and grabbed his hand. They walked into the main living area and looked out over the mountains. There was glass on all sides of them and the view looking out was spectacular. Majestic mountains to the side, the green valley far below, the sunlight reflecting off the entire view. There was a simple, sleek kitchen area and then a couple other rooms off of the main room and that was it. He invited her in to sit down and they enjoyed the view for a moment.

"Wow. That's quite a view to look out at every day. I'm pretty jealous."

"I spend less time here than you probably think. It is amazing, but cold and lonely. Needs some more life to give it some vibrancy. Know anyone interested in spending some time here?"

"Not really..." she joked. "Why would anyone want to spend time here? View sucks. Company stinks. Need I go on?"

"Does that mean yes?"

"Yes, to what? Are you asking me something?"

"No, I mean, maybe, should I be?"

"You're a very confusing man sometimes. One minute I think I know you, the next, you get all mysterious again."

"I feel like everything is happening for a reason. At first I was shocked to know that you had called and were even interested in talking to me. Then you show up here, out of the blue and it really caught me off guard. Then you keep coming back and show interest in things that never interested you before. I'm trying to grasp all of this, but I can't see this ending any other way."

"Meaning what? Are you asking me something? I am not sure where you are going with all this. Bringing me up here to reveal some big top secret thing that no one knows about. Is this the big secret? You and me? What's going on?"

"I have not planned any of this, but I think I'm going to do what feels right, like I always do. So, yes, Lucina, will you spend the rest of your life with me?"

Lucina was at first flustered and confused. But then realizes he was serious and then her emotions begin to shift to joy.

"I can't believe this is happening. Are you sure about this? Are you asking me to marry you, like, officially and everything? I'm not sure if that is what you are talking about?"

Landau breaks off into a laugh. "I guess. I don't really care how you want to go about doing it. Sure, let's gets married. I don't think you would be here now if this wasn't something you were considering. I love you and can't imagine life without you at this point, so, if you want to, let's do this together."

"I still can't believe that Landau is asking me to marry him. I never thought I would see the day...".

She jumps into his arms and hugs him with all her might. She has tears in her eyes and they begin to kiss.

"Would you like to see my bedroom?"

"Yes, please..."

Not wanting to get too far off task, they finished their celebration and then got ready to continue the tour of the complex. Landau led the way back out through the courtyard and into one of the buildings. It was odd to Lu that there was what appeared to be a research building so close to his living quarters. Once again their was a security clearance and then they entered into a much larger building that was designed for a completely different purpose.

They walked through a long hallway that opened up onto a balcony that went all the way around a series of different glass rooms connected to each other. Three walls of these rooms were glass, while the outside wall appeared to be glass also, but was black instead of clear. There were various sitting stools throughout these rooms and not much else. The rooms were actually not square but connected together in a circle of sorts. It appeared that they formed the shape of an octagon making eight different rooms. They were all connected by glass doors and what their purpose was she had no idea. They looked down upon the strange area and Lu looked at Landau with a curious look.

"You'll see. Let's go downstairs and get a better look."

They went down a staircase and entered a door that appeared to be on the outside of one of the rooms. They could see into the room through a tinted glass wall. There were all sorts of monitors and sensors that seemed to be set up for observing whatever was going on in the rooms. The walls were see-through on one side only. Landau walked up to a computer and a virtual keyboard popped up from the desk in front of him. He touched a few buttons and the tinting or coloring on the glass wall looking into the room faded and made the glass looking into the room bright and clear again.

"This is where the magic happens."

"What exactly is the magic?" Lu inquired with a hint of wonder.

Landau spoke to the computer. "Please set up quantum particle sensors." A three dimensional image popped up in the middle of the room out of what appeared to be a laser output and appeared to show the chair sitting empty in the room in front of them. It was like watching a 3D television. It was a square about 20 inches in all dimensions. Lu walked around the box in sheer amazement. This hologram type image somehow showed that the air around the chair seemed to be vibrating at a different rate than the chair. It seemed to be showing the chair and the air on a molecular level. It was very difficult to describe.

"Watch this."

He then walked into the room and sat down on the chair. As he walked into the room the hologram showed him vibrating at another rate and the air around him apparently to be affected by him. As he began to talk it was apparent that he was affecting the room all around him and the sensors were showing all of it on the image.

"Wow, that is amazing. But, what is it?" Lu was obviously surprised by what she saw and wondered what this was showing. It was like some sort of infrared sensor, but was measuring more than heat.

"We know that there is more to us than what we see Lu. We created a sensor that would measure everything down to the molecular level and display it in a way that our naked eyes could interpret. What you see is what it looks like to see the world through a high powered microscope. Light waves and energy can be measured, but what we are truly looking for cannot be measured. Tell me something wonderful."

"I love you!" she shouted.

As she said this the energy around Landau began to vibrate again differently and then radiate outward from him like a pebble hitting a calm pond and making waves. Her heart began to race and she smiled uncontrollably.

"Oh my gosh. What just happened?" she exclaimed.

"Cool, eh? What did it look like?"

As he talked, more waves radiated from him but not like a moment ago.

"It is hard to describe, but the air all around you just swelled outward and radiated like an echo away from you."

It just occurred to her that the other rooms were for having more people to monitor simultaneously and observe what would happen.

"Are these other rooms for other people?"

"Not just for other people but for how the other people are all connected. How we are all connected in a way you would not believe."

He walked back into the room and told the computer to begin recording. He grabbed her by the hand and brought her back out into the room.

"Kiss me." Landau said to her.

She leaned in and gave him a big long kiss. Then she wrapped her arms around him and hugged him.

"Are we trying to get a big reaction on that monitor?" she joked.

"Sure. Whatever we want. Let's go see what happened. I've been wanting to do that for quite some time now."

They walked back into the room and Landau told the computer to replay the last couple minutes. The screen went back and began playing as they walked into the room. As soon as they walked into the room the air waved and even their bodies were clearly vibrating at a whole other level than before. As they kissed the waves clearly began to vibrate together at the same speed and it appeared as though something else was happening. It was almost as if the fabric of space was opening up into another dimension.

"What is happening? Is that something you have seen before?"

"Oh, yes. And so much more. What we have tapped into here is just a glimpse of our human potential. It is like finding a whole new species, one that never existed before. Yet, here we are."

"What are you doing with this information? What does this mean?"

"We already are doing something with it. We are applying it. We are using it for the benefit of mankind."

"I'm not sure I follow."

"You will, the tour is not over."

"Well, so far, I have to admit, I am impressed. I had no idea what you have been up to up here in your hideaway lair. Really, this is not what I expected."

"We have known for a long time that there is more to our connection than we can see. It's just that no one has ever taken it seriously enough to try and take it to another level. We all know when we "feel" energy between two or more of us. We have all experienced love or any heightened emotion, but we all just pass it off as just that, an emotion. But what is an emotion? What is love? What is it when you listen to an inspiring talk or see a great movie or read a life-changing book and you experience more than what your five senses tell you you are feeling? There is more to it and we all know it, but no one has ever delved into it deeper on a scientific level. We have studied people meditating, when one might think that those vibrating waves would be quiet, but they do something quite the contrary. And, the secret to all of this is when there is more than one person meditating...together."

"Can I see it happen? What does happen?"

"I want you to see it for yourself. It will blow your mind."

They leave the glass rooms and head towards some other buildings with all sorts of apparent research facilities. They begin to see some people walking around heading for their appointed positions to begin their day doing whatever it is they do. They walk through some other similar rooms that are individual glass rooms instead of the ones connected. They leave this building and enter another building through a glass walkway. The entire system of buildings is connected by tunnels or walkways so that they do not have to technically leave any of the buildings whenever the weather gets problematic. There are also some outside garden areas along with plenty of trees and various vegetation. They are beautiful, and as is everything in Genisova, it was designed with a purpose. This building is already buzzing with a few people working around a particular area. In front of them is what appears to be a crude droid-like robot. The scientists in the room are asking it questions and doing some tests on it.

"Is that a droid?" Asked Lu.

"As are a lot of other teams throughout the world, we are also working on artificial intelligence. It is a very big concern for many because of the potential problems it could present. We here at Genisova agree to some extent, but feel as though, if it is going to be designed by someone we think it would be in better hands here where we feel like it won't be used for the wrong reasons."

"How is it going so far?" She inquired.

"It is coming along fairly slowly. The droid part is very challenging. It is extremely difficult to replicate all of the movements that a human makes, or any animal for that matter. The intelligence part is a whole other matter. We have already developed "robots" for our own use in space once the space station is begun. They will increase the speed at which we can build the space stations for they can be outside in space with no need for all of the human elements we need. They will need to be controlled individually remotely, but we can do that from anywhere, even here on earth, 24- 7. Our people will work in shifts telling them what to do and things will move very quickly. There will be some humans in space all the time helping to deal with any problems that arise. They will stay there for only a few days at a time and then return to earth for the next shift to take their place."

They continue to watch as the scientist asks the robot a question and it answers in a manner uncannily like a human. Lu's face makes a look like, whoa, that was freaky. Then the droid begins to move and it becomes very apparent that it is not a human. It is still fairly stiff in its movements and is cautious as it is walking. There is still a long ways to go with this part.

"How long before these things take over?" she kids.

"Apparently, not that long. They are in most ways more intelligent than us, but lack most importantly many human elements, like the ability to think during high stress times. They lack the true ability to make original decisions."

"It is amazing and scary at the same time."
"Truly, it is."

—∞—

They head back to Landau's house and have some lunch. They discuss many things while sitting at a table that overlooked the valley. The view was breathtaking. The blue sky was now dotted with puffy clouds here and there. She was overwhelmed with emotions and still trying to process everything that happened and all that she had seen so far.

"What's next?"

"I would like to take you back to the glass rooms to watch a little more of what is going on over there. It is very difficult to see everything that goes on here in one day, but you can get a glimpse of it."

They finish their lunch and then head back over to the labs. There are several people already there seemingly already doing what Landau was hinting at. There were two people in two separate rooms right next to each other that had one big room on the other side of the dark glass wall. This room was obviously for observing both rooms at the same time. Lu thought she recognized both of the people sitting in the two different rooms.

"Hey, don't I know those people? They look very familiar."

"You have seen them around town. They are both quantum physicists. They are on the same team working on some of the most difficult questions of our time. Let's watch for a moment and see what happens."

They were facing each other in the separate rooms and were quietly meditating. The air surrounding both of them was vibrating at different wavelengths. You could see the difference in the hologram. They were different but nearly the same. They had both been meditating for nearly a half an hour. As they sat and watched them the wavelengths began to match up more closely. It was mesmerizing. Slowly the vibrations began to sync and vibrate together so that you could not tell them apart. Then something completely unexpected happened. There began to be a spiral in between them that looked like a far off galaxy. The air began to appear to open up and create a void of sorts. There was now what seemed to be a faint glow surrounding the hole and emanating outward back towards the two physicists.

Lu looked up at the room and saw just two people sitting in the rooms with their eyes closed, acting like nothing out of the ordinary was happening. Then, as if something more could happen that would blow her mind, she suddenly began to feel the hairs on the back of her neck stand on end and she felt what she thought was some sort of electric current running through her body. She glanced over and Landau and he smiled back at her and nodded his head up and down as if to signify that he felt it, too. How could this be happening? What was happening?

Her eyes were watching the hologram and seeing something happening that she could not understand except through what her eyes were seeing. Now she was certainly feeling something physical to match what her eyes were witnessing. She was speechless, yet she was overcome with a feeling of joy beyond belief. It was indescribable. This continued for nearly another 30 minutes without interruption and then the scientists slowly awoke from their trance. They both got up and stretched and walked into the room where Lu and Landau and the other researchers were sitting. Landau looked at them and introduced Lu to them. They both shook her hand and said welcome. One of them asked her what she thought about all of this?

"I am so curious about all of this What are you feeling as you are going through something like this? Did you have intentions of connecting with your friend over here while you are doing this?"

He replied, "I am not sure where to begin with answering your questions."

He looks over at Landau for some guidance or help in any way. Landau motions to him that he will take over for a minute.

"Let me explain a little bit of what is going on here before he answers your questions. We have separated entangled particles and recorded their invisible connections for quite some time. How is this possible? What is the connection? Why can't we see it or measure it? How can two separated particles communicate with each other instantaneously over distances impossible to cover in zero time? It is impossible yet it still happens. The answer lies in the way we think about the answer. We need to think literally outside the box. Outside the box of our dimensions that we can see. An unknown dimension has to be there, we just don't know where it is."

"We are all so sure of things that we cannot explain or prove, but we still know it to be so. Consciousness resides in this dimension, but there is more to us in another dimension. What you saw today in there was a glimpse into that other dimension. It is invisible to the naked eye and most of our senses, but we can still sense it somehow. You and I both felt something, even though we cannot explain it, we are still sure of it. How is this so, you may ask? How can a separated particle from my own body sense something at the same time I sense it? My nervous system does not course through a tiny particle that is no longer connected to me, yet it can still register awareness of some sort at the same time I do? How is this possible? It is connected in this other dimension?"

"Is there consciousness in a tiny particle that comes from me? Is consciousness born into the union of a sperm and an egg when a baby begins forming in utero? Does it take consciousness from their mother or father or both?"

"Where does it come from?" This is the question we all must ask. "Where does it come from? Do we all continue to look away with a blind eye or do we look it in the eyes and finally realize that we already know the answer to this question that all pretend is unknowable?"

He pauses for a moment.

"I believe it comes from this hidden dimension I speak of. The one we all know exists, but refuse to look deeper into. What you saw today was two people looking deeper for something."

Lucina had no idea what to say. It was so much to digest and understand. She agreed that there had to be more to us than our basic senses tell us, but what it was she did not know.

"So all of this is about looking for an unknown dimension? That's the big secret?"

"The secret is learning how to know that dimension. Let's ask our friends here now what they experienced."

The one scientist began, "We have both been working on solving a problem in science that neither of us knows how to solve. When you run into a roadblock in science you need to seek an alternate route to the answer. When you meditate you can begin to tap into another source of information that lies hidden from your everyday senses. When you meditate together with another person trying to search for the same answers you are, we found that you can open up a door into another realm. It is not easy and takes an inordinate amount of time and focus. What you saw here is the end result of months of work on tapping into this hidden part of our being. Most people would laugh at what is going on and call it foolishness, but look around you and see all the wonders of this method. When more than one person tries to open up this portal into a source of knowledge, you can see things you never saw before."

The other scientist chimed in. "We have been searching for the mysteries of dark matter and dark energy forever. They are hidden from our view even though we know they are there. Scientists have been so set on searching for the answers to this riddle within our known universe and dimensions that they have never stepped back and searched elsewhere for the answers. Together we have opened up a whole new approach to solving problems. Answers seem to come as quick as we come up with questions. When we tap into this dimension we can see things more clearly. We now see that the answer to dark matter and dark energy lies outside our universe. Why would any scientist think that the answer to this problem lies outside our own universe when we have no proof that something outside our universe even exists? When you begin to think from another dimension you realize that a separate entity outside our universe could and does have an affect on our own existing universe. These other universes account for the mysterious dark matter and dark energy that affect our own universe. We have not found the tools to measure things in other universes, but that doesn't change the fact that these places can and do exist."

Lu is trying to take all this in, with the little bit of knowledge of our universe that she has. "So, you are telling me that when you meditate together and are focusing on solving a problem, you can come up with the answers more easily?"

"Something like that. Not so much that the answer just pops up on a screen for us both to see, but it is difficult to explain unless you actually experience it. Let's say it helps you focus better and taps in to a source of creativity and imagination that leads you closer to the solution. It is like asking God for a big hint, if that helps make it any easier to understand. I'm not really able to explain it any better."

"Just think about all the different problems we have come up with answers for here at Genisova. We cured cancer for one. Technology, medicine, food solutions… The sky is the limit. It is a new way of approaching problem solving. It truly is unlocking the potential of the human mind and spirit."

"Wait a minute. The people who discovered the cure for cancer used this method to find it?"

"Doesn't it now make sense that they would?"

Landau now began to sneak back into the conversation. "If you truly believe that everything in life happens for a reason, and everything is in a divine order, then you begin to realize how we need to be able to take our level of problem solving to a higher level, or we are all going to die. Humans are on a path to destruction unless something changes. The inability to approach thinking in this way would have left us to our doom. People are too preoccupied with their external world to search this deep into our internal world. This does not mean that we have new amazing superpowers, but instead that we now have a path to a higher level of thinking.

"There is so much more to see and learn in this world and this universe. There are an infinite amount of problems to solve and they will just become more complex and difficult as we begin to increase our level of intelligence. Just look at how much more a child of our own time knows than a well seasoned master of a time long passed. The level of intelligence will just continue to increase and our capacity for this information will also continue to grow. As you can see, the path to this new dimension is not an easy one. One cannot just read in a book how to do this. It takes years of practice and then even more to master anything remotely close to this. For this reason, it is important that everyone here masters the basics of meditating and looking inside of oneself to begin to see a glimpse of this other dimension. We already have quite a few that have mastered this process, but we hope that someday it will become commonplace among us."

Lucina felt like it was all beginning to make some sense finally. She realized that just this morning she was thinking about how everything in her life had happened for a reason and had led her up to this. She couldn't help but laugh in wonderment as the day's events unfolded before her and presented themselves in magical form. What was this mysterious dimension that these incredible people were tapping into? Was it is true that they had found a cure for cancer, which would seem to be proof of something extraordinary going on? Could it be true that this was the beginning of something big, something that would change the fate of humanity forever? Was all this happening in order to save humans from the sun? Somehow she felt like it all made sense. She couldn't explain how she knew, but she just did. Everything was going to be okay. It would be a long and most assuredly difficult path, but people would survive. Humans would live to venture into the next frontier of space and whatever that holds.

—ɯ—

They were finally ready to begin setting the space station into orbit around the earth. The goal was to get a main living portion up and running and then add on the rest of the space station. It would be in the shape of a giant wheel. It would spin slowly, creating an artificial gravity that would be necessary for living in space for long periods of time. This main station was successfully built in place and able to sustain humans so they could continue building the rest of the spokes of the wheel. As time went by, the people of Genisova got more and more excited about the future. The rest of the world really began to take notice and the pressure on the government to build other space stations was ramped up.

People who had considerable money and power were getting very worked up. There were threats on the people of Genisova from various different places saying that it was not legal to keep others from coming on board the space station. The Council of Genisova had actually worked very closely with the government in making sure that everything they did was in regulation. This open communication helped them continue to move forward. The debate heated up over the technology that Genisova had developed and whether or not they should share the information. The Council was considering giving away some of their secrets but would not do so without something in return. For one, they would use this knowledge as leverage to help further their own cause. The government was trying to get them to give up the information for free, but the Council was not having any of it.

The proceeds from this information and the material things sold could help in maintaining the costs of the space stations indefinitely. In the meantime the space station became bigger and bigger news. The world began to take more notice, and since the space station was in open space for everyone to see, people everywhere could see it. Literally, people with high powered telescopes could look up at night and see the space station being built. There were videos of the space station being built on You Tube. The conversations around the world shifted to the future of mankind and what would become of us. There were other space exploration teams that were making plans for moving to Mars and other moons first. These teams continued towards their goals and pressed the government for funding and stressed their reasons for going to moons or planets instead of a space station.

There were valid reasons for doing this, but there were many variables that could not be accounted for yet. For one, no one had ever been to any of these places and they were still much, much further away. They were vying for government funding and trying to become the savior of mankind. Suddenly, what was once just the next great human adventure had now become the hope of mankind. Or, they would have you believe. Actually, Genisovians knew that one day the space stations would not be all that we could rely on and that we would need to move on to the next planet or moon. Or, hopefully the next star in the galaxy, somehow, some way. But, a planet or moon was not as sure of a thing in the near future, so they bet on the space stations. Quicker, easier, more manageable. Resources available, for at least a little while, on Earth. Essentially it was buying time, until the technology and our knowledge increased and made the further distances more possible for humans.

Genisova was developing a better way of thinking for the future, so the jump to the next frontier would be feasible. They were also preparing people for life in space. People were being trained physically and mentally for something like this. Many, but not all, of them knew this as they were going through it.

—⚞—

Eventually Sarkovia discovered what was going on up in the mountains. He was told about some of the incredible breakthroughs in medicine, science, and other technologies. He was not told the reason Genisovians believed these revelations were occurring. They left that up to him to see if he could make the connection on his own. He never did. He just assumed it was luck, and a bunch of smart people who were given a ton of money to figure out these challenging problems. The researchers at Andromeda One actually brought him to witness their experiments and showed him their results, and he still was not phased. The scientists there were actually thinking it may even convert him to want to become a member of Genisova. After watching a meditation session, he just shrugged his shoulders and said, "What's the big deal? I don't get it. You built this super expensive facility in the most isolated area for that?" They all just smiled and said, "yup."

Andrew and Fiona finally went on that date, and even though she continued to play hard to get, Andrew had all the patience in the world. He had to work hard enough just to get that first date with her. Dating was not really all that much of a priority for many people of Genisova; however, it did happen. Fiona was just extremely preoccupied with everything going on with the Council. She didn't have to make up excuses, she was just too busy to find a moment. When he finally pinned her down to getting lunch at some point, he held her to it.

"Geez, you are impossible to get in one place for more than a minute," Andrew said with exasperation.

"I know. There is just so much to be done, as you know. Dating is not really that high up on the priority list right now, as you could guess."

"Well, I'm just glad I actually won this meal time out of your day. I don't even know where to begin. Doesn't it all just seem so overwhelming? I mean, when you step back and look at all that is going on in the world today, in our lives here. I am surprised there is not more chaos going on out there in the world."

"We predict that there will be. Level heads will prevail for some time, but as the climate begins to change and the ill affects begin to take their toll on people not prepared, it's going to get worse. Imagine, if all the earth lived in the Sahara desert right now. What would become of everyone? People would get desperate and take much greater risks for survival. It's coming, just be glad you are here."

"Are you going to go up there? Do you want to go up there?" he asked.

"That is a good question. Those of us on the Council don't really talk too much about what we as individuals will do someday. I imagine for the most part we will split time everywhere. We will continue to oversee everything and that will entail checking in on wherever the people may be. We don't plan on just getting it started and then letting it go. People depend on the council to help run things properly. There will actually need to be more people in charge eventually, as this all continues to grow."

"Okay, but do you want to go live up there?" he persisted.

"Hmm, well, no one has ever asked me if I wanted to. I guess, I would have to say yes. Partly because I have lived here on earth and I think it would be an amazing adventure to live in space and to partake in it and make it work. There will be so much to do up there to keep things going smoothly."

"Where are you from, originally? I feel like I know you pretty well, on the surface, but have no idea who you really are. Give me some background. Its date question time," he said with a smirk.

"It's been so long since I thought about my early life. I have been so focused on making this place become what it is today. I grew up in a small town in the Midwest. Middle of nowhere. Parents both worked. Mom was a nurse, dad was a computer engineer in a neighboring city. He was gone a lot. Mom worked crazy hours. I have two siblings, an older brother and younger sister. Both married with kids and spread out across the country. After I moved away, the family spent less and less time together. We all just became busy with our lives. Our parents kept busy until they retired and now enjoy the simple things in life. I still do go visit them occasionally. I haven't seen my siblings in years. We talk every now and then, birthdays, maybe. Christmas, maybe. I have never been married, although in a couple serious relationships, as you know. I see my life here as a calling. I am happy, although, maybe deep down when I have time to stop and think about it, I probably am a little lonely. But, then again, here I am, on a date with you."

"Yes, you are. And what a lucky boy I am."

"If you say so," she said and smiled.

"I do say so. You are a pretty special person. I mean, look around. You are in charge of people and what goes on here. That's huge. Maybe the rest of the world doesn't know it, but someday they will. Someday, they are going to write books about all this. This will be part of history because this is what is going to save history, if you know what I mean."

"I'm glad you see it that way. And, I do like you, so far, what I know of you, that is. What's your story, since we are sharing?"

"City boy, born and raised. New York. Surrounded by all that goes with it most of the time. It really is a different way of life. People, in general, are different. Their focus is different. They are very occupied with the status of all parts of their life. Car, clothes, friends, job, you name it. I was there. I wanted fame and fortune as much as the next guy, or girl. I got to hang out with some pretty big names and famous people. Many of their lifestyles were just out of touch with reality. I just don't know any other way to describe it. They had different priorities. Not much their fault, if I stop and think about it now. They were mostly products of their environments. Everyone trying to get ahead and make as much money as they can and have the most things and have the most fun. It's contagious, if you are around it too much. You feel like it is the normal way of life, and then, get this, you feel like everyone else who isn't playing along in this game, this way of life, well, they just were clueless losers. They were less than you and you knew better than all of them. Funny thing is, now that I have a clearer head, I think they may have it backwards. But, like I said, when you are in that environment, man, it is hard to get out of it. Hard to turn away."

"That is an interesting perspective. What about your family? What were they like?"

"Mom and dad divorced when I was in high school. My brother lives in the city still. He works for a financial company, doing God knows what to make a decent living. Its dog eat dog in his world. I still stay in contact with them for the most part, but was never really that close with any of them. Fragmented relationships mostly. I could go on, but it would be pretty boring considering where we are and what we are doing."

"I like to hear about people and their stories, especially those that I choose to sit and eat lunch with amidst my busy schedule." She smiled and looked into his eyes.

"Okay, then I will continue on with the story of my boring life…"

"Don't be a smart Alec" she kidded back. "Tell me something, a favorite memory from your childhood, anything. Give me a glimpse of something."

He sat and seemed to be in deep thought for a long while.

"My parents really did love me and my brother more than anything. It is amazing how the love of your child trumps anything. They couldn't love each other to save the world, but they would not hold back for us. My mother's parents lived a couple hours out of the city on a small farm. Once a month we would pile in the car and head out of the city for a reprieve and go spend the day with my grandparents. Once in a while, when my parents were getting along, we would spend the night. It was like a whole other world. There were these odd, small rooms upstairs and the basement was like an antique treasure chest. We would play hide and seek up-stairs and go search for treasure in the basement. I remember they had this cellar stocked full of canned food and soaps, like they were getting ready for another depression or something. There wasn't much room in that old farmhouse and it was so old, but we all found a cozy place to sleep. Just grab some blankets curl up close to the fireplace and all your problems, faded away. It was the best, ever. If I could bottle up that memory and just hold it close to my heart and never let it go, I would."

He had gotten so lost in his story that he was taken away, back to that farm from his childhood, just for a moment or two. He looked up and thought he maybe saw a small tear in the corner of Fiona's eye.

"That makes me happy and sad all at the same time. I think we all have memories like that from our childhood. We cling to them and save them with all our might. There is such an innocence and purity from the memories of childhood. I often times wonder, why our memories can be so strong at certain times. How is it that they can evoke such intense emotions from something that happened so long ago? It really is amazing. We truly are special creatures and blessed to be able to have such memories and feelings inside us."

They both just sat in silence for a few minutes, seemingly both caught up in some time gone by that they both didn't want to let go of.

Andrew broke the silence, "I do wonder what love for a child feels like. I never really considered myself parenting material, but I think a lot about my parents' love for me back then. It really was powerful. I'm not sure that type of love is something I want to miss out on in my time here on earth, or a space station, for that matter."

"Are you saying that you want to have kids? On a first date?" She caught him in the trap and giggled a bit.

"Oh, no, I mean, maybe, yes, not with you, um, oh boy, that was not where I was trying to go with that…"

"It's okay, I know. It's very sweet, really."

They had both finished eating their lunches.

Fiona broke the silence and said, "I need to get going. Shall we do this again sometime?"

"Oh, uh, sure, absolutely. Yes. When?"

She leaned over and gave him a kiss on the cheek and whispered, "I like you," then walked out the door. He stood there, again, with that feeling, again. But, something inside of him told him this was a good feeling, and things were going to work out exactly like they were supposed to.

Jacob had cruised through his phases of Genisova and had embraced all facets of his new life. He loved being introduced to all the different classes and so many different ones had interested him that decided he wanted to learn a new trade. He had inquired about mechanical engineering and then asked if they offered any higher level classes, as in college. They, of course, had an accelerated mini version of college in different areas. They would subcontract different professionals to come in and teach any of the subjects they needed help with. Information was so accessible these days that anyone could learn just about any profession through computers. They actually had virtual professors for most classes and you could simply order up whatever you wanted.

He had spent most of a year studying to become a mechanical engineer. In the meantime he was in charge of the custodial services all around the campuses of Genisova. He had worked closely with the existing engineers at Genisova in building a recycling program for virtually everything that was disposed of throughout the villages. There was practically no waste at all. This process began with the design of all products produced at Genisova. When things were manufactured for whatever purpose they had, the people thought about what would become of the excess parts. Whatever wasn't used would need to be recycled or repurposed in some way. For everything else they could not get rid of, they consulted with an outside corporation that would figure out what to do with it. These were things like biohazardous waste or other toxic chemicals that they were not allowed to dispose of.

Just like the rest of the group he entered into Genisova with, he had found his place. They each came in from different backgrounds and situations and they had all found their way. Like each and every person that had ever come to Genisova, they had all taken a unique path and figured out what they were supposed to be doing and what their purpose was. It really was not much different from life on the outside, except people here were solely focused on just finding their purpose. There were no worries about making ends meet financially, where to live, what car to drive, and all the other extraneous stresses that people go through every day of their lives. It was a paradigm shift for sure for most all of the people when they first came to Genisova. No money and all the dilemmas it brings.

It is a sacrifice in some ways, to not be able to potentially make a lot of money and all the things that it brings. People who make a lot of money can live a pretty nice life. However, it is also true that many people who make a lot of money can become consumed with the things that money buys. They often end up living above their means and it actually turns into a stressful life, instead of what could have been an easy life. Those who saw this opportunity to take money out of the equation of life were wise. It involved being able to let go of many things that most people cannot. Jacob was someone who was not making a lot of money and had very little to lose by coming to Genisova. He actually had much to gain.

All of his basic needs were taken care of and the stresses of worrying about having a steady job and paying the bills were gone. He could now focus on himself and reaching his potential. He now had the opportunity to live on a space station with the rest of the Genisovians that had made this adventure with him. People with inordinate amounts of money were willing to pay millions to get a spot in space, but were turned away. He had studied hard and was on his way to becoming an engineer. In the meantime, he did his part and helped the cause. It wasn't long before Landau showed up one day while he was studying in the library and asked him if he could have a minute of his time.

"Hi Jacob, how are you today?" Landau began.

"Just studying for one of my exams. How are you?" He replied.

"I've been watching your progress closely and I was wondering if you were interested in checking out a new research project we've been working on."

"Absolutely."

"That's what I thought," Landau said with a smile.

Year 2050

The first parts of the space station were ready to be placed into orbit. It had now been 12 years since Genisova began. The space planes had been perfected and had made many trips into space and back without any problems whatsoever. The day of the first liftoff was to be celebrated and everyone at Genisova was going to cut loose a little. All the fruits of their labor were finally being realized. It would now take approximately five more years to complete the space station and have it be fully functional. It would be a slow process but also an exciting time. Once the center station was completed, people could actually start to live there while they continued to build the rest of it.

The constant spinning of the space station would create artificial gravity minimizing some of the effects, but it would not completely eliminate them. People would still have to exercise and do various things to counteract zero gravity. It would be one thing to put a few well trained astronauts into space for an extended period of time, but another to put an entire population up there. Things were bound to happen that were never accounted for. Someone would develop diabetes, someone would develop high blood pressure, someone would develop eye issues, and on and on. Eventually there would need to be a full-time hospital up there, but for now, they could just triage someone and then get them back to earth at some point.

There was a big watch party and the first lift off was a success. The space plane was a large cargo holder and was carrying quite a few crew members along with the initial pieces of the space station. It was placed successfully and the journey into the next frontier had begun. In time, the space station began slowly to get pieced together. The main control center was in place in one of the Langrangian points and the droids they had created were now working away in space, building the rest of the spokes of the station. This was a new process so there was a learning curve at first, but eventually they got the hang of it. The droids had basic functions and could understand some basic commands, but mostly served as an able bodied robot outside the existing space station that could keep putting the pieces together. This enabled humans to work from inside the space station or even from earth almost around the clock.

Everything at Genisova continued on at a steady pace and without much drama to speak of. The rest of the world however, continued to escalate in its drama. There continued to be much debate as to whether or not putting space stations up in the sky was even worth doing. There were so many issues with the idea that most countries decided to focus more on solving the issue here on earth. And the issues were beginning to arrive. The sun was now showing certain signs that it was changing. There was now little debate over the fate of the sun. The average temperatures began to rise around the world and the measurable radiation was increasing. Governments started to work on ways to save planet earth from the sun. People from the United States began defecting to Canada at such an alarming rate that the Canadian government had to increase their restrictions on people trying to enter.

Of course, people were trying to move away from the equator all around the globe. The glaciers were now thawing at an incredible rate and Antarctica had now become the hottest real estate on the planet. The sea levels around the coasts of the world were beginning to rise. The human race was in panic mode. Global councils were formed to work on the problems, but because of the different geographical locations it was a very difficult task. A country that was located anywhere near the equator was virtually doomed much more quickly because of their location. This made it difficult to negotiate plans with everyone equally. There was much conversation about how to protect humans from the radiation as well as how to adapt to the temperature changes.

How the changing sun would affect the food supply was probably the biggest concern. If crops began to fail, where would the world's source of food come from? Humans could adapt in small concentrated locations, but what about the masses? This is where the panic set in. Many people who felt like they would not be "saved" were becoming more volatile. In many countries this was causing problems. Not only were governments having to try and work on solving all of the issues related to the sun, they were also having to deal with people from lower socioeconomic situations being rebellious. Crime rates continued to soar and homicides were at an all time high around the world. The wealthy, on the other hand were a whole other issue. Private enterprises began to pop up all over the place welcoming anyone who could afford the salvation they were preparing. They were also buying up land in the model of Genisova and beginning to create new little cities of their own.

They were juggling the idea of a space station in the sky, but like most governments they looked at it as a last resort. The main difficulty here was that many of the people interested in this idea were extremely wealthy and were very opinionated. They felt like if they were going to spend all of their money on this new project then they should have a considerable say in what was going to happen. No progress could ever be made towards building one. Instead, they began to build gated communities inside glass domes. These were billion-dollar projects, but to some extent they had real viability. These may work short term but long term was the problem. Where was the food going to come from? Thankfully, farmers around the world began to realize this and they actually began to develop backup plans for the future. Companies began to pour research into how to develop food substitutes that could be created using certain crops that were more resistant to the changing climate and radiation. The bottom line was that crops would need to be grown under protection from the UV rays because they would not grow well otherwise.

Large storehouses were being built to begin storing away vast amounts of food. People were certainly beginning to think about how they would survive in the future. The people of Genisova had already thought ahead about this dilemma. They had already purchased a large area of fertile land further north and were now in the process of creating a greenhouse of sorts to help filter out the harmful rays of the sun. As the climate got worse, people looked more and more to Genisova as a consultant to help come up with a solution. At this point, Genisova was so busy with building their space stations and trying to protect their environment on earth, that they had little time or desire to help anyone else. The way they saw it, if people wanted help they could come and join their already existing solution. Otherwise, they had little motivation to help them.

However, some people felt like they should help and that Genisovians were discriminating by not just allowing anyone to enter in, even though they did. People felt like it was unfair that they had to go through their "process" and that it was their constitutional right to be able to walk in and have a spot on the space station or in their city. There were also many, including some in Washington, who felt like they needed to share their secret technology that apparently was helping them be so successful at their mission. Experts around the world began to analyze what they were doing and came to the conclusion that they were using some extremely cutting edge technology that did not exist anywhere else in the world. Materials, fuels, foods, and several others on the list of suspicious things going on. The Defense Department was trying to make a push to try and obtain some of the information they were withholding from everyone.

Landau and the Council did feel bad for the rest of the country and did not wish ill upon them, but were not sure how to go about giving them information. Should they let them have full access or try and control it? It seemed as though the government was mostly inquiring about the composite material used for building the rockets and space station and the type of fuel and energy they were using for them. In the end they decided to maintain the rights to these materials and simply let the entire world have access to them. They contracted with factories on the outside of Genisova to manufacture the material and the energy source. This way, they would now be able to reap the financial benefits of their creation.

This eased the government over for a while, but eventually they came back for more. Even the government was in a panic mode of sorts. They were feeling the pressure from the general public more than ever. People were marching in the streets demanding that the government do something to help save them. They had many opinions but no on really knew what the right answer was. Many people just wanted to try and save themselves, go alone, but they knew they couldn't do it. Eventually everyone would need help with something. Someone could build a giant dome and live inside it, but eventually you would have to go out. You would want to go out of it and partake of life with the rest of the world. The question was, what would become of the rest of the world? Would there be grocery stores to go buy food at? Restaurants? Libraries? Shows? Sporting events? The orchestra? What would become of the rest of the world when the sun would unleash its wrath on earth? This was the fear that was slowly settling in on people's minds and beginning to take its toll on them.

—⚏—

The reason Genisova continued to be so successful amidst all the chaos in the world, was because they had a well thought out plan and everyone was on board to work towards that goal. People looked at this city and thought: why couldn't the government create something like this for the rest of the country? It would seem to be fairly easy to replicate some of the basics that were going on, but there was too much disagreement about what to do. The problem was so widespread and everyone had a different idea about how they wanted to solve the problem.

The idea was proposed to try and build giant towers that shields could be hung from to help block out the UV rays and then people could still function beneath them. The temperature would not be rising too much all at once, so it would be hotter, but people would be protected to some degree. They would just have to figure out how to stay cool. Then hope that in future another plan would be developed. Many hoped that the people of Genisova would perfect their plans and then everyone else could just replicate those plans and begin to move off the planet. But the main long-term problem was food. How long could food be harvested from earth?

Hopefully long enough to figure out how to get food from another planet or moon. It became the central focus of the global council for dealing with the dilemma of the sun. They believed they had enough time to survive until they could figure out a way to keep making food from the ground we walked on. While all this continued, Genisovians carried on towards building the space station and creating their own 'umbrella' to protect their people on earth.

Landau and the Council advanced their work on group meditative practices and expanding their collective consciousness. With time, the rest of Genisova slowly began to discover what was going on and wonder what it meant. What was this new dimension they were tapping into and how would it change the course of humanity? How did this new form of communication work, and what unseen mysterious power were they tapping into? The excitement level was at a new high-combined with the progress on the space station. Landau continued to experiment and see to how much deeper they could dig into this hidden realm.

Was there a connection between this unseen dimension and the one that connects entangled particles? There were some amongst the Genisovians who began to wonder if there was a higher power at work here. Or, was this a way of communicating with God or some divine consciousness? Many who meditate already believed that this was a path to God. But this seemed to be somewhat more quantitative, a bit more tangible, for a lack of a better word. They began to experiment with more and more people to see to what extent they could break down barriers. It became apparent to everyone that there was a collective consciousness that existed in a realm that we'd had very little access to in the past. Clearly, people here and there had harnessed this realm, but it had never been explored with a concentrated effort by a large group of people with modern technology trying to unravel the mystery.

There was evidently some physical energy, invisible to all of our human senses, that was the fabric upon which all of reality was painted. The only part of a human that could begin to see this was the consciousness hidden within all of us. It has been there since the beginning of time and we have had obvious signs and symptoms that it was there. It is the reason we look for a God at all. Without this hidden source of energy within all of us, we would not even begin to search for something more. It is what many call the spirit or the soul or love, but whatever label you slap on it, it still resides within all of us and everything we see. It pulls us towards it.

For most of our history we have looked at it with wonderment, but then just shrugged it off as something unattainable. People such as Jesus even hinted at it by saying things like, "all of these things and more you will be capable of." Just like people see the signs and symptoms and just ignore them, people ignore sayings like this. If Jesus said we would capable of all this and more, than why don't we believe it? Why don't we try to do 'this and more'? The questions began to swirl: what other applications could this new source of knowledge have? What were the limitations? What would the rest of the world think when they found out about it? It would only be a matter of time before the word leaked out and people began to have their opinions about what it means or if it is truly happening at all. Was it all just a figment of their imaginations?

People like Suzi and Andrew had similar reactions when they found out about it. They both felt like it was part of the big secret behind Genisova and that it was the reason for all the discretion that seemed to continually be a part of this place. It now made sense why they required all members to learn how to meditate and delve deeper into their soul. If someone wanted to be able to participate in these group meditations, then they would first have to master their own individual meditation. The more experiments they did with this type of group meditation the more they realized that it was not a very exact science. There would be sessions where very little to nothing would happen. And this happened all the time. Especially when there were newcomers to the method.

With more than two people it would get a little trickier to understand the meaning of the sessions. People would leave sometimes more confused than clear as to what they were supposed to ascertain from the session. But, when it worked, people came away from it with a clearer vision towards what they were working on. They would say that they had tapped into a level of creativity that they did not know they were capable of. They were going to need this ability to help solve some of the many problems that they were going to confront on earth and up in space. Mohammed was not sure what to make of it at first. He was still very firm in his faith about God, but was not sure what this meant. Was this truly another level of communicating with God? He was fascinated and it certainly inspired him to try and get a chance to participate in the project. He wanted to try and get a minute alone with Landau so he could inquire what he needed to do to have a shot at trying this. By chance he saw Landau making his rounds one day in their department and he couldn't help but say something.

"Hey Landau, I was wondering if I could have a second of your time?" he began.

Landau, who was pretty keen on people like Mohammed, said, "Sure, what do you need?"

"I was just wondering what your criteria are for prospects for your new meditative experiments."

"We don't really have any criteria, but I have recently noticed that there have been many inquiries such as this."

"Oh, I am so sorry, I didn't mean to come across like that. I am just very interested in finding out more of what it all means."

"What do you think it means?"

"Well, I am not sure, but I am curious to talk to some people that have experienced it. Is there anyone I know that has been through this already?"

"I assure you that everyone here knows someone that has already experienced this."

"So, there are a lot of people that are involved with the project?"

"Mohammed, we have been here for over 12 years now, and we have been working on things like this since the very beginning. Do not be surprised by anything that you find out is going on here."

"So, can I ask you what you think it means?" Mohammed said seriously.

"I am not sure that I can explain it very well with my own words. It is something that is probably best understood by being experienced."

"So, are you saying that I can experience it then?"

"Well, it's not so simple, my friend. You see, it is not something that you just sign up for, show up, and then you get your magic ticket. The people who are having any results from this process have been spending inordinate amounts of time working on it."

"Can you tell me anything, a glimpse of what they experience? Do you think they are talking with God?"

"I see, this is something personal for you, isn't it? I wish I could give you some answers that would satisfy what it is you are looking for. Your faith is strong, this I know. As strong as anyone's here. You would think that would be enough, right? It should be that simple, I know. But, it's not, is it? We are always searching for more. We want to know more and it drives us forward. People have asked these questions for as long as we have been able to dream them up. But, humans have been at a standstill for quite some time. We are so smart in so many ways, but thinking with these beautiful brains has distracted us from the our true potential. Do you know what that potential is Mohammed?" Landau looked him straight in the eyes with the most loving look that was possible.

Mohammed looked back at him somewhat frightened and unsure of himself. He wasn't sure what to say for he wasn't sure the answer.

"I don't know. Love?"

Landau just laughed and put his hand on his shoulder like an old friend. "You know, Mohammed, I really do hope you get to come soon and spend some time with me. I can see it in your soul that you are almost ready to delve deeper into this."

"How will I know that I am ready? Am I ready?" He inquired.

"You are so close. Is there something you are looking for the answer to?" He paused. "Don't tell me. Just think about it and bring it with you when I come and get you." He smiled and the walked over to another friend of his and began asking him some questions. He wondered if his friend was ready. What was this silly thing that he was so curious about and was it true what people were saying about it? Time would tell. He went back to work and resolved to make it happen one way or another.

—⚇—

Landau and Lucina had surprised everyone at Genisova when word got out that they were engaged. It actually made the news outside and brought even more attention to Genisova. They had fallen back in love and, yet, they still marched forward in this process of survival with all the people around them. Landau was a new person, but still focused and determined to carry on like he had before. The space station continued to grow and was nearly completed. Time went by and eventually it was ready for people to begin living up there. The world looked on in amazement and wondered what would happen to those who began to live up there. The world was changing, but it had not reached a point of being unbearable. Agriculture continued to adapt to the surroundings and it was still sustainable for the time being. Like all humans, having foresight to actually make change was difficult. People only focused on what was happening right in front of them and everyone just assumed we would adapt. Little did they know that many of the crops were beginning to struggle to the point of no return.

Many areas of the world were in an extreme drought. The water levels throughout the world had dropped to a level of no return. Companies were now desalinating water from the ocean and selling it at a premium to people. The world got back to basics in many ways with water and food and shelter from the sun being the primary concerns for all. For the wealthy it was not as much of a burden, but for the middle class on down it began to create problems. People had to modify their lives to account for all the new expenses. The crops that became more challenging to grow became expensive; consequently, all the foods that were made from those crops did too. Bottled water could cost $10 and a bag of flour could cost $30. The climate changes also affected just about all aspects of the weather. It created even more extreme conditions. Tornados, hurricanes, tsunamis, earthquakes, torrential rainstorms, droughts and every type of weather you could imagine. It was getting worse.

Life for most became more about survival than enjoyment. Focus had changed back to mere necessities in life. True humanity became more apparent everywhere you looked. Sensible people realized that chance of survival for all would be better if they worked together to help solve problems. They looked at places like Genisova, and even though they didn't agree with their philosophy, they could recognize the benefit of working together to solve a problem. For others it created more disarray and their lives began to spiral downward. Some of these angry people became organized with other desperate people and wanted to take their anger out on those who seemed to be more resilient to all the changes going on.

Many religious zealots and other extremists became more and more dangerous as their hope dwindled. Places like Genisova became increasingly more likely to be attacked by these vigilantes. It was only a matter of time before enough of these desperate people cooked up schemes to try and inflict damage to those who were being more successful than they were. It was very difficult for anyone to get inside Genisova from the ground, but through the air was slightly easier. This is where the attacks began and continued to get worse and worse. A couple deranged lunatics flew an airplane over Genisova and dropped several makeshift bombs on a couple buildings. There were casualties and extensive damage to the buildings. This prompted the Council to actually seek additional protection from the government. They had given Sarkovia a considerable amount of information and felt like they were due something in return. The spread of violence had reached even peaceful, harmless places like Genisova and it was only the beginning. It was a sign of the times to come for the rest of earth for the foreseeable future. The world was beginning to spin out of control. There were pockets of hope here and there, but the overall sentiments of the people of earth was despair.

Year 2140

Master Seisha went back to her home after her lesson that day and reflected upon how her day went. These children being raised on a space station in orbit around earth lived such a different life than almost the entirety of humanity. Many of these children did often wonder what it is like to live down there with the trees and grass and dirt. Looking out into space at this big beautiful planet was quite a view. What they did know did know that it was a highly volatile place to live and difficult place to survive. They were told very little that would ever convince them to want to go and live there. Maybe visit to see what it was like, but never to stay. Too much turmoil. It was a fighting and harsh way of life. The sun had become an enigma unlike anything the earth had ever witnessed. The radiation had wilted everything in its path and without protection it eventually destroyed everything it touched.

Humans continued to move away from the equator and this created so many problems in itself. Countries already had boundaries and so those furthest from the middle of earth— Canada, Russia and Antarctica became the most populated places on earth. The changes to earth were so incredible and widespread that humans had to completely adapt or die. Those who were less attached to their worldly possessions and were willing to up and do whatever it took, were much more successful at surviving. Many species of animals and plants became extinct and only the more hardy species endured. Adapt or die. Anarchy spread throughout the world and the boundaries of all countries became less discernible. The sheer number of people migrating to other areas was impossible for any government to stop, and the foundations of society began to crumble. People left their lives and jobs in order to survive. Most all urban areas anywhere near the equator fell to ruin. Any major products manufactured near these areas were either no longer produced or they were nearly impossible to get. The ramifications of this alone began to cripple large parts of society. It was chaos right out of Armageddon and only the fittest would make it. Many believed it was Armageddon.

But to those of Genisova, it was merely a new challenge and the dawn of a new age. Many major leaps in human advancements came in the face of adversity. This just happened to be the most difficult one while humans inhabited the earth. There had been many other major catastrophic events that wiped out most all of the life on earth, but this one was different because this occurred while humans were alive. And, as far as they could tell, life was not going to ever be easier on earth. It would continue to get worse. The only way to survive was to begin the adventure to other planets or moons and even, eventually, other galaxies.

Master Seisha thought about her great grandfather, Landau, and the vision he'd had so long ago. He had created an opportunity for survival, and a chance to thrive, for those who believed in his ideas. Humans still survived down there on earth, but it was not a peaceful or enjoyable life. It was merely survival. He had opened his gates to anyone willing to enter. And for those willing to make some sacrifices, they were taken care of and protection from the sun awaited them. More importantly, he had expanded the human consciousness by searching for and finding the dimension that lies hidden outside of our everyday senses and yet somehow touches all that we know.

There were now three cities of Genisova on Earth, and all continued to function harmoniously and successfully. Life was definitely different from when they began, but the people who lived there were glad to be living there instead of outside in the rest of the world. The means of acquiring materials from outside of Genisova became much more difficult and in many ways impossible. Humans on Earth had to continue to adapt and change in the name of survival. The basic necessities were all they had sometimes. Life on the space stations was also very different and challenging in many ways, but it was peaceful and stable. There were now several million people who lived between the cities and space stations of Genisova. They were nearly ready to begin a journey to the moon Titan, of Saturn, and begin a colony there. They had already colonized Mars and were continuing to improve the conditions there so it could also be a viable option for humans.

The increasing temperature from the sun was making changes on all of the planets and moons throughout the solar system, and the future outlook was good for someday living on one of these new frontiers. The core temperature of Mars was warming up almost enough to melt the ice and create water. Changes like this were occurring all throughout the solar system. The technological advancements continued to keep up with all of the various challenges that presented themselves to the Genisovians. This was in large part due to their ability to tap into a new dimension and the insights it brought. Those who had mastered the art of this form of communicating at this higher level earned the label of Master. Meditating had become a normal everyday practice for everyone in Genisova. Children were raised with this practice instilled in them from day one. It was not a foreign thing to them ever. It helped to create peace and tranquility throughout the people and kept everyone focused on what was truly important—survival.

Life was different now from what it was like 100 years ago. On earth, people did not live lives of luxury and materialism anymore. The prosperity (along with the greed) of capitalism no longer existed in any way, shape, or form. The rich and glamorous lifestyles no longer were attainable. There were pockets of wealthy people here and there that tried to succeed in living this type of lifestyle, but it was still very arduous. The people of Genisova were happy and thankful to be alive and safe. There were plans for another space station, the largest of all, that would be able to harbor as many as a million people. It would take years to build, but would be a city in the sky. There were shuttles that could taxi people between stations and earth, if need be, and the plans were to push out away from the sun further.

Seisha sat on a stool facing a window looking out at earth and began to close her eyes. She had a vision of the universe and beyond. She saw humans traveling through different dimensions to faraway galaxies and exploring new planets. She saw people communicating with one another without saying a word, just by thinking the thoughts. She looked within and felt these things to be true already because she was able to see through time and be one with everything at this very moment. She could see the energy that coursed through the fabric of the universe and connected everyone and everything together. More than anything, she felt love and its power, and how its presence was beneath all that was. There was no mistaking it. Scientific advancements would continue to amaze and mesmerize people with all their grandeur, pushing humans forward and to the boundaries of the universe, but that feeling deep down inside of her, and inside all of us, would prevail. There would always be times in our lives that we would lose sight of this truth, but it would always be there, waiting for us to come back around to find it and eventually, become one with it.

Printed and bound by PG in the USA